Rollo Duchamps-Avery, the high-spirited second son of the eleventh Earl of Rossingley, is not in his father's best books. After one misdemeanour too many, the earl ruins Rollo's idyllic summer by packing him off to the wilds of rural Norfolk, arranging for him to stay with the Duke of Ashington's loathsome brother.

Lord Lyndon Fitzsimmons has an aversion to houseguests. Shunned by polite society for crimes far wickeder than anything Rollo could dream up, all Fitzsimmons wants is to drink himself into a stupor, tend his beloved hydrangeas, and take potshots at tin soldiers.

If only his inquisitive young visitor, with his pretty little head of wispy blond hair, his stupidly coltish legs, and his knack of always being where Fitzsimmons would rather him not, would leave him in peace.

This third book in the Rossingley Regency romance series features the fourteenth Earl of Rossingley's lively second son, Rollo, and the Duke of Ashington's disgraced brother, Lord Lyndon Fitzsimmons. This book can be read as a standalone.

TO BEGUILE A

BANISHED LORD

REGENCY ROSSINGLEY, BOOK THREE

FEARNE HILL

A NineStar Press Publication
www.ninestarpress.com

To Beguile a Banished Lord

First Edition, November 2025

ISBN: 978-1-64890-906-1

Also available in eBook, ISBN: 978-1-64890-905-4

CONTENT WARNING:

This book contains sexually explicit content, which may only be suitable for mature readers. Depictions of alcohol use, suicidal ideation, and mental health issues.

To Sebastian

Chapter One

Rossingley Estate, Summer, 1825

I must not swive the stable boy (again).
I must not swive the stable boy (again).
I must not swive the stable boy (again).
I must not…

"Crocodile tears won't save you this time, Master Rollo."

Pritchard's lisping note of triumph was unmistakeable. "No matter how prettily you shed them, you've pushed your papa too far. He is provoked beyond measure."

"He'd be his usual fine and dandy self if you hadn't gone running to inform him."

"My primary role in the Rossingley household is to serve the earl," answered Pritchard, as prissy and prim as ever. "Not his licentious offspring."

Rollo harboured an ugly notion that his father's valet had been waiting a long time for this moment, possibly since when Rollo, at age four, had sprinkled rich, resinous lily pollen amongst Papa's meticulously folded white linens. It had been the opening salvo of a rather jolly dislike of each other.

"You're relishing this, aren't you, Pritchard?"

"Tremendously," Pritchard confirmed.

Escape flitted across Rollo's mind, but only for a second. One step ahead, and perhaps recalling the time Rollo had feinted past him and sprinted away across the lawns, Pritchard had brought along reinforcements in the form of two burly footmen stationed on either side of the library door. The window, alas, was closed.

Rollo shot a pleading look towards Kit Angel — Papa's divine and terribly understanding paramour — currently decorating the settee, who shook his head. Everybody was loyal to Papa to a fault, and it was damned annoying.

"Sorry, old chap." At least Kit sounded genuine. "For what it's worth, I tried to talk your father out of it. Some of us enjoy having you around."

What did he mean by *having you around*? Rollo wasn't planning on going anywhere, unless swallow diving headfirst out of the nearest window and running for the hills until Papa had calmed down counted. And talk him out of what?

Before Rollo could further parse Kit's words, Papa himself swept into the library, dressed in his favourite chartreuse silk banyan and pearls. Rollo coveted both immensely. As always, the eleventh earl was impeccably turned out, though this morning, his flamboyant attire sat at odds with the discomfiting, frigid set of his mouth. Rollo barely dared meet his pale eyes; when his mouth looked as grim as that, his gaze could freeze a lake.

"Rollo, my darling."

Rollo winced. Only a fool would mistake the endearment for anything other than an affectation.

"Yes, Papa."

The ice-chip eyes glittered. "You know why you're here, I assume?"

"Yes, Papa."

Experience taught Rollo that short answers tended to be met more favourably. Unfortunately, his smart mouth had a lamentable tendency to act independently of his mind. "Writing out *I must not swive the stable boy* one hundred times was a significant clue. The lack of hot water in my room this morning more subtle. But no less vexing."

The faintest ghost of a smile twitched his father's lips, gone in an instant. Even in the midst of a scolding, Rollo still appreciated he had the best of fathers. Most would have introduced his arse to the switch long ago.

"Do you have anything to say for yourself, Rollo?"

Rollo straightened his shoulders. Might as well be hanged for a sheep as a lamb and all that. The importance of standing up for himself had been instilled in him from a young age; Papa could hardly complain now he was reaping what he'd sown.

"Yes, Papa. Several things, actually."

Papa sighed. "I'd expect nothing less."

"Firstly, my wrist aches." Rollo waggled it to demonstrate. "I have indelible green ink stains on my second-favourite blush waistcoat, and I'm still frightfully chilly. And, for the record, Ellis was an able, willing, practiced, and — dare I say — extremely encouraging participant."

"Naturally, he was; you paid him two pounds!"

"And it was very well deserved."

"And then a further crown, on account, for future favours!"

Goodness, Pritchard had been busy. Rollo shot him an evil look, though in having his financial transactions laid out so bluntly, his bravura hung by a thread.

"At risk of repeating myself," Rollo ploughed on, "I considered it money well spent. Ellis has several strings to his bow."

"Evidently."

His father's fine blond brows knit together. The line between standing up for himself and cheeking Papa was a fine one; Rollo had a sneaking suspicion he might have tiptoed across it.

"Darling Rollo," began his father, a layer of frost coating each syllable. "For all I care, our stable boy could have the whole string section of London's prestigious Philharmonic Society tucked behind the fall of his breeches. And you could have twanged every single instrument."

Rollo had been on his knees attempting exactly that until he'd been discovered by the second groom, who'd blabbed to the head groom, who'd gone tittle-tattling to Pritchard.

"Nevertheless, as you are well aware, there is nothing I detest more than fortunate, well-heeled members of society taking advantage of those in their employ." With an irritable flick of his hand, Papa waved away Rollo's attempt to defend his actions. "That Ellis was willing is an irrelevance. You placed the man in a devilishly awkward position, and I simply will not tolerate it. Have I made myself crystal clear?"

"Yes, Papa," he replied meekly. "Sorry, Papa."

"And so you should be."

Yet to be mollified, his father folded his arms and began pacing in front of the fireplace. "The simple truth remains. Our loyal servants are out of bounds. I distinctly recall this being made perfectly clear to you when you returned from Eton last year. Did I not?"

Rollo hung his head. "Yes, Papa."

"If it had been your first demeanour and you had been totally in the dark, then, of course, I would instruct you on how a Duchamps-Avery should behave. It would be remiss of me not to. But, as it is, the fact that you stand here, arguing the point after all I've…"

Ahhh, to begin the day with one of Papa's sweet lectures. Rollo didn't need to tune in for the rest. He knew how things ran. Their disputes were well rehearsed operatic duets, composed of increasing exasperation on Papa's part, Rollo feigning abject apology, a discourse on how a Duchamps-Avery should conduct themselves, ending with a loving embrace and a promise to do better. As usual, Pritchard and Kit had been making a fuss over nothing. Rollo would bow his head a few times, continue to appear suitably repentant, and ride this one out.

Content in the sure knowledge he was loved, Rollo's thoughts drifted. In a few moments, Papa would fizzle out and decree his penance. Idly, Rollo wondered what it might be. Papa was nothing if not creative. Over the years, Rollo's punishments had ranged from counting all the earwigs in the orangery (aged five, he was discovered hiding in the coal cellar after two hours of searching) to scrubbing the scullery steps with a toothbrush (for convincing his twin brother, Willoughby, that eating crushed pinecones would allow him to see better in the dark). Willoughby casting up his accounts the next morning during the church sermon aside, some of Rollo's so-called punishments had turned into rather good fun. Like the time he was consigned to digging over the vegetable patch and unearthed an adder, which had slithered over Pritchard's foot.

"To that end, Rollo, it is high time you had a firmer hand. My own father, rest his soul, oft quoted that a rose bush must be heavily pruned in order to produce the best blooms. And, on this occasion, I believe he was speaking with the weight of wisdom. Don't you agree?"

Papa's lecture appeared to have taken a horticultural detour. "Er…yes?"

"Excellent." His father clapped his hands. "Therefore, Dobson will accompany you when you depart for your trip to Norfolk this afternoon, see you safely settled in, and return to collect you in three months' time."

"D-Dobson will…what?" Rollo's happy flights of reminiscence screeched to a halt. *Did…did he…did…?* "Sorry, Papa, I must have misheard. Did you just say Dobson's accompanying me to *Norfolk*?"

"Got it in one, darling. You are clever. To Goule Hall, to be precise. On the edge of the Broads, between some hellish backwater named Stokesby and another provincial bog going by the name of Wroxham, I believe. A delightful, if not a tad isolated, property belonging to the

Ashington estate. The duke's twin brother, Lord Lyndon Fitzsimmons, remains in residence after spending an enforced period of seclusion there a couple of years ago, whilst he…ah…reflected on several episodes of…ah…poor behaviour in and around the *ton*. I shall spare you the details. Suffice to say that in comparison, dear boy, your antics are those of a rank amateur."

This Lord Lyndon Fitz-something-or-other could have kidnapped the moon from under the noses of the sun and the stars for all that Rollo cared. "And this…this Goule Hall is in Norfolk?" he clarified, aghast. Perhaps, somehow, his father was confusing Norfolk with Mayfair.

Alas, no.

"Unless the hall has been excavated and deposited elsewhere since the duke and I corresponded less than a week ago, then yes."

"And Willoughby is coming too," Rollo decreed, praying if he said it with enough confidence, that would somehow make it true.

His father shook his head. "On the contrary. Willoughby will be travelling to London with me. I plan to use the time you are apart to begin schooling your brother in the rudiments of my business affairs." He flashed Rollo an evil little smile very much like Rollo's own, displaying all of his sharp pointed teeth. "And perhaps take the opportunity to do some shopping, pay a visit to my tailor, and so forth."

Ugh. That was a low blow. Rollo didn't give two hoots for learning about business. Willoughby would inherit the title and all that nonsense, anyhow. But how he adored their family shopping expeditions! Much more than Willoughby ever did.

Pritchard made an odd noise, quickly covering his mouth with his hand. Knowing the blasted valet, the whole thing had been his bloody idea. He'd always enjoyed having the earl to himself. Rollo would have said so, too, if every ounce of his not inconsiderable intelligence wasn't fixated on desperately seeking a way out of the barren wasteland now known as his immediate future. Because, from where he was sitting,

Norfolk already seemed horribly like a fait accompli. Three months. Three *summer* months. Stuck with a dull, ancient lord, in a draughty old hall in the middle of effing nowhere. They might as well just shoot him with a musket ball now and be done with it.

He tried one last time. "Ha ha, very funny. But…really, Papa? Norfolk? Cold, flat, windy Norfolk? Even Bonaparte wasn't exiled to *Norfolk!*"

"No." The earl tilted his white-blond head, so like Rollo's own, in gentle acknowledgement. "But then, my dear, Napoleon Bonaparte wasn't a spoiled second son of an earl, caught swiving one of my stable boys when he'd been given explicit instructions not to manhandle the servants. Pritchard? Ring for Dobson, if you would be so kind. I do believe Rollo's valises are already packed."

Chapter Two

My dearest Willoughby,

Papa is an ass. You were paying an afternoon call to Miss Lavinia when we left. He didn't even allow me to track you down and say farewell. Needless to say, three days sharing the landau with Dobson has been insufferable. On his return to Rossingley, please ensure somebody acquaints him with a bar of soap.

God, I miss you already.

We rode into the county of Norfolk two hours ago, yet still no sign of Goule Hall. Dobson has family around here. He says Goule isn't on the way to anywhere, an end in itself. For all that his breath is foul, I think he may be onto something. The landscape is bleak, a never-ending cycle of green marsh and grey saltings, with limitless skies and a church tower on every horizon. Though sobering, it imbues me with an incredible urge to do peculiar things, such as hunting for wild garlic or skimming stones across the marshes. Mostly, however, it makes me want to demand that the landau turn around.

I am being so terribly brave, despite everything.

PS In your last ode to Lavinia, you may wish to revisit the definition of iambic pentameter.

Your Grace, I write to thank you for permitting me to spend the summer at one of your country homes. I am truly blessed.

MANY YEARS AGO, Rollo's papa had a very *special* friend named Charles. Like Rollo, he was also terribly brave—a soldier. After fighting Napoleon's finest on the battlefields of La Coruna, he returned home alive, only to sadly perish a few years later of consumption. Willoughby and Rollo never knew him particularly well because they'd been away at school, but Papa grieved his loss as if a cloak had been cast over the sun. Then, a couple of years later, Kit came along, and Papa went back to being his usual incorrigible, annoying, adorable self.

The point being that if ever Rollo were in the doldrums, Papa would remind him that something terrific might be waiting just around the next corner. And if not that corner, then the one after, or perhaps a corner Rollo was unaware even existed until he stumbled around it. Though peeved at his father's decision to send him away, and still smarting from his humiliating dressing down, Rollo would do his best. He'd spend his three months at this blasted Goule place, and even if, privately, he believed that making the best of things was a damned poor way of dealing with them, then that was what he'd do.

Despite padding his brain with optimistic, courageous intent, as the landau rounded a sharp bend in a rutted track, affording him his first glimpse of Goule Hall, Rollo concluded his special corner had yet to reveal itself.

"If this place ain't haunted," declared Dobson, leaning towards Rollo to get a better view, "then my prick's a kipper. I reckon I can hear the creaks and bumps in the night from all the way out here."

Rollo breathed through his mouth for a few seconds; after three days in the confines of the landau, he concluded Dobson had a rotten tooth. Though, if his member really was a kipper, then it would explain the unfortunate odour.

"Nonsense," Rollo said. "You've been listening to too many of Cook's silly stories. There are no such things as ghosts. Old houses simply make strange noises. When the wind blows and the windows rattle and such."

All the same, as the stark flint façade loomed closer, he wrapped his travelling rug a little more snugly across his lap and vowed to lock his bedchamber door that night. And then he vowed to stop harbouring mean thoughts about people. It was not a nice trait in him. Dobson was a good man. He'd also fought for his country. Big and strong, too, which was why Papa had selected him for this errand. Thieves would think twice about waylaying their carriage. The smell alone would be a deterrent.

"Anyhow, I think it's a pretty house," Rollo lied, staring up at the three-storey, double-fronted hall. Cut in severe straight lines, as though someone had taken a sharp knife to it, the hall defiantly stared back. Half-hearted curls of smoke puffed from two of the chimneys. Considering it was the first week of June, the country air still carried a chill. "Good. The fires have been lit."

Even the slate-grey chimney pots appeared precisely drawn, four on the front aspect of the roof partnered with four identical ones on the rear, as if ready to join hands and dance a terribly sedate, terribly depressing minuet.

As the carriage drew closer, Rollo picked out more odd details. The unwelcoming front door, for instance — too narrow — as if squeezed in as an afterthought. The ornate gables swooping down on either side of each window, like elaborate fringes disguising plain faces. On another house, they would have been a delight; on this one, they only drew attention to the meanness of the window proportions. In contrast, immaculate gardens flanked the property. Dobson sniffed noisily.

"It's as ugly as a mud fence," he declared.

"It's romantic," Rollo contradicted stoutly. "And evidently well cared for."

"Nope." Dobson shook his head. "Needs knocking down. And a pretty penny spent building another in its place. Mebbe this lord ain't got enough blunt to do it."

"The Duke of Ashington is one of the richest men in the country." Rollo's own father was possibly the only man richer. "And generous too. I daresay his brother's portion is more than enough."

Rollo hadn't anticipated a large welcome party, and Goule Hall didn't disappoint. He knew and liked the Duke of Ashington well enough. The man occasionally dined with his father at the earl's London house. Pleasant, handsome, and unassuming, he talked to Rollo like a man, not a boy, about serious things, such as politics and the poor. The duke's youngest brother, Lord Francis, lacking the duke's natural timidity, was an absolute hoot. If Lord Lyndon, the duke's twin and Rollo's imminent host was anything like his brothers, then Rollo wouldn't be feeling quite so down in the mouth. Except, as a gleeful Pritchard had informed him, the lord was none of those things. He had a reputation as a drunk, a rakehell, a gambler, and the possessor of shocking ill-temper.

So what? Rollo told himself crossly, adjusting his gloves and donning his hat. He could be quite loutish himself if he chose. Perhaps this Lord Lyndon person was simply unhappy. Perhaps he hurt others because he was hurting himself. It must be hard having a revered duke for a twin brother and playing second fiddle all the time. Especially when said duke never put a step wrong. Why, Rollo could relate to that. He adored Willoughby, though they were as different as oil and vinegar.

Aside from the crunch of his boots on the pristine pebbled drive-way, Rollo stepped from the carriage into a deathly silence, not broken by even a dog bark or the crow of a bird.

"I do hope they're expecting me." A note of alarm crept into his voice. "I'm famished and ready for a hot bath."

"Mebbe the bunting is strewn around the back," replied Dobson with a mean little laugh. Rollo ignored him.

Papa had written, and the duke had confirmed. Rollo had seen Ashington's slanting penmanship himself when he'd still prayed the duke had erroneously substituted the word Norfolk for Mayfair. He assumed the duke's instruction had been passed on to the household at Goule Hall, but what if the letter had become lost or…

The first of Rollo's valises hit the ground with a dull thud, swiftly followed by another. Even those noises failed to alert anyone inside the house. Dobson and the driver had arrangements to pass the night at a local inn before heading back to Rossingley; already they were discussing directions. Feeling a long way from home, Rollo wished that Willoughby were by his side. And that he was a little older.

The first member of the household Rollo encountered did nothing to put his mind at rest. One minute, the front door was shut tight, and the next, it opened wide, half-filled by the most fragile-looking butler Rollo had ever seen.

"Sir?" he queried in a voice so wavery Rollo would not have been surprised if it was the last word he ever uttered.

"Rollo Duchamps-Avery," declared Rollo, stepping forward. And then added with a confidence he most certainly didn't feel, "Good day to you. I'm to be a houseguest of Lord Lyndon. My father is a dear friend of the duke."

There was a pregnant pause whilst the butler looked him up and down, then peered beyond him with the air of a man hoping another visitor might appear. Rollo squared his shoulders to make himself look more impressive. An enduring challenge when one was short of stature and as slender as a willow. Even more so at the end of a miserable three-day expedition.

"My father being Henry Orlando Fitzwilliam Albert Duchamps-Avery, the Earl of Rossingley," he elaborated firmly.

The servant squinted up at him, then nodded as if rearranging his expectations. "Ah. Then a very warm welcome to Goule Hall, sir. Do come this—"

A crashing sound rent the still air, as brief as it was sudden. As far as Rollo could tell, it emanated from somewhere deep inside the house.

"Good heavens!" He cupped a hand to his ear. "Was that a…" Another splintering noise stilled him.

"I'm Berridge, head butler here at Goule. At your service, sir."

Perhaps the butler was a trifle deaf.

Rollo tried again. "Forgive me, but that sounded awfully as…as if someone was pitching rocks through panes of glass?"

"Oh, no." Berridge ushered Rollo inside, relieving him of his hat and gloves. "That's just his lordship and his old toy soldiers in the drawing room. You'll soon get used to him and his ways."

Not a single part of that response allayed Rollo's concerns whatsoever. "His ways?"

"Yes, until you work some magic on him, obviously. Begging your pardon, sir, but you're a bit younger than I was expecting. Your man can bring your things inside the back way."

Greaves, a younger, fitter footman, showed Rollo up to his bedchamber, along two sets of stairs and various passages. His valises appeared at about the same time, and Greaves set about unpacking and arranging Rollo's belongings whilst Rollo drank in the monotonous views from the window. At least his room was decent and his mattress comfortable. Though the large oil painting hanging above the bed was atrocious — a bird of some description, or possibly a large-gilled fish. Either way, the poor creature was half gutted and in its death throes. *Dejected* declared the title in the lower left corner. Personally, if he were being disembowelled, Rollo's vocabulary would be far riper.

Curious art aside, the household staff seemed to know what they were about. More importantly, if Rollo overlooked the hall's generally forbidding air, nothing untoward suggested it was haunted.

"His lordship prefers to dine alone," Greaves explained as if that were a perfectly natural thing to do when one had an expected houseguest. Rollo didn't have much experience for comparison, although his father wouldn't have dreamed of it. "Though hopefully not for much longer, now you've arrived. Dinner will be brought to your chamber, sir, in about half an hour."

A little later, alone, washed, and in fresh clothing, Rollo steeled himself to count his blessings. The alternative was to burst into tears, and that just wouldn't do at all. Far too self-pitying. After all, his bedchamber was well-proportioned, and the water in his basin plentiful and warm. The door had a working lock, and his belly filled with tasty venison stew. He was in good health and much loved.

Regardless, a lonely tear trickled down his cheek. There was no shame in feeling homesick, he told himself as he wiped it away. Willoughby, Papa, and Kit would be in the informal cosy drawing room at Rossingley by now, reading, playing cards, or simply chewing over the matters of the day. And Rollo's favourite chair would be empty.

Determined to push those thoughts aside, he reflected instead on Berridge and Greaves's peculiar comments. *Work magic*? What on earth had Berridge meant by that? What were they expecting from Rollo? And playing with *toy soldiers*? Was his host wrong in the head?

As it was far too early to turn in for the night, Rollo rang for

Greaves. "I'd like to meet my host," he informed him. "If his lordship is available."

"Certainly." Greaves nodded, though Rollo detected hesitation. "Lord Lyndon generally retires to the drawing room after dinner. Allow me to escort you."

Once more, Rollo traipsed behind the footman along unfamiliar corridors. This time, Greaves pointed out a few useful interior landmarks along the way. When he came to a halt outside a forbidding oak door, he gestured to Rollo.

"You may enter, sir," he advised, clearly reluctant to do so himself. "I have no requirement to present you. His lordship doesn't stand on ceremony."

Nonetheless, after the man gave a small bow then left him loitering there alone, Rollo felt obliged to make some sort of effort. He couldn't simply barge in. Instead, he scratched on the half-opened door, a little feebly if he was being honest. Then, annoyed with himself, he scratched again more boldly. And as no response was forthcoming, he pushed it wide.

In most ways, the drawing room was unremarkable, much in keeping with the interior of the rest of Goule Hall. It seemed a little dated, perhaps, compared to stylish London drawing rooms, yet the heavy furniture and rich carpets still spoke of centuries of Ashington money. Uninspiring oils adorned the walls—portraits of ancestors in the main, though he spied another peculiar animal disembowelment hidden amongst them, probably by the same inept artist.

Feeling bold, Rollo took a pace forward. Though neither hot, cold, nor draughty, the room smelled of stale alcohol and used lamp oil. In anticipation of the last of the daylight, someone had lit a couple of oil lamps, and the embers of a fire burned in the grate. In all, it was reassuringly familiar. As a boy, Rollo had whiled away many an interminable hour in similar spaces belonging to his father's wide circle of acquaintances.

One feature, however, drew his eye and held it: A man, sprawled on a low settee and facing away from the doorway. His booted feet rested on a worn pouffe, and a tumbler of dark liquor clung precariously to a narrow armrest. Rollo jerked his head around, hoping Greaves might be hovering to perform the introductions, but the servant had vanished.

If the man occupying the settee was aware he had a visitor, he gave no sign. Frozen to the spot, Rollo found himself caught in a dilemma. Did he retreat and postpone presenting himself to his host until tomorrow? Or take another step forward and boldly announce his arrival?

"You're either in or out. There's no in between."

Rollo jumped with a little squeak of shock. He clapped his hand over his mouth so another didn't escape.

"Make a decision, boy. I don't care what. Just stop standing there like a bloody simpleton."

Lord Lyndon Fitzsimmons, Rollo presumed. Pritchard hadn't been wrong about the ill temper.

"My lord," he responded, voice quivering.

"Eh?" The man gave a vulgar sniff. "Speak up."

Rollo dug his fingertips into his palms and gritted his teeth. To beat a retreat now would look rather like cowardice. He was the son of a distinguished earl, for heaven's sake! A Duchamps-Avery, no less. Time to begin acting like one.

"My lord," he tried again, a fraction clearer.

In place of acknowledgement, Lord Lyndon brought the tumbler to his mouth and drank deeply.

"My lord," Rollo repeated. Much better. "Good evening to you. I'm…"

"Rossingley's pup." The words spilled over one another, thickened with whatever was in the glass. "Welcome to purgatory, pup."

Unsteadily, Lord Lyndon replaced the tumbler on the armrest, then lifted a child's wooden bow from his lap. Rollo watched, with mounting alarm, as Fitzsimmons plucked a slender arrow from a heap piled next to him. Fumbling, he notched it in the gut string, raised it vaguely level with his eye, pulled back, and fired. *Thwish!* A pewter toy soldier leaped into the air. Tumbling from the mantelpiece, it clattered to the floor and skidded to an ignoble death against the log basket.

Lord Lyndon emitted a satisfied belch. "And another loyal man fallen."

"Um…jolly good shot," remarked Rollo. Because what else could he say?

The next shot went wide, the arrow pinging into the plaster wall of the chimney breast before skittering to the floor. As did the next, issuing the remaining members of the battalion a reprieve, but at the cost of a small glass ornament.

"Oh!" yelped Rollo as a shard landed on his coat. He sprang back. "I say! Are…are you—"

A fourth arrow was clumsily notched. Hurriedly, Rollo retreated a few paces, unfamiliar uncertainty stealing his voice. That one was on target, as was the fifth. By the sixth, Rollo's apprehension had turned to puzzlement with a hint of annoyance. He didn't care for wanton destruction. Had Lord Lyndon forgotten he wasn't alone?

Yes, it seemed, because a second later, he lurched to his feet. At first, as he staggered over to the fireplace, Rollo assumed it was to pick up the fallen debris. Instead, Fitzsimmons ignored the crunching underfoot, widened his stance, and, after some rummaging around behind the fall of his breeches, proceeded to release a fountain of piss into the hearth.

Mortified, Rollo stared down at his feet, the sizzling of hot coals filling his ears and discomfort burning his cheeks. He was no angel himself, but this lord behaved like a heathen!

As a puff of black smoke spiralled out of the fireplace, Lord Lyndon turned to study Rollo from over his shoulder. "Care for some brandy, pup?" He waved in the general direction of a collection of decanters. "I take my liquor neat. One needs it, living here."

God, yes. The entire bottle. "No, but thank you, my lord. Sadly, I was not born into this world with a taste for hard spirits."

"No man ever was." Fitzsimmons belched. "But this world drives a man to it. You should persevere. There's no sound like the plop of brandy in a glass. And no feeling like that first powerful violent impact when it hits the mark below."

"I'll…um…take your word for it."

Rollo's hot gaze flickered up to where the uncouth lord still merrily voided his bladder into the fireplace. His linen-shirted back was broader than the duke's. He had a coarser shape all round, more muscled, like the form of a man who worked the land. The shirt clung to him, tighter than it should, as if it used to fit properly, as if he hadn't always been this way. Though, as Rollo's expert eye tracked down to his solid arse and thighs, he wagered the lord would still cut a fine figure in the *ton*. He'd have to improve his manners first, obviously, and do something with the wild, unruly mane of hair hanging in long coppery flames down his back. A decent cut would be a start.

Finished at last, the lord shook himself. Thankfully, he was safely tucked away when he turned to examine Rollo properly.

"Cat got your tongue, pup?"

"Well…yes. I'm…yes."

That Lord Lyndon and the duke were twins was evident, despite the contrasting hair and manners. But where the Duke of Ashington's dark eyes were warm and kind, verging on timid, his brother held Rollo trapped in two black, arrogant pools.

Fitzsimmons shrugged. "Your father always has enough to say for himself."

That was true, at least, and those mocking words inspired Rollo to a few of his own.

"He certainly does, my lord. Papa is never afraid to speak in the name of honesty and self-dignity against boorish and ungentlemanly behaviour and...and sheer bad form."

He raised himself to his full five feet six inches. "And I'm not a pup. I'm nineteen years of age, and I am Rollo Sebastian Lucien Duchamps-Avery, second son of Henry Orlando Fitzwilliam Albert Duchamps-Avery, the respected, eminent Eleventh Earl of Rossingley." He finished with a brusque nod, though his knees quaked. "And I assure you, my lord, I no more wish to impose upon your hospitality than you wish to have me here. So, on that note, I'll bid you a good night."

Chapter Three

My dearest Willoughby,

It is a harsh, proud landscape, Norfolk. Largely uncultivated, nothing but marshland and flat, flat peat bog, stretching right to the edges of the earth. This wild roughness does not ask to be loved, which is a jolly good thing as I detest it. In fact, every brown ditch and each muddy puddle serve to remind me of my host, Lord Lyndon, whom I have only cast eyes upon once. He has an interesting face, memorable rather than handsome, though his well-favoured features are of no consequence be-cause he is ill-mannered, uncouth, and untamed. Frankly, both the ton *and the even-tempered Duke of Ashington are better served without him. Notwithstanding, I shall endeavour to be unflappable, represent all that is good about the Duchamps-Averys, and make Papa proud. In a word, I am determined to draw out the best in him; I fear I shall go mad otherwise.*

PS I swear to God, the bell pull in the breakfast room is shaped like a hangman's noose. I am yet to use it.

PPS Your latest ode to Lavinia was your most divine attempt yet. Rhyming grind with behind in a poem to a lady? Scandalous! Needless to say, I adored it. It has been the only bright spot in a desperately dreary landscape.

Dear Papa. I am in good spirits and have settled in nicely. I am acquainting myself with the routines of the household. Lord Lyndon is proving to be an interesting host. He possesses an unrivalled sense of humour.

FIVE DAYS PASSED, during which his lordship was nowhere to be seen. Five interminable days of Rollo eating alone, mostly in his bed-chamber, interspersed with picking up and putting down books far too weighty and dull to command his attention. Sporadically, he wandered past the drawing room; once or twice, he even cupped his ear to the firmly closed door. He detected occasional *thwumps*, and despite his bold intentions, decided he was best off out of there, in case one of those inaccurate arrows should fly in his direction.

When restlessness and ennui got the better of him, he paced a route through the well-tended gardens, too fearful to venture much beyond. What with one gloomy marsh very much resembling another and spending too many hours with only his cheerless thoughts for company, Rollo entertained visions of finding himself utterly lost out there. Of dying young and lonely of exposure, thirst, and starvation. Or, even worse, being eaten by some ferocious, bog-dwelling monster.

The indoor servants provided his only means of company. Thankfully, there wasn't a tempting, comely male amongst them, except for the fresh-faced stable boy. Rollo made certain to give him a wide berth.

A fear surpassing even his dread of losing his way in the marshes was his father sending him to a place even more hellish than Norfolk. Such as Scotland, for instance.

Never very far away, the butler, Berridge, and Greaves, the footman, were almost overattentive to his needs. So much so that by the third day, Rollo had the distinct impression his movements were being closely monitored. Given his past demeanours, both at school and as a trouble-seeking lad frolicking around Rossingley, that wasn't an entirely new experience. But out here, it all felt very different. As if they were watching and waiting for him to do something. Though, for the life of him, what? There was *nothing* to do. Rollo was far too old to fall from a tree or set a fire under his bed. More to the point, if exile was to be a new line of punishment his father planned on meting out more often, then Rollo was determined to keep his halo well and truly polished at least until he reached his majority.

"Where…um…does his lordship disappear to every day?"

Rollo directed this question to Cook. So fed up with his own company, on day four, he decided he was still boyish enough to get away with hanging around the kitchen. A sound decision, as Cook rustled him up some hot scones and the comfiest seat by the stove. In fact, the exceptional standard of the food at Goule Hall was the sole positive to report back to Willoughby. Cook's sponge pudding even rivalled the one they used to serve at Eton. On consideration, the whole Goule Hall experience was reminiscent of the one endless term he spent at school without his twin, left behind and recovering from scarlet fever at home. Every letter Rollo penned had focused on food, his lumpy bed, and interminable days hunched in the library.

"His lordship is everywhere," Cook replied in an enigmatic, singularly unhelpful fashion. The fat spider casting a web across the corner of Rollo's bedchamber window (the second most interesting thing at Goule, after his absent host) was more forthcoming. Honestly, when

Rollo resolved to take his father's punishment like a man, he'd no idea it would be so…stagnating.

"And…um…everywhere would be…"

"Here and there. Doing good by folks, mostly."

Rollo almost choked on his buttered scone. "*Good? Really?*"

Cook smiled a gap-toothed smile at him. "I'll be bound. It occupies him most of his days."

A slip of a kitchen maid, stirring a big pot of something that smelled heavenly, looked over her shoulder and rolled her eyes. When Cook turned elsewhere, Rollo threw the girl a wink. She'd get nowhere batting her lashes at him, but allies were always useful.

"I'm surprised you're not spending more of your days together," Cook added.

"Are you?" Had she met Lord Lyndon? The man wielded poor temper like a broadsword.

"Oh, yes. The sooner you get started, the sooner we can all go back to how we were before and sleep easier in our beds."

Get started with what? Planning my trip back home?

Rollo contemplated her words, mesmerised by the fleshy woggle of her upper arm as she beat a bowl of eggs into submission. Their own cook at Rossingley was an alarmingly angled woman, while Goule's cook was all soft curves and rosy cheeks, exactly as a cook should be. The homesick part of him wanted to curl up in her lap and let her rock him to sleep.

"If you don't mind my asking, what is it about his lordship that's keeping you awake?" *And what am I expected to do about it?*

"Because he's not himself, is he, sir? Hasn't been for nigh on several years. Any fool can sense that."

"Oh. Oh, yes. I see." *About as clearly as a blind beggar*, he nearly added. "If you don't mind my asking, how is he…um…normally?"

"Well," she began, in the way of someone who had been dying to be asked. "He was a scamp the likes of which I'd never seen when he was so high." She indicated a tallness not far from Rollo's actual height, then smiled dreamily. Evidently, Rollo had alighted upon her favourite topic. "The family spent every summer here when the boys were nippers. Young Lord Lyndon was always getting under my skirts, pinching all manner of sweet treats from the larder when my back was turned. He liked his liquorice, so he did. He'd stare up at me with those big brown eyes. Like a bleedin' spaniel he was. Never refused him anything."

"And now?" Rollo prompted.

"Oh, I still can't say no to him." The woman nursed a *tendre*, that much was clear. Or for the old Lord Lyndon, at least.

"But..."

She sighed. "But now, nothing keeps him occupied except tending the gardens and doing good by others."

"*He* tends the gardens?" Rollo spluttered. "His lordship?"

"As much as anyone else," she confirmed with a note of pride. "Best blooms in the county, I reckon. Born to work the soil, he was."

"But...but..." Rollo shook his head. Was the fabled Ashington wealth built on a lie? "Doesn't Lord Lyndon employ people for that sort of thing?"

"He does, but it's him that decides what goes where. And he's always happy to get his hands dirty. It gets him away from that desk and out of that drawing room."

"Oh."

Now Rollo's opinion of the man was even more confused. Reconciling the oaf who pissed in the fireplace as the architect behind the design of those wonderful flowerbeds, never mind *doing good by folks* and once being a sweet, innocent boy was headache-inducing.

"Why...why does he spend so much time alone in the drawing room? Why...why—" He searched for the correct diplomatic phrase.

"Why is he so…so solitary?"

Cook's gaze flicked across to the girl who had ceased all pretence that she wasn't listening, and her face turned stony. "Since he came back here for good, there are all sorts of stories. Some folks reckon he fell in love and had his suit rejected. Or got too fond of the liquor. His father, bless his soul, liked a tipple too. Or maybe him and his brother fell out. You know what twins be like."

"I do," Rollo exclaimed. "I'm one myself. But…" He and Willoughby had never quarrelled. They'd wrestled each other, built forts, hunted pirates, and kept each other's secrets as if cast from stone, but never quarrelled. Aside from penning execrable poetry, Willoughby was the finest twin brother a chap could ever wish for.

"And what do you believe, Cook?"

Again, her eyes shifted to the girl. "It's not my business to say."

Rollo waited. In his experience, that phrase usually heralded the opinion of someone who had very much decided something *was* their business.

Nodding to herself, Cook wiped her hands on a towel. "I think the poor soul never recovered from what happened down at the lake."

Chapter Four

LYNDON LEANED AGAINST the window frame, watching the young man map out the perimeter of the gardens, on foot, for the second time that day. Slight of build and fair as a wisp of barley, from this distance the Honourable Rollo Duchamps-Avery cut an insubstantial figure. He plodded with his head down, occasionally brushing at the sedge on either side of him with a stick. If he sought exercise, and if Lyndon was more inclined to graciousness, then he'd have informed him there was an excellent, circular route leading from the stables over to Beccles Ridge and back. But the youth seemed reluctant to wander too far. Goodness knew why; the marshland didn't fight back. And Goule was a far cry from London. There were no pickpockets or doxy's lying in wait to catch the unwary. Loitering about the house and gardens, occasionally prodding at the undergrowth with a stick, he was about as much use as a square wheel on a curricle.

Pup. The lad hadn't liked being called that one bit, and had told Lyndon so, for all he was frit. He'd stamped his prettily booted foot and flashed his prettily coloured eyes. The spirited Earl of Rossingley's son, through and through. A force to be reckoned with a few years from now, once his soft edges had been filed away.

His visitor stooped to smell a summer bloom, the movement efficient and elegant. He had a pretty nose too. In fact, now he thought about it, Duchamps-Avery was far too extravagantly pretty all round. Like a damned chit.

And then he disappeared out of sight, behind a hedge. A sudden thought curdled Lyndon's belly. "He doesn't ever wander as far as the lake, does he?"

"No, my lord," answered Berridge, tidying away the shaving things. Lyndon didn't care for a valet; in London he hadn't the funds, and now, even though his brother, Benedict, had restored the entirety of his generous income, he'd since discovered he valued his privacy too much.

"Greaves says he rarely strays from the gardens."

"Good. If he enquires, suggest to our visitor that he takes a stroll somewhere else."

"Yes, my lord." Berridge hesitated. "The gentleman guest doesn't know the area at all. He seems a bit fearful of the marshes. Perhaps… perhaps you might accompany him sometime?"

"So that he can interrogate me?"

"I couldn't possibly comment, my lord."

Lyndon smiled at his wily old butler. They had both guessed the real reason behind Benedict prompting this boy's visit. Two years had elapsed since Lyndon's banishment to Goule, and he had not encouraged visitors. Once Benedict had restored his allowance, Lyndon could have returned to the *ton* whenever he liked. But that would have required courage — courage to look his brother in the eye, to apologise, and admit they shared the same inclinations. Inclinations he'd used against Benedict, to torment and shame him, to almost bring down the Fitzsimmons name.

How could Lyndon acknowledge all that, when he hardly had the courage to admit it to himself?

Nonetheless, kindly, forgiving Benedict and their younger brother, Francis, would be fretting.

"This fresh-faced Rollo Duchamps-Avery makes a perfect, innocent spy, don't you think?"

As Berridge sought a tactful response, Lyndon waved him away. "You can't comment, blah-blah. I know. But this little scheme has clever Rossingley's fingerprints all over it."

"Yes, my lord."

If he were still a gambling man, Lyndon would wager the only person who hadn't pieced the scheme together was Rossingley's boy himself. Well, true to form, Lyndon wouldn't make it easy for them.

He waited a few minutes, but the boy didn't reappear.

Lyndon turned from the window. "I can take things from here, Berridge. Thank you."

"Will you be requiring Fury saddled up to visit Mr Elliot?"

"Certainly. Thank you."

*

BY THE SUMMER of his second year sequestered in Norfolk — latterly being of his own volition — Lord Lyndon Fitzsimmons's daily routines had been well established. Ablute, breakfast, pay a visit to Will, take a constitutional through the grounds in the company of his sketch pad, then dinner in his bedchamber. Followed by brandy-induced oblivion. Sometimes, he deviated and supped port wine, yielding the same result.

For the first few weeks after Lyndon's expulsion from society, Benedict had sent a man to keep tabs on him, to check he hadn't turned Goule into a den of iniquity, or that he wasn't, as many would have wished, stone-cold dead in a ditch. Given Lyndon's reputation as a former rakehell of the highest order, no doubt Benedict expected his spy to return laden with tales of prodigal womanizing, lavish debts, and stories of Lyndon selling off the family heirlooms to settle them.

Though it pained Lyndon to admit, his brother's punishment had been a wise one. Enforced solitude and the bracing Norfolk air, coupled with the sick humiliation of admitting all his failings to his oldest friend, Will Elliot, underlined what Lyndon already knew and had desperately tried to fight. That causing merry hell wasn't for him. Depraved vices and scheming to bring Benedict down didn't banish his demons any more successfully than pious prayers and abstinence. Whatever peace and absolution he craved were not to be found in the gambling houses, racetracks, and ballrooms of London. Nor had he found them in bawdy house beds or with his nose between the breasts of buxom ladies. Much to his chagrin.

Thus, after a series of dull reports, Benedict's man ceased coming.

*

FOR A SHAMEFUL period immediately after the lake accident, Lyndon had struggled to look Will square in the eye. His breathing would become unbearable, as if by merely looking at what had befallen Will had shattered every single one of his ribs.

Because, all too freshly, Lyndon remembered his beloved farm boy as he was before the accident, when Will's long, thin face and direct gaze used to sit atop a firm and active body. A boy who thought nothing of tossing a dozen bales of hay into a cart without pause for breath, or ploughing four furlongs in between supper and nightfall. He remembered when Will's lips would smother Lyndon's own with deep, desperate kisses.

These days, Will's fine body was ugly and twisted. A lifeless arm hung loosely across his lap. Spit dribbled down his sagging chin. The physician surmised he'd banged his head and bled into his cranium, whilst the village healer insisted he'd *upset the balance of the veil,* whatever that meant. Yet despite all that, Lyndon now had no trouble looking at him at all. The other, more finely made man was still inside, of course, his clever mind miraculously intact. But with a heart as broken as Lyndon's. Though they never spoke of it.

"Hot weather's coming," Will slurred, by way of greeting. Will's speech had markedly improved over the decade or more since the accident, or maybe Lyndon had become more adept at deciphering his liquid vowels. "There was a heavy dag at dawn."

"I'll have to take your word for it," answered Lyndon with a smile. "At that godforsaken hour, I was still examining my eyelids."

Crossing the simple room, he laid a hand on Will's thin shoulder then bent and kissed him, once on each cheek, and then, as fondly, on his smooth forehead. Straightening, he arranged his offerings on a tray, poured a mug of ale, and brought both closer to where Will was propped awkwardly against a heap of cushions.

"Some of Cook's leek soup," Lyndon declared, setting the tray down. He eased Will into a better position. "And an excellent cheese."

Messily, Will began feeding himself. Knowing better than to offer assistance, Lyndon prodded the fire, then set about arranging candles for later, for when the light grew dim.

"I hear you've got a visitor up at the house."

For a person never receiving his own, Will was mightily well informed. Lyndon paid his housemaid's sister a few shillings to keep a daily eye on him. He might as well put a full-page advert in the Norfolk Chronicle.

"Yes. The Earl of Rossingley's youngest son," Lyndon confirmed. "Sent by Benedict to spy on me." *To cure me. Cheer me. Save me.* Or something like that. "Got himself in a scrape at home; he thinks he's been sent away as punishment. But I know his father and my brother better than that."

"Kind-hearted," managed Will, stumbling over the words. "Your brother."

"Yes," Lyndon said shortly. "Yes, you're right."

Will slurped and chomped through his food. The sound didn't bother Lyndon. In fact, he scarcely registered it. Saliva pooled at the corner of his old friend's mouth, and every few minutes Lyndon dabbed at it with a cloth. That didn't revolt him either, though guilt rolled through him that he'd once recoiled from it. A more agonising way to pass the meal would have been remembering how a once-perfect Will would nibble on strawberries, the sweet juice coating his lips. And how he'd once shared a handful of them with Lyndon. And how his grey eyes had fixed intently on Lyndon's mouth as he took the soft fruit, then kissed him around it.

Ah, God. Lyndon dabbed again, wiping a dribble of soup from Will's shirt. Going over that mawkish, fustian nonsense was of use to neither man nor beast. In a moment, he'd clear away the dishes, help Will use the pot, then settle him into bed for a rest. Some afternoons, Lyndon read aloud to him. Will struggled to turn the pages and had an insatiable desire for gothic novels. Lyndon regularly replenished his library accordingly. Today, however, Will was too weary. His turnips needed a hoe — Lyndon would get on with that for an hour or so instead. The sun shone, he had an afternoon to kill, and for all he was a lord, Lyndon had two arms and two legs in full working order. He'd put them to good use.

And so the afternoon trudged onward, much like the last, with manual labour keeping the circling blue devils at bay. Perhaps Lyndon didn't need to be saved. Didn't need to be rehabilitated in polite company. Perhaps this was his role in life, his penance for evermore. To be the mad, bad brother, living out in the wilds. Drinking alone, surrounded by fine gardens and amateur sketches, with no one to show them off to because nobody cared. Cleaning spit from an invalid's mouth. Shooting at pewter soldiers. Who on earth imagined a lad barely out of short trousers could alter any of that?

Chapter Five

ON THE MORNING of the sixth day, Rollo delved into his meagre stores of bravery to wander as far as the Fitzsimmons family's private chapel. According to Cook, no one had set foot in the place for years, even though it boasted a rare collection of ancient hymnals. As he caught himself almost looking forward to this venture, Rollo reflected on how far he'd sunk.

English summertime was having one of those dilemma days, the weather gods undecided whether to bathe the land in blazing sunshine or blanket it in cloud. Twice, Rollo had removed his topcoat only to reshoulder it, tearing a shirt sleeve on an errant bramble in the process.

The tangle of paths seemed as unconvinced as to where they were heading as the weather. When trees obscured the ugly gables of Goule Hall, Rollo prayed he'd memorised sufficient landmarks to find a route back. Nothing too terrible could befall him, could it, whilst on the way to a place of worship?

Once more, Goule didn't fail in its ability to disappoint. The chapel was small and lonely and, if the sinewy ropes of ivy clawing their way around the heavy oak door had any say in the matter, going quietly back to nature. Towering blue-marbled elms shaded it from the sunlight, stretching their arms in benediction over a small gathering of the Goule dead, marked by a row of humble crosses. No mighty Fitzsimmons were buried here in this boneyard reserved for countryfolk — the thatchers, gardeners, cooks, and maids — only simple remembrances of simple lives hard won and ultimately forgotten, now sunken into the ground and buried under a web of weeds.

As Rollo picked his way to the door, two larger grave markers caught his eye. A little off to the side, they stood out as newer and cleaner than the rest and adorned with real headstones to boot. Larger mounds of earth rose up, the surrounding grass plucked of foliage. Squatting, he rested his hand against the cool limestone to inspect the weathered inscriptions. *Henry George Elliot. 1774-1812. Mary Elliot. 1776-1811. Together with God, for eternity.*

Rollo's skin prickled with momentary sadness. Both relatively young and, judging from the neat banks of earth, still loved and remembered, more than ten years hence. In a sombre mood, he made his way inside the cool, modest chapel, still wondering what the loving couple had succumbed to. Terminal boredom, perhaps, stuck living out here, with only ancient *hymnals* for interest. Five of them lay pinned in glass cases but falling apart anyhow. Oh, the thrill of it.

*

A GIRL WAS busy in his bedchamber when Rollo returned, shaking out the sheets and turning back his bed. He recognised her as the same one from the kitchen. *Lucy*, he recalled. More importantly, she was someone with whom to converse.

"Begging your pardon, sir." She bobbed a neat curtsy. "I can come back and finish, sir."

"Don't rush on my account," said Rollo, taking up a stance by the window. "Carry on. I don't mind."

The clouds from earlier had scudded to wherever clouds went, leaving behind nothing but a washed clean expanse of blue sky. A warm breeze floated through the window as nature set herself up for one of those long summer evenings created for dancing, picnicking, and romantic assignations.

Alas, not for Rollo. Nor for the poor couple buried under the sod.

"I was hoping to catch someone," he said. "There's a rent in my shirt sleeve. From the brambles down by the chapel."

As was proper, he'd replaced his topcoat upon entering the house. He gestured towards the area of his upper arm. "Here."

"I can mend that for you, sir." Another bob of the head as Lucy smoothed the bedsheet flat.

"A proper Jill of all trades." Rollo smiled at her. "I'd be much obliged. Thank you. But I don't want to keep you from your kitchen duties. I'd hate for you to get into trouble with Cook."

She tucked in a linen corner with practised efficiency. "Kitchen work, cleaning, mending. I do it all, sir. There's not that many of us manage the place. No need, seeing as there's only his lordship most of the time. He's not one for entertaining."

"So I've gathered. More's the pity." He hesitated, then added, "He's a rum fellow."

Unfortunately, Lucy did not rise to the bait.

"His lordship only keeps one riding horse and a matched pair for the carriage," she prattled on. "So the stable lad, Jack, he does the gardens too." At this, Rollo detected a faint flush to her cheeks. "He's Mr Greaves's son," she added.

"The gardens are a credit to him." Rollo treated her to his most winning smile and was rewarded with another blush. "And to his lordship."

"That they are, sir. His lordship often lets Jack's cousin help, even though he's not right in the head. Pays him too." She busied herself plumping a pillow. "He's kind like that. Mr Berridge, in charge, he's been here since he was a nipper. His da was head butler before him, when the old duke was alive, and the Fitzsimmons used to use this as a summer place. Most nobs would have got rid by now, seeing as he's too old to do things proper. But our lord would never. Cook and Mr Greaves have been here seems like forever too."

"Is that the extent of the staff?" Even for a rarely used home, it seemed a bit thin.

"A couple of girls come from the village to help clean and launder once a week," she explained. "And an under footman, too, to help out Mr Berridge. But as I said, nobody visits here except for his lordship." A small frown creased her pretty features. "He's never stayed this long before though. Used to come with friends for parties and the like. Shooting parties—a great big rowdy crowd of them. He's stopped with all that, looks like."

"Is he a fair master?" Rollo returned his gaze to the window, attempting not to seem too invested. Not only was the elusive, solitary Lord Lyndon Fitzsimmons by far the most fascinating thing about the place, but by Goule standards, this was fast becoming a conversation of epic proportions. At this rate, he'd have some content worth reading in his twice-weekly letters to Willoughby.

"I should say so," said Lucy. "Though I don't know any other; I've been here since I turned fourteen. But Berridge and Cook are as loyal to him as stars to the night. Won't hear a word said against him. Worry about him every hour, too, the pair of them; Berridge says he won't retire until he's seen him settled."

"Do you?" Rollo asked, curiosity getting the better of him. "Worry about him? Are you as faithful too?"

Perhaps Lucy had no idea there were nobles out there who didn't squander their evenings shooting at pewter soldiers and drinking the county dry. Dozens of them, decent chaps who rode and clubbed and boxed and courted ladies. Even a few like his own father, a noble accomplishing all of those things whilst discreetly living alongside another male.

She contemplated him. "I wouldn't go so far as to say I'd take a pistol shot for him, like Berridge would. But he's a good man, as far as nobs go. So I daresay I wouldn't mind him being a bit happier, like." Hesitating a fraction, she added, "They all hoped you'd come and talk some sense into him. Except..."

"Except I'm a disappointment," Rollo finished for her, smiling again. "Too young. Not worldly enough. They were hoping for someone to take him in hand. It's all right. I'm not offended. In fact, I'm in full agreement. I don't think I'm the man for the job either."

Lucy sighed. "We'll just have to put up with his unhappiness a bit longer then, won't we? Mr Berridge will never retire."

"What did his lordship used to be like?" Rollo pressed. "Was he really as charming as Cook says?"

Lucy nodded. "When I was a nipper, he was all that and some. Everyone said so. And even though Lord Benedict was good and kind and never put a boot wrong, Lord Lyndon was always the servant's favourite. He had a way with him, see. Used to coax the birds from the trees. The local lasses didn't stand a chance; they all used to fancy him rotten. Him and young Will were here, there, and everywhere, getting into scrapes, then getting out of them on their wits."

"Will?" Rollo turned from the window, just as a bell rang out in the hallway. "Who's Will?"

"A friend. Local lad." Her head jerked up at the bell. "Goodness, it's that time already. That'll be Cook calling. She'll have my guts for garters if she hears I've been gossiping. Now, sir, if you leave that shirt out, I'll see it gets mended."

Chapter Six

My dearest Willoughby. Wish me luck. I'm venturing into the drawing room. For armour, I have only my fortitude and my wits. If I am an absent correspondent over the coming days, send for reinforcements!

Dear Papa. Lord Lyndon and I pass most of our evenings in the drawing room. He has an insatiable interest in the first regiment of the Coldstream Guards. Fascinating!

WITH A VAGUE feeling of déjà vu mixed with a much more well-defined trepidation, Rollo scratched at the drawing room door. Inside, all was quiet. Perhaps his lordship wasn't there this evening. That would be typical of Rollo's luck — the first occasion he plucked up the courage to join his host was the one evening his host was elsewhere. In which case, he'd sit awhile with a book. If nothing else, it would be an evening spent contemplating a different set of four walls.

The back of Lord Lyndon's head greeted him, his long wavy hair falling about his shoulders like sheets of rust. So absorbed in whatever he was doing, the man hadn't heard Rollo open the door, obliging Rollo to fake a ridiculous little polite cough. A flurry of activity ensued as Lord Lyndon thrust whatever occupied him under a cushion, yet not before Rollo caught a glimpse of paper and a crayon.

"Good evening, my lord." He prayed his voice sounded surer of itself out loud than it did in his head. "Might I join you in a glass?"

"Does Papa allow it?" answered his lordship gruffly.

"I think we established my age at our last meeting, my lord."

Whilst maturity was not on Rollo's side, his steely aristocratic forebears were. He absolutely would not be cowed even though his palms perspired and his tone tended towards the waspish, especially when anxious, like now. Rollo had a feeling Lord Lyndon wasn't much for waspish men. Too bad. Another evening spent alone in his room might turn Rollo stark raving mad.

Lord Lyndon shrugged as if it mattered not what Rollo did, which Rollo suspected wasn't far from the truth. Daringly, he helped himself to a snifter of port; the lesser of the two evils on offer. Even more daring, he took a seat, uninvited, on the settee opposite his host.

In excruciating silence, they both drank. Rollo tried not to peer at a corner of foolscap sticking out from under a cushion whilst his host toyed with the little wooden bow in his lap. A neat row of pewter foot soldiers on the mantel mutely observed them both. Sipping cautiously, Rollo reflected on small mercies. He had not been used as target practice, and Fitzsimmons wasn't watering the fireplace.

Fully aware it was the sort of dull pronouncement a maiden aunt might make, but unable to bear the silence any longer, Rollo offered, "May I say this is a very nicely proportioned room, my lord. It is well-positioned to catch the evening light." His gaze landed on a harpsichord half hidden under an embroidered throw. "Do you play?"

Lord Lyndon's dark eyes followed the direction of his gaze. "No. Nor does anyone who comes here. Instrument's as useless as tits on a bull."

If his lordship was endeavouring to be especially boorish, then he was succeeding. He swigged from his glass, making no move to wipe away the trickle of red liquid running down his chin. Then he put the empty glass down and picked up the bow properly, testing the string.

"How do you occupy your time here at Goule, my lord, if I may be so forward as to enquire? Do you read? You have a splendid library."

"No."

"What about keeping abreast of newssheets and such?"

"No. Full of half-truths and lies."

At breakfast, Rollo's father could frequently be heard bemoaning the same. "Then your time must be taken up with estate matters."

"No."

"Billiards?"

"No."

"Do you ride? Fence? Box?" An air of exasperation crept into Rollo's voice. Really, the man was quite insufferable.

"Fencing is a sport for simpering foreign dandies." He swigged again. "I ride women, and I box inquisitive young pups."

Fine. If that was the game his lordship wanted to play, then Rollo would prove himself a worthwhile adversary. "Goodness, then you must be terribly bored," he countered, "Seeing as there is a paucity of both here at Goule. No wonder you've resorted to child's play."

That provoked a reaction at least, in the form of an almighty put-upon sigh. "Remind me how long I have to tolerate your presence?"

"Another ten weeks, two days, and —" Rollo glanced at the long-case clock. " —approximately eleven hours assuming I make an early start." He threw Lord Lyndon a wry look. "Believe me, you're not the only one counting."

"Have you filed your first report yet?"

"What? What report?"

Lord Lyndon took another long swallow. "Your report on my welfare. You've been sent here to poke around. To spy on me. On behalf of my brother."

"I've been sent here to do nothing of the sort," Rollo retorted, flummoxed. "I'm here to reflect on my own poor behaviour, repent, and vow to do better. A lesson I've already absorbed." He wrinkled his brow. "Another ten weeks feels quite excessive."

"You send out regular letters though." Lord Lyndon sounded as if he'd caught Rollo out. He raked his fingers through his pile of arrows, deciding which to select. They all looked the same to Rollo, and by that, he meant equally lethal. "Twice weekly. To your brother and your father. In addition to penning one to my brother, the duke."

And this man had the audacity to accuse Rollo of being a spy? "What of it? I merely wrote to His Grace thanking him for his generosity in affording me this wonderful opportunity to spend my summer basking in your exquisite company. Regarding my father and brother, my letters—"

"Reports," cut in his lordship emphatically. "Not letters."

"Letters," Rollo insisted. "To my brother I write dull, endless letters, filled with nothing. I describe Norfolk, in other words. And to my father, I pretend that I am having a marvellous stay. He tolerates most sentiments; however, lamenting one's privileged situation when less fortunate people are starving in the streets is the exception."

It occurred to Rollo that the four walls of his bedchamber weren't so terrible after all. Except that when he made to rise, he suddenly found himself at the menacing, pointy end of a nocked arrow. Level with the blunt fletching, one of Lord Lyndon's half-closed, heavy-lidded eyes lined the thing up directly at him.

"Stop that at once! I'm not one of your pewter soldiers!"

"No." His gaze swivelled towards the mantel, then back to Rollo. "I have no need to question their integrity."

"Nor mine." Fuelled with rage, Rollo raised himself to his full, unimpressive height and addressed the man, doing his darndest to block out the weapon now fixed directly at the centre of his forehead. His heart beat fit to burst out of his chest.

"My lord," he began, his voice trembling. "I am a Duchamps-Avery. From a long line of distinguished Duchamps-Averys. My family can be traced back to the Domesday Book and far beyond. Whilst I am not the wisest, oldest, largest, or strongest of my line, I have the heart of a lion and the backbone of a…another very large creature. You will not accuse me of spying on my host, you will not piss in the fireplace in my company, you will not question my integrity, and most of all, you will not point that beastly, pathetic children's weapon between my eyes.

"I have no idea why you are so obnoxiously miserable, nor why you waste your every evening alone in this drawing room in a drunken haze. Frankly, I do not care. But I shall tell you this. As God as my witness, how a man chooses to run his affairs is his own private business. And whilst I believe you to be of questionable character and barely clinging to sound reason, my father and your brother shall never hear of it."

And on that note, he flounced out. Before his knees gave way.

Chapter Seven

My dearest Willoughby. I fear Fitzsimmons is quite insane, and it might be catching, given that I'm voluntarily returning to his lair tonight. The man is a ferocious beast – I'm playing with veritable fire. I'll have no one but myself to blame if I get burned. Yet there are secrets to be unearthed here at Goule, Fitzsimmons the most intriguing of them all. Only by provoking him will he reveal his true self.

Papa. Lord Lyndon has a riveting interest in archery. And an impressive collection of hand-carved arrows.

SUMMONING EVERY OUNCE of nerve, Rollo once more positioned himself on the settee, with Lord Lyndon slumped in his usual chair opposite.

"Waving the bow at you was poor form," his host announced,

directing this microscopic sliver of insight to the fireplace. Rollo waited for an apology to follow. It did not come.

"Waving?" he prompted. "Or purposefully lining me up in your sights?"

"The latter." Lord Lyndon sounded as far from apologetic as a man could get. "I do not relish house guests, and I was half-cut."

"Your explanation is a poor excuse," replied Rollo coldly. "Though I suppose one must amuse oneself somehow here in Norfolk. What with the never-ending…nothingness. It's enough to drive one to insanity."

"At the risk of being a contrarian—" Lord Lyndon took a measured sip of his brandy. "—I find the loneliness and solitude here at Goule clears my mind. Norfolk possesses a soaring majesty. Perhaps you are too much of a simpleton to see it."

The man was toying with him, Rollo realised. Needling was a game. If Rollo said black, his host would counter with white. Lord Lyndon, a rich, bored aristocrat, for reasons unbeknownst, harboured a deep-seated anger towards Rollo, the fireplace, toy pewter soldiers, and possibly anything and anybody else with the temerity to approach him. The man was lonely, unloved, and unloving. And with that flash of insight, and the secure knowledge that Rollo was none of those things, his habitual boldness returned.

"Forgive me for being so brash, but I don't believe you," he said. "I believe you tell yourself that story. But the truth of the matter is, like me, you've been exiled to this godforsaken place thanks to even poorer form up in the *ton*. And whereas I am swallowing my bitter pill with good grace, my lord, you are mightily furious about it."

"Exiled?" The man gave a coarse puff of laughter. "Hardly. And Goule Hall is *my* bloody house! My brother may be the largest landowner in England, pup, but he has no say in the running of these few hundred acres. Our grandfather entailed this particular property to me!"

"Then I stand corrected." Rollo nodded primly. "But deduce that your grandfather can't have been terribly fond of you."

"On the contrary again," answered Lord Lyndon with a note of triumph. "Goule was his favourite of all our family residences, and he wanted it to be used. And…and enjoyed." He made an exasperated grunting noise. "And I have no idea why I am explaining this when frankly it is none of your concern. And, whilst we're at it, take it from me—you have not been sent here for deflowering a virginal butler."

"A stable boy," Rollo corrected. "And many years after his flower first came into blossom, I assure you."

Harrumphing, Lord Lyndon tossed back his brandy. "Exactly. You're here because Benedict requested that I accept your presence as a favour. In order for you to spy on me. And I'd wager you lack the bodily strength to deflower a dandelion."

"Attacking my slender physique is a low blow, my lord. My smallness is beyond my control, just as your height and admirable musculature are beyond yours." As Lord Lyndon's expression turned to smugness, Rollo clenched his fists. "Perhaps your vicious tongue is too. As for the accusation of spying, I believe we established, yesterday evening, that I am doing no such thing. Foremost, because you are not interesting enough. But answer me this, my lord. If you aren't exiled and your brother would welcome you back to society, then why the devil are you still here?"

That dart hit home. "I could have left months ago," Lord Lyndon insisted haughtily. In his lap, his hands twitched, no doubt seeking his bow. "I'm here by choice, I assure you."

"If that is the case, to what purpose?"

"None of your concern."

The lord stuck out his bottom lip as he examined his nails. He then poured himself another generous drink, not offering the same to Rollo. After that, he toyed with the bow and huffed a couple of times. The whole pantomime reminded Rollo of himself, except when he was much younger, and Pritchard or Papa scolded him for some terribly minor incursion and filled him with impotent frustrat—

"You're sulking, aren't you?" Rollo burst out. He nodded rapidly. "Yes, that's it. That's why you're still here. For the last eighteen months or longer, you've been sulking. The longest sulk in the history of sulks."

"I am not!"

"Yes, you are. Even now. Sulking!"

"No, I'm not!" Lord Lyndon gave a withering snort. "At this precise moment, I'm waiting for violent urges to subside by being quiet and observant. For instance, I'm quietly observing how you move. Incessantly." He waggled a finger at Rollo. "Seeing as one is in the mood for questions, pup, answer me this. Are you merely a fidget, or are you suffering a dose of the clap?"

That was rich coming from a man famous for his bedchamber exploits. Or at least he was according to Pritchard's version of events, which were always subject to embellishment. But instead of snapping back with a healthy retort, Rollo bit his tongue. He would not take the bait. He would not allow Lord Lyndon to bring out the worst in him. Instead, he would rise above, like the air in one of Cook's light sponges, and in the spirit of a true Duchamps-Avery.

Rollo wasn't above dangling a little bait himself though.

"In that case, if you are not sulking, as you insist, then I shall have to guess as to why—of your own volition—you have chosen to lay low here in Norfolk."

Pressing a finger to his lips, Rollo pretended to ponder. "Did you swive a stable boy too? Is there a law written down somewhere that the correct punishment for swiving a stable boy is a three-month stretch of solitude in Norfolk? It's perfectly understandable if you did. There's something irresistible, don't you find, about those tight breeches, the close confines of a sweaty dark stall, the…

"Certainly not."

"Perhaps the groom, then? You prefer your men slightly older?"

"No." An uncomfortable expression flitted across Lord Lyndon's handsome features that Rollo hadn't seen before. "My carnal desires do not lie in that direction. Not at all. And they never have. Not one bit. I am a ladies' man, through and through."

Lord Lyndon's big hand clenched around his brandy glass. His cheeks flamed so brightly they almost matched the vibrant tone of his hair.

Most interesting, Rollo thought.

"My lord doth protest too much," he goaded.

"Poppycock! And it is only by dint of your papa's wealth and breeding that you dare make such a boast yourself. You know as well as I that sodomy is illegal, abhorrent, abnormal, and unnatural."

Rollo grinned at him. "Jolly good fun though." He received a foul look. "And nothing is illegal until you get caught. My papa taught me that."

A glimmer of amusement crossed the lord's lips. If Rollo had blinked, he'd have missed it.

"Perhaps the gardener's wife, then?" Rollo pressed, wanting to entice it again. "Yes, surely that's it. You strike one as a man of more...*vanilla* tastes, yes? Plain, unadventurous."

"An attraction to the appropriate sex does not make one unadventurous." Lord Lyndon's expression returned to its usual glare. "And I do not employ a gardener."

Rollo answered with a grin. "That's right. I gather your comely stable boy tends the gardens. He sounds like a chap in possession of several talents. Perhaps I should pop along and introduce myself. Wouldn't want to step on your toes though."

"Put your bravado away, pup," Fitzsimmons's rich, throaty bass warned. "Your dear papa would tan your hide. And we both know it."

Lord Lyndon's eyebrows furrowed into a single line, and Rollo's loins stirred. Perhaps he'd teased him enough for one evening. Though there was something undeniably attractive about hearing that crabby voice growl 'tan your hide'.

Rollo moved swiftly on. "The ostler, then? His wife? His mother? His grandmother?"

At Lord Lyndon's increasingly murderous stare, he clamped a hand over his mouth, as if aghast, and spoke in a hushed whisper. "I'm aware how lonely one can get out here. But—and as you insist you are an adventurer, not—surely…not one of the…the horses?"

Lord Lyndon's throat generated another rumbling snarl that, frankly, a man had no place making outside of a bedchamber. Not that Rollo was disposed to pointing that out.

"Not all delinquencies in life revolve around damned swiving, pup."

"Don't they?" Rollo batted his eyelashes at him. "Oh, righty-ho. In that case, I'll change tack. How about I run through all the possible—"

The lord made a frustrated moan somewhere between a sigh and a despairing lament. "If only your silence were as voluble as your voice, Duchamps-Avery. Did your dear papa not school you in the benefits of it?"

"He taught me that one should never be afraid to ask questions and have an enquiring mind."

"And evidently an interrupting one too." Lord Lyndon frowned again. It was like watching Zeus gathering thunderclouds. "Listen to me carefully, young man, as I am not in the habit of repeating myself.

"I came to stay here at Goule, *exiled*, as you insist on dramatically referring to it, as the culmination of several misadventures over the preceding few years which served to slight the good Fitzsimmons name. Beginning with a duel in 1821, whereupon I limited myself to removing a slice of gristle from the Marquess of Fording's left ear. It was that or end his life. A little later the same year, I ran a curricle into Lord Horsham's privet hedge. Behind which Lady Horsham was having an illicit liaison with Sir John Pimperne. Their amour did not survive his broken foot. The following winter, I bilked Tuffy Bannister out of one hundred pounds. In the spring of the same year, I bilked him out of two hundred more and used it during the autumn to drink White's brandy stores dry. Furthermore, two years ago, I stole a quantity of Ashington silver, then pawned it to pay off gambling debts. In addition, I fed my brother's prize stallion a bucket of sand to ensure it lost at Ascot, but not before placing heavy bets against it winning. For a hippophile such as Benedict, that was the final nail in my coffin."

Rollo, undeniably impressed, was hungry for more. "Sounds like you came here for a jolly good rest after all that lot." If his companion would stop pointing his silly little bow at him and treating him like an imbecile, they might get on splendidly. "So, during your sojourn here, you've turned over a new leaf?"

"Not quite." Lord Lyndon threw him a threatening smile, dark as a demon. "I'm currently plotting another dastardly act."

"Ooh! Really?"

"Yes. My most glorious yet."

Goodness, the man was beautiful when he smiled. Even when it had an evil twist to it.

"Am I to be privy?"

"Most certainly. In fact, you have a starring role." The lord smiled again, and this time, Rollo's cock gave a little twitch in response. "I'm going to shoot an annoying young man. With this child's bow and arrow. Through the heart. Because he won't. Stop. Pestering."

A sixth sense whispered to Rollo that he'd poked the devil enough for one night. Uncurling himself from the settee, noting the manner in which Lord Lyndon fleetingly appraised him before looking away, and not sure what to make of it, he performed a mocking bow.

"No mention of swiving though, my lord, amongst your long list of antics. Very interesting. No wonder you're so damned miserable."

And on that note, he scarpered before he could receive a sharp arrow in the backside.

Chapter Eight

ABHORRENT, ABNORMAL, AND *unnatural*. A story Lyndon told himself for years. A sour lie that didn't improve with repetition. And no matter how hard he tried, he failed to squash the truth.

Ah, William, all those years ago, what did you start?

Stretched out in his bed with nothing but bitter memories for company, Lyndon sighed. Images of the Duchamps-Avery boy's slim thighs, crossing and uncrossing, played on his mind and thickened his cock, though he'd die rather than succumb to relieving the ache. Damned fidget, the pup was forever drawing attention to every bleeding lean inch of them, dredging up every single one of the urges Lyndon tried to suppress.

The boy was a sodomite. He'd freely admitted as much and flirted like an alley cat, his flirtation loosely wrapped up as taunting. He flaunted his effeminacy, and Lyndon had found it thrilling. The boy himself was thrilling, from his long pale fingers pressed against lips ripe as spring blooms, to his pale glittery eyes, so like those of his acerbic, clever papa's, yet softer, more forgiving. Kinder.

Naturally, Lyndon had not flirted back.

*

A FEW DAYS later, not content with hounding Lyndon's evenings in the drawing room, the confounded boy appeared in the bloody study. During the middle of the afternoon! Lyndon didn't recall inviting him to join him there and made that perfectly clear by picking up his bow and declaring war on the 1st Royal Dragoons, temporarily on a reconnaissance mission on the fifth shelf of the bookcase.

"You have the run of the whole bloody hall, you know." His grumbles landed on deaf ears.

According to Berridge, Duchamps-Avery had spent the morning pruning the roses on the front lawn — as if they weren't already perfectly pruned. Dressed in a mulberry silk banyan of all things — the bloody tulip — paired with mulberry kidskin gloves. Thank the lord, he'd changed into a sky-coloured topcoat, which was an improvement, though tailored within an inch of its life, mind. The youth was slim as a crayon. Both hands around his waist would have Lyndon's fingertips joining at the back like a bloody corseted chit.

A yellow rose — one of Lyndon's perfect yellow roses — sat in his buttonhole. Bloody dandy. Berridge reported he'd requested ratafia with his supper of an evening, Lyndon's expensive French liquor apparently not to his liking. Ratafia was a stupid drink, a prissy, made-up concoction for folks who couldn't stomach their brandy neat.

Ignoring his uninvited visitor as he arranged those damned spindly legs on Lyndon's window seat, Lyndon shot six infantrymen dead and mortally wounded Major General William Ponsonby.

He wagered the youth would last five minutes before interrupting his military advances. He managed seven.

"Missed," Duchamps-Avery declared with undeniable satisfaction in his tone as an arrow pinged off the side of the fourth shelf and clattered to the floor. "Too far to the left."

"Are you suggesting I swing farther to the right?" Lyndon waved the bow in his general direction. To his credit, the boy didn't flinch.

"I'm suggesting that you attack opponents who have the capability to fight back. Or perhaps, while away your hours on this earth doing something less…idle? Less…lazy? Laziness is the indolent parent of boredom, Papa always says."

Papa had rather a lot to say about everything. "I'm not lazy. On the contrary. I'm simply incredibly motivated to do nothing. And anyhow, you'll be pleased to hear that, at two o'clock, we have visitors joining us for tea. Indolence and boredom will seem like El Dorado, in comparison. Trust me."

The news had the young fool positively wriggling with excitement. "Visitors? Who? Who?"

"A dull, local squire named Simpson. Damp-handed sort of fellow, though rich as Croesus. Thinks his pots of blunt give him carte blanche to call us friends. New money, of course. No family to speak of, and a dreadful northern accent. The man has worked for his fortune. Coal mining or some such grubby ghastliness."

"Papa owns several northern cotton mills. He says one should never condemn another on the basis of their lowly birth, and that there's nothing wrong with—"

"Save me from bleeding hearts, pup." Trust bloody Rossingley to be all for the advancement of the great unwashed. "Even worse than Simpson's inability to correctly pronounce simple words in everyday parlance, he's bringing along his unmarried, bovine daughters. So we can forget a boozy lunch followed by a few hands of baccarat. We'll be nibbling on cucumber sandwiches, drowning in a vat of tea, and discussing the latest hat styles coming out of Paris this season."

He suspected his guest could make an informed contribution to conversations regarding the latter.

"Ooh! Unmarried!" exclaimed Duchamps-Avery. "How thrilling. Is their father hoping you develop a *tendre* for one?"

Lyndon smiled pityingly. Hell would freeze over first, especially as overnight, he seemed to have come down with a full-blown *tendre* for Duchamps-Avery's lean, taut thighs.

"He's hoping, yes. I also suspect he's heard I have an aristocratic young guest and is hoping you develop similar feelings for the other." Lyndon flicked his gaze over the elegant brocade hemming the youth's immaculate coat. Goule Hall had never hosted such a dainty, effeminate creature, and he included women amongst his reckoning. "The man's an eternal optimist."

Duchamps-Avery clapped his hands with joy. "This spectacle, I can't wait to see. The mysterious, brooding Lord Lyndon being wooed. And wooing in return. Tell me, do you growl at the ladies like an irate bear *before* you impress them with your archery skills, or do you save that treat until after?"

Lyndon deigned not to respond. And anyhow, one wasn't required. The boy was too busy examining his attire.

"Perhaps a different cravat," Duchamps-Avery declared, plucking at a floral necktie that wouldn't have been out of place on stage at the Paris Opera. "Something brighter. And my emerald topcoat. With the little gold swirls of piping, here and here." He nodded, satisfied, then fixed those irritatingly clear eyes on Lyndon. "What say you, my lord?"

Lyndon harrumphed in the manner of his father and grandfather before him. "I say I never trust a man who dresses like a concubine at breakfast and then changes into a highwayman's outfit at tea."

The pup laughed at that, flashing his showy, perfect teeth, which had not been Lyndon's intention at all. And then, with the grace of a damned gazelle, the pup raised himself from the settee.

"You and your little jokes, Lord Lyndon. You hide your humour under a bushel, you know."

Those gazelle legs propelled him to the door.

Alas, the words flew from Lyndon's mouth before he had chance to put a halt to them. "Why do you insist on walking like that?"

"Like what?" The boy turned back, more a fluid pirouette than a turn.

Lyndon huffed again. "Like...like..."

He made an ineffectual gesture with his hand, not sure what he was encompassing but wishing to buggery he'd kept his trap shut and that a wash of crimson wasn't climbing his cheeks. "Like a damned pantomime horse," he growled.

Then he snatched up his bow and decimated the commander of the 39th Foot Regiment.

*

OVERLY TALL AND spikily thin, Reginald Simpson had the lugubrious air of a haunted pencil. Naturally, young Rollo had to position himself on the settee close to him, contrasting like a dazzling ray of bleeding sunshine. Albeit sunshine mixed with a sharp gust of hurricane, a gust most often directed in Lyndon's direction whenever he said something the pup deemed insufficiently gracious.

Even more infuriatingly, the boy appeared to find Simpson's company charming. Especially when the girls' father insisted on relating all the local goings-on in Goule village as if Lyndon had expressed avid interest. Which he most certainly never had.

"The vicar has had terrible lumbago," Simpson commented, "for over a sennight."

"Poor man," responded Lyndon with all the empathy of a footman wielding a fly swat.

"My grandfather always found oil of lavender rather effective,"

Duchamps-Avery piped up. "Used to rub it all over. Liberally. I've even tried it myself, once or twice. It can't be beat, massaged in deep after an overenthusiastic, hard ride."

"Why doesn't that surprise me," Lyndon drawled and, for good measure, scowled.

Ignoring him, Duchamps-Avery showed all of his excellent teeth again. One of the daughters fanned herself rapidly. "Pass on the message to the vicar that if it's too difficult to procure in these parts, then I can ask my brother, Willoughby, to send some. It would be no trouble at all, isn't that right, Lord Lyndon? One must do one's best for the clergy, must we not?"

"Ugh."

A lengthy discourse on calfskin versus kidskin gloves followed, a topic dull enough to bore Lyndon's breeches off. As his numerous and uninvited guests conversed amongst themselves, or rather, spoke over one another, he made himself terribly busy with Cook's moist seed cake.

"How fares Will Elliot?" enquired Mr Simpson in a hushed tone. Naturally, within half a second, the room fell quiet enough to hear a bumblebee belch. "Is he..." The man paused, no doubt suddenly aware of the tension ratcheting up in his host's jaw. His daughters schooled their features into appropriately sympathetic expressions, whilst bloody Duchamps-Avery cocked his head like an inquisitive magpie.

"He's fine," Lyndon declared stoutly, and Mr Simpson and his daughters audibly exhaled. "Absolutely fine. Coping admirably as usual. Nothing to report, as ever, nothing at all."

"Who is William Elliot, may I ask?" enquired Duchamps-Avery.

"A friend," said Lyndon shortly, in a tone not far from murderous. His personal relationship with Will Elliot was not for public consumption. The fact that the man scarcely left his home for fear of being scorned by the local ignoramuses was nobody's business but Will's. Whilst the Simpsons didn't fall into that category, their polite interest remained unwelcome.

"You've made an excellent job of his vegetable patch, my lord, if I may be so bold," chirruped one of the daughters. Nanette? Nancy? Noni? Something uninspiring beginning with N. "We rode past only yesterday and halted to admire it. It is a credit to you that you roll up your sleeves, where lesser and less important men would—"

"It's nothing," Lyndon lied, as if he hadn't nigh on broken his back hoeing the half acre of stony ground before planting more potatoes, carrots, and turnips. Although he'd snap his spine in two before rubbing it with oil of bleeding lavender. With a bit of luck, they'd change the subject. The pup was far too attentive. "Trifling work of minutes, nothing to it, nothing at all."

From the eager lean of his body, Duchamps-Avery was building up to probe further. Fortunately, Simpson got there first with a change of subject.

"I wish to take advantage of this luncheon," he said, "by bringing you up to date on the progress of our charitable works, my lord."

Lyndon scowled. Any subject except that. "Really?" he said through gritted teeth. If Duchamps-Avery listened any harder, cocking his head like that, he'd have his own back problems. "Are financial forecasts a suitable topic for young ladies?"

"My daughters are fully versed in all of my charitable and business endeavours, my lord," answered Simpson, gazing proudly at his offspring. "So that they may use my money to continue to expand them further, independent of their husbands' wishes, when I fall from my mortal coil. And whether, at that point, my girls are married or not."

"My papa would be thrilled to hear you say that, Mr Simpson," chipped in the pup. "He is well-versed in the writings of Mary Wollstonecraft and is a firm supporter of the advancement of the rights of women." Duchamps-Avery clasped his delicate little hands together as if he'd just anointed the entire Simpson clan with holy water. "But pray,

Mr Simpson, do tell me more about your charitable venture. And you say Lord Lyndon is involved?"

Lyndon had never seen Simpson's drab features so animated.

"His lordship has campaigned tirelessly," Simpson said. "Without his backing, the whole project would never have got off the ground!"

"Nonsense," Lyndon cut in. "My small involvement in the whole thing barely warrants mentioning. I was simply fulfilling my Christian and civic duty. Anyone in my position would have done the same."

"But with respect, my lord," countered Simpson, "no one did, did they? For five years, I sought permission to build this institution, cap in hand to every councilman, clergyman, and squire this side of Ely. None came forward until you. Your modesty is an example to us all."

Lyndon's attempt at a self-deprecating laugh sounded more like a snarl. Not that any of his guests noticed.

"I'm hanging on the edge of my seat, Mr Simpson," simpered an agog Duchamps-Avery. "Pray, what is it that my humble host has done to warrant such fulsome praise so that I, too, may congratulate him?"

"Ugh." Lyndon drank deeply from his wine.

"You are no doubt unacquainted with the ways of rural Norfolk, Mr Duchamps-Avery," began Simpson. "But the folks around these parts are very set in their ways. Most still believe that to be permanently debilitated or lose one's abilities to reason are afflictions from God."

This pronouncement received a round of despairing head shakes from his daughters.

"Punishment, as it were!" Simpson continued. "And the Church isn't much help in promoting the truth. Only a man as locally respected as Lord Lyndon could persuade the council and clergy that these poor creatures haven't been sent a divine message or some such nonsense but are deserving of our charity. Thanks to his immeasurable aid, my mission has now dug the foundations and put up the outer walls on a property at the edge of Norwich town. We will be able to house twenty-five of the poor and afflicted with the proper care they require."

Duchamps-Avery's pretty little mouth hung open, his eyes out on stalks. His infernal papa and Benedict would have wind of it by the morrow evening at the latest. As he probed Simpson for more details, and Simpson readily obliged, Lyndon miserably picked at the crumbs on his plate. The last thing he wanted — deserved — from his brother was praise. Not after everything he'd done; Lyndon could build fifty such buildings with his own bare hands, and it wouldn't be enough.

Give him a conversation about hat ribbons and calfskin gloves any day.

Thank heavens Mr Simpson made no further mention of William, the spur for the whole damned thing. And thank heavens for seed cake.

Finally, Simpson ceased his unnecessary eulogising, and Duchamps-Avery remembered his manners sufficiently to twist in his seat and engage the shyest of the Simpson girls.

"Tell me, Miss Nancy, how does this enchanting corner of Norfolk fare regarding summer diversions?" He threw her another of his beguiling smiles, and to Lyndon's alarm, he experienced a prickling of resentment that it wasn't in his direction. "Parties, dances, and such? You and your dear sister strike me as precisely the sort of charming ladies a young swell like me should be escorting to them."

More gratuitous pleasantness ensued as Miss Nancy and the other one cooed and sighed and waxed lyrical about local knitting societies and an operation to rescue a litter of abandoned kittens. Lyndon tore at a third helping of seed cake, deciding it was too dry after all, even though his cook was the best in the county, and it wasn't dry at all, just…

"A summer dance here in Goule village? This Saturday? How marvellous! Of course, Lord Lyndon and I would be delighted to accompany you both. In fact, nothing would give his lordship more pleasure. We were only saying at supper yesterday that we really should make more of these lovely, long, warm evenings. Weren't we, Fitz?"

Fitz? *Fitz*? Supper? The damned cheek! A swift current of wrath swirled inside Lyndon's head as four sets of eyes turned expectantly towards him. One set gleefully twinkled like bloody stars. *Fitz*? Never mind taking a pop at Duchamps-Avery with blunted toy arrows. Once their dear guests departed, the pup was going to find himself blasted to hell and back with his father's old musket. Lyndon didn't do summer dances — nor winter ones, when it came to that — and he most definitely didn't accompany unmarried provincial squire's daughters anywhere.

"Well, Fitz?" the bloody Duchamps-Avery boy repeated, his stupidly pretty eyes still lit up like Vauxhall pleasure gardens. Eyes used to getting their own way. "Shall we escort these fine ladies to the dance and show them how it's done?"

Mr Simpson's sombre mien instantly rearranged itself into the sort of self-satisfied expression only seen on the faces of fathers of daughters anticipating not one but two wedding breakfasts.

"Ugh," Lyndon managed.

"Sorry, Fitz, old chap." Duchamps-Avery aimed the full force of that impossible smile in Lyndon's direction. "Didn't quite catch that."

Lyndon's jaw tightened. Every morsel of his being projected his displeasure. How was this boy so utterly oblivious?

"Yes," he barked, making the ladies start. "Yes," he repeated in a more moderate tone. "The summer dance."

Chapter Nine

My dearest Willoughby. You'd think we were preparing to walk the plank, not attend a country dance. Fitzsimmons is mooching about the place as if I've stolen his favourite battallion.

PS Thank you for the verse. I take issue with "She is lovely as the hawthorn tree. And with a glance could shatter me." I adore you, Willoughby, with every fibre of my being, I really do. But have you smelled hawthorn? It's reminiscent of a decomposing corpse. Surely Lavinia's parfum is an improvement on that!

Papa. Our social whirl continues apace with a village dance.

BELOW STAIRS, EXCITEMENT for the forthcoming fête was palpable. And in striking contrast to the all-pervasive, funereal whiff upstairs, where Lord Lyndon stalked the corridors with a face like a cat licking piss from a nettle. When not baking, steaming, broiling, and doing whatever else was required to produce such excellent dinners, Lucy and Cook could be found trimming their Sunday-best outfits with gaudy ribbons and practicing the quadrille with two brooms as makeshift partners.

Tucked into the comfiest kitchen chair with his boots propped on a pair of firedogs, Rollo was a more than willing seamstress.

"So, everybody in Goule attends this dance, yes?" With a length of lemon-yellow satin draped across his lap, he made short work of banding a straw hat.

"And all the folks from the cottages up on Beccles Ridge too. Proper grand affair it is, seeing as the Fitzsimmons foot the bill. They have done since my da was a boy."

"By 'the Fitzsimmons', do you mean Lord Lyndon?"

"Since he took up living here full time these last two years, yes. His father before him — " She pulled a face. "He wasn't much for looking after the village, the old duke — no one liked him very much. And Her Grace was even worse. But he always coughed up for that."

In comparison, his son sounded generous to a fault. "So, the Fitzsimmons are always in attendance?"

Cook shook her head. "The old Duke and Duchess, never, even if they were summering at Goule. And his lordship hasn't been seen at the dance since he were a lad." She lifted her head from her stitching to give Rollo a toothy smile. "I wasn't sure you were up to the job when I met you, sir, begging your pardon. But you've started putting the sunshine back in him. You've got a way about you, if you don't mind my saying."

"I have done nothing, Cook. It's all down to Mr Simpson's visit."

The woman shook her head. "He's been more like his old self all this past week since you've been joining him after dinner. He likes the company."

Rollo chuckled, recalling yesterday evening's hour after dinner. For the first quarter, Lord Lyndon pretended Rollo wasn't there. For the second, he poked at the fire whilst grumbling about the smoke his efforts produced, and for the remaining half hour, greeted every single one of Rollo's attempts at civilised discourse with a pained noise and a look of intense annoyance. He also watched very carefully when Rollo removed his coat (thanks to the roaring fire) and loosened his cravat, though Rollo kept those fascinating details to himself.

"I'm afraid you have been misinformed, Cook. We spar continually. I assure you he loathes me like young fruit facing a late frost."

His audience was unimpressed. "All I'm saying is, he's got much more of a spring in his step. He's beset by the blue devils if he spends too much time on his own or with Mr Elliot."

That name had cropped up at dinner with the Simpsons. "Who is this Mr Elliot? Mr Simpson asked after his welfare."

"An old friend of his." Cook and Lucy exchanged a look, and Cook crossed herself. "His lordship looks out for him."

"Will he be at the dance too?"

Lucy smirked. "Not unless they move the dance to his front parlour."

"Hush, girl." Cook gave the housemaid a disapproving look. "It's bad luck to gossip about the afflicted. My da used to run down old Dick Cooper something rotten — he had a hunchback — and my da had two fits of the apoplexy and died. So there."

Rollo could have pointed out that a case study of one was hardly scientific proof. But judging from the sage manner in which Lucy chipped in with a similar tale about her now deceased aunt and a boy with six toes on both feet, he held his tongue.

"That rose pink is delightful, Lucy," he remarked instead as she held her handiwork up against her. "You shall be the belle of the ball!" And then, because naughtiness ran through his veins, added, "Will Jack, the stable lad, be attending this marvellous festivity?"

"Yes, he will," interrupted Cook. "And he'll be keeping his wandering hands to himself unless he wants to feel my rolling pin up against his arse."

Kings and paupers shared more common ground than a *ton* soirée and a Norfolk country dance. For a start, the rural affair promised to be ten times more fun. And dazzlingly bright. The *ton*'s latest, muted sartorial styles had not reached Norfolk, as evidenced by the array of ladies' costumes, patched and decorated from any of the previous five decades. Most menfolk stuck to Sunday best—dark breeches and clean linen. In his lavender tailcoat, intricately detailed at the collar and cuffs, Rollo was easily the brightest peacock on show.

"Lucy, my dear, you are a vision," he exclaimed, taking the serving maid's arm. In lieu of a smart London ballroom, they were crammed into a dusty barn festooned with so many green boughs and garlands of summer blooms, Rollo felt he'd been transported back to the orangery at Rossingley. "Young Jack has not dragged his eyes away since we danced that polka."

"And I'd have danced it with him if Cook wasn't bleeding watching me like a hawk."

Rollo pouted in pretend dismay. "Then I shall insist she partner me for the jig, sweep her over to the far side of the barn, and distract her with a thorough ravaging." He waggled his eyebrows at her. "Whilst you are ravaged by young Jack."

He delivered a flouncy little bow, making her giggle. "But first, I must have a stern word with our dear patron, Lord Lyndon. He appears to have entirely forgotten that the purpose of a dance is to dance and make merry."

They both looked over to where Fitzsimmons loomed beside a pillar, a little like a pillar himself. Rollo heaved a sigh. Since arriving at the dance, two things had become perfectly clear. One: Lord Lyndon danced as stiffly as a longcase clock and with similar levels of enthusiasm. Two: Lord Lyndon was still sulking, fond of rout cakes, and so many shades of devilishly handsome dressed head to toe in forbidding black, that when his polished mahogany eyes, flecked with bronze, landed on Rollo, he forgot to breathe. Fitzsimmons wore formal attire the way others wore their own skin, the fabric moulded to his masculine frame as if affixed there by God's hand. A few of the ladies present weren't immune either. A whole cluster trailed in his wake, not that the man took the slightest notice.

"My lord," Rollo began as he sidled up to him. "As fetching as you are, slouched against that foliage, you might use the next dance as an opportunity to practise the art of conversation. An area of allure in which, sadly, you lack proficiency."

Lord Lyndon treated him to the sort of intense glower that would make a lesser mortal crumble (and by that Rollo included everybody not blessed with his superior Duchamps-Avery lineage). On Rollo, it had quite the reverse effect, especially coming from this man whom God had constructed, as far as Rollo could tell, from a lush sheet of granite.

"I'm not against talking to people, in general," Lord Lyndon declared with his usual lazy disdain. "I simply prefer to interact as infrequently as possible. My tongue has a regrettable tendency to utter words best left unsaid. Is there something wrong with that, pup?"

"Nothing at all, my lord. But do you have to make it quite so obvious? You almost smiled two days ago. It took ten years off your age! That furrowed groove between your eyebrows entirely disappeared." Rollo indicated to the perfectly smooth spot between his own brows. "If you repeat the action again tonight, you could easily pass yourself off as no older than thirty years."

The furrow deepened. "I *am* no older than bloody thirty years! I entered my thirty-first year not two months ago!"

Rollo's blue eyes widened as he feigned shock. Gadzooks, this man's nerves were easy to prod. "Good heavens! Did you really?"

"Yes!"

Safe from bows and arrows, Rollo treated him to a condescending pat on the arm. "Then you're a mere stripling, Fitz. Go forth! Drink, dance, and woo. You're the guest of honour! Put on a show!"

A tick started in the lord's strong jaw. "I am not a performing seal. And, unless your cheeks want to feel the back of my hand, I strongly suggest you refrain from calling me Fitz."

Rollo hooted with laughter. "That all depends on which cheeks you have in mind. *Fitz*."

He was still chortling to himself as he weaved through the crowds in search of Cook, his next dance partner, and refreshment. As fun as needling the lord was, it mostly served to remind him how handsome he was, how infuriating he was, and how Rollo would relish crawling across that broad chest—no doubt covered in as much delicious, thick, reddish hair as the man's whiskers promised.

"Is this what you're looking for?" A pleasant-looking chap, cleanly but shabbily dressed, proffered a cup of punch. "Take one. I have two."

"Gladly," Rollo replied. "And thank you, sir. Much obliged. I would drink it with you, except I have an important engagement with the dancefloor and that delightful lady over there."

He pointed to where Cook appeared to be giving Lucy a piece of her mind, then turned back to the man.

"Perhaps later, then," the man answered.

As his knowing gaze raked over Rollo, it occurred to him that he might gain a little more from this evening than simply sore feet and some new friends. Even though a little voice at the back of his mind warned him his father wouldn't approve, and discretion had been drummed into him since his very first episode with the stable boy. But then his father was at Rossingley, wasn't he? Three days ride away from a rural Norfolk barn dance. What he didn't know couldn't hurt him.

"Yes, perhaps we could share a cup later," Rollo agreed. "Somewhere...um...quieter?"

The man's lips twisted into a slow smile. "I might just hold you to that."

Being flung around the dancefloor in Cook's sturdy hold reminded Rollo of when he was a young boy, placing his feet on his father's bigger, booted ones and whirling across the ballroom at Rossingley whilst one of his father's chums bashed out a tune on the harpsichord. He thirstily tossed back his new friend's fruit punch, already quite giddy from it. After keeping Cook occupied for two dances, he moved on to the Simpson girls, who were a veritable delight. As were their cheery coterie of pals, especially as they pursued curmudgeonly Lord Lyndon with the determination of a pack of starving terriers cleaning out a henhouse. They all had first names like Ann and Emma and Jane and Mary. And Ann and Ann and Ann. He quite lost track after his third cup of punch, though it mattered not a jot.

Rollo himself wasn't immune, especially as he'd been grandly introduced to them all, but when it came down to it, the main prize was the wealthy, brooding lord of Goule Hall.

"He's frightfully dark, isn't he?" gasped Nancy as Rollo swung her in a pirouette. "I am not sure there is a single lady on this earth capable of taming him."

"He is untameable," agreed Rollo. He glanced up to where Fitzsimmons stood, arms folded across his magnificent chest, and quite alone. He'd watched their progress across the dancefloor since the dance had begun, his sulky gaze stroking across Rollo's skin like a living, visceral thing. He shivered. "Ensnaring him would be like caging a panther or a lion. Turn your back on him for a second, and he'd devour you whole." *How wonderful.*

Nancy sighed. "Though my father wishes it other, I fear he is not the marrying kind. Perhaps that is a blessed relief."

*

WITH ALL HIS dancing duties thoroughly executed, Rollo stepped outside for air. Resting his back against the barn wall, he breathed in the cool night. As much as he adored a decent rout, he was melting from the fearsome heat.

After a minute, another fellow appeared, no doubt bent on the same. They nodded to each other, and Rollo started. What with Cook and Fitz and entertaining the girls, he'd quite forgotten the man who'd offered him a refreshing punch.

"Jolly warm in there, isn't it?" Rollo declared, dabbing at his forehead with his silk pocket square.

"That it is," agreed the chap, doing the same with a cotton rag. After a beat, he added, "Enough to make a man want to unload a layer or two."

"Quite."

There followed a pregnant pause during which their eyes met and held as if the man had posed a question and now waited for Rollo to answer more fully.

Rollo's belly lurched with a flutter of anticipation. One of *those* types of questions. Probing and suggestive but wrapped in a bland pleasantry, just in case the situation had been misjudged. For all he was young, Rollo was an old hand at this game. The man's appraising glance transcended both social class and location, a glance understood by Rossingley stable boys, Rollo's Latin master at Eton (before pushing Rollo to his knees), and thruppenny bit mollies, as well as high *ton* nobs. Men sharing Rollo's tastes were everywhere and ripe for the picking if one knew the signs. And this country chap had properly mastered the art with just the right degree of heat not to attract unwanted attention. An unspoken invitation.

Behind his trouser fastening, Rollo's cock swelled, a pleasant reminder that, since the stable boy incident, one of his basic human requirements had been wholly overlooked.

"There's a nice little copse up that slope yonder, you know," the man murmured with a jerk of his chin. Very deliberately, he tucked his rag away, drawing far more attention to the pocket near his groin than strictly necessary. "Views stretching across the Broads for miles. With a lovely cool breeze coming over the ridge."

"Local, are you?" Rollo queried.

"Familiar with this land as my own name," the man confirmed. "Always a fresh breeze up in that copse. Quiet, too."

Rollo knew better than to ask that name, in the same way he knew better than to offer his own. That wasn't how these things worked.

His mouth watering, Rollo drank in his new friend's spade-like workman's hands and the strength in his thick, scarred forearms. What with Lord Lyndon looking good enough to eat but regrettably not on the menu, and more weeks stretching ahead than he cared to record without the relief of another man's attentions, only a fool would look this gift horse in the mouth.

"Is that so?" he replied. "How appealing."

The man nodded. "I reckon." He stared straight ahead, a few coarse whiskers on his chin outlined against the moonlight. Though possessed of a fine, strong shape, his profile was far from classical; at some point his nose must have been broken and never reset. Pockmarks littered his cheeks, and he had the thick ears of a fighter. In summary, he was nowhere near as tempting as a certain ill-tempered lord, but comely enough.

And Rollo was desperate. "A popular beauty spot, is it?"

"Nope." The man made a deliberate popping sound on the *p*, drawing Rollo's attention to his moist, ripe lips. "Nobbut me goes there this time of night."

Neither spoke after that, the gauntlet well and truly laid down. Now it was simply a matter of waiting for the other to make the first move. The man smoothed his hair whilst Rollo adjusted his cuffs. Then, without turning, the man subtly inclined his head.

"I might take a look now," he said, "before the sun totally sets. It only takes three or four minutes to get there." He doffed his cap. "Good evening to you, sir."

"And to you I extend the same," offered Rollo pleasantly.

Rollo's gaze was lazy, his body relaxed and unmoving, as the man, hands thrust in his pockets, sauntered away from him. When he was nearly out of earshot, Rollo called, "Three to four minutes, you say? I might follow and take a closer look."

As darkness descended, he shadowed at a distance, taking his sweet time. For all the world looking like a man with nothing more on his mind than seeking cooler air or a quiet spot for a leisurely piss. Ahead, the man ascended the shallow grassy slope, his sturdy arse filling his breeches. By now, Rollo's cock was leading the way, and he gave it a discreet rub. Summer country dances had a lot to commend themselves, he decided.

"*Psst.*"

Waiting behind the first thicket, the man was of the same mind. With a low chuckle, he grabbed Rollo and hauled him up against him. "I like me a bit of class. Chance don't come along very often." His rough voice filled with need as he ran one of his coarse hands over Rollo's bulge, giving it a firm squeeze. "And the class around these parts is rarely as pretty as you."

"Then you're in luck, my friend," breathed Rollo, his own hands busy at the man's breeches. "And if you care to look, you'll find that I'm pretty everywhere." His hand landed on its objective — thick and stubby and ready to go.

God, he'd missed this. As his senses filled with the bitter scent of sweat mixed with arousal, he ground against the warmth of a firm thigh. The length of the man's hard cock thrust into Rollo's hand; he hummed his approval as the man's thick fingers eagerly pushed inside Rollo's drawers. Out of both necessity and desire, it would be quick. Already Rollo's mind had placed his shaft against the man's, already he imagined their warm, wanting bodies pressed up close, that big, callused hand clasped around the both of them. If he held back his crisis, then the man might even be willing to drop to his knees and —

An unexpected flurry of cold air gusted against Rollo's privates. At the same moment, a strong hand clamped around the scruff of his neck, slicing through his shriek of protest and nearly lifting him off the ground. Like a rag doll, Rollo was tossed aside.

With an indignant yelp, he staggered back into the undergrowth. "Hey! What—"

He tripped, landing on his arse with a hard thud.

"Ouch! What...what the blazes?"

A few feet away in the dark, a short scuffle ensued. From his agonised yell, Rollo's new countryman friend was on the losing end of it. A thumping noise, a harsh curse, another pained grunt, and it was all over.

"Be gone with you," a deep voice thundered. An all too familiar one, unbidden, unwelcome, and unneeded. Not that its owner gave two shakes of a duck's tail about that.

Another sharp thump heralded another pained curse, and then Rollo's brief companion was off, crashing through the brush and swearing as if he'd trodden on an ant's nest.

"And if you show your face up at the Hall," the voice thundered again, "there'll be hell to pay!"

A profound quiet ensued, during which Rollo recovered his breathing, picked spikey blades of grass and twigs from the seat of his trousers, then crossly clambered to his feet. Dismayed, humiliated, and damned livid enough to kill came nowhere near to mining the depth of his annoyance.

"Gods teeth!" he hissed, seeing as the other was in no hurry. "Care to explain why you chose to spoil my evening's diversions?"

Fitzsimmons loomed over him, still impeccably attired, not a hair out of place, and hardly out of breath. "You have dirt and a leaf on your sleeve, pup," he observed and made to brush at it.

Rollo batted him away. "Because you put it there, you damned bacon-brained half-wit." He prodded Fitzsimmons in the chest. It was like prodding a sheet of iron. "Answer the damned question."

The lord fixed him with a blunt, haughty stare. "You and that man were about to commit acts unseemly at a country dance."

"Which is precisely why I left the country dance and traipsed up to this bloody thicket, a good way beyond the country dance. And even if I was, what business is it of yours anyway?"

"You…you belong to me. You're in my charge; therefore, you're my business."

Rollo glared, long and hard, at this great hulking creature, his smug arms folded across his substantial smug chest and his thick, expressive, smug eyebrows knitted together like two fearsome devil horns. Underneath them, flat brown eyes glared back at Rollo with a cool intensity the younger man failed to match. If Fitzsimmons had presented a smaller target, Rollo would have bunched up his fist and planted him a facer, right on his self-satisfied sneer of a mouth. Instead, he smoothed his hair and straightened his cravat, trying for all the world to behave like a chap in the company of nobody but his valet.

"I'm nineteen years of age, my lord," he spat with as much contempt as he could muster. "I'm in no one's charge, and I belong to nobody. And you're not much of a Latin scholar."

For the briefest of seconds, the lord appeared nonplussed, allowing Rollo to conjure up his most chilly stare, worthy of his father's repertoire.

"If you were," Rollo explained, "you'd know that interruptus *follows* coitus, and not the other way around."

As a cutting riposte, it fell horribly short of the Earl of Rossingley's icy standards, but for a young man with his now very limp cock waving in the breeze, it could have been a lot worse. Satisfied he'd removed most of the foliage from his coat, Rollo poked himself back inside, taking his own sweet time. The lord's eyes flicked down, then just as swiftly flicked away. The faintest tinge of colour stole across his cheeks, and Rollo's hand stilled at the fall of his trousers. *You belong to me*, he'd said. Surely...surely not.

"Oh, I see," Rollo said softly. "It's like that."

A dry twig cracked underfoot as he took a pace closer to where Lord Lyndon stood rooted to the spot. As if pulled by a magnet, the lord's dark eyes again dropped to where Rollo's fingers still loitered.

"You like what you see, Fitz?"

"I see nothing," he snapped, "except a foxed young fool about to shame his father's good name."

"My father's good name is none of your business either." Employing the same wide-eyed innocent stare he'd used with great success on the countryman not fifteen minutes earlier, Rollo gave himself a slow, deliberate rub. "So why do you appear so discomfited, my lord? Am I to believe you want some of this too?"

Lord Lyndon shoved him away, hard enough to send him careening back into the undergrowth. "You're a damned fool, pup, messing with a man like Ralph Hart, and not fifty yards from where any person could spot you."

"A man like what? Oh...you mean..." Recovering his balance, Rollo gave a sly wink. "...a man that you...have a *familiarity* with too? Is that it? My sincere apologies if I'm trespassing on your territory, *Fitz*."

"Your insinuations are insanity, boy," hissed the lord. "I am only acquainted with Ralph Hart because his family were the gamekeepers on Ashington land for over one hundred years until that lazy oaf got himself the sack."

Rollo nodded slowly. "I see. Then your reason for such disapproval must be because he shares the same tastes as myself. Or is it because he is one of the lower classes? Gamekeepers? Stable boys and the like?" He tutted. "I'm sorry, Fitz, would you prefer I stick to only pleasuring swells like you?"

"Damn your eyes!" Venting an angry roar, the lord grabbed Rollo by his cravat. His hot breath gusted against Rollo's cheek, and Rollo's nostrils filled with the sharp musk of brandy, cologne, and clean, solid man. "I mean leg-shackled men. Ralph Hart was born and bred in this village. He's a wife and three brats at home. He's a drunkard, a sodomite, and barely holds down bits and bobs of honest work as it is. Drives the mail coach once a day from Beccles to Norwich — rumour has it he thieves from it when opportune; mail certainly goes missing more often than not. He scrounges a bit of gavelling work at harvest, and not much else. The man's the devil's own trouble, but do you want his brats turfed out and in the workhouse?" His warning finger was inches away from Rollo's face. "Because I'll tell you this much, boy. That's what will happen if Ralph Hart gets caught messing about with the likes of you."

Pushing Rollo away from him, his lips twisted into a sneer. "Your prancing, frolicking ways might be all the rage in the *ton*, or at your beloved Rossingley, where every last man and his bloody horse is a damned invert. But not here. Not here in Goule. The folks won't stomach it from one of their own. They still have a quack healer in the village. Not fifteen years ago, a woman was stoned to death accused of being a damned witch."

"He approached me," cried Rollo.

"Ralph Hart can approach the King of bloody Siam if that's what he wants! But if rumours get around that he's a sodomite, then he's out of a home and a wage. And over my dead body will the Fitzsimmons or any guests of the Fitzsimmons be a part of it. I'm not having his wife and brats on my conscience, and neither will you. And I'd wager all the tea in bloody Siam that your wonderful, damned *papa* would be of the same damned opinion."

Rollo glowered at him even as hot tears pricked his eyelids. Ye gods and damnation but his lordship was right. He could almost hear his dear papa's voice in his ear, whispering more or less the same words because God knew he'd never stoop to shouting. But of all the people to put Rollo in his place, did it have to be this bloody man? Had Rollo learned nothing from writing out endless lines? From being sent to this godforsaken backwater with his tail between his legs?

"Some bloody hellraiser you are!" he lobbed back, but it seemed to land on deaf ears. Lord Lyndon had already turned his broad shoulders away and now descended the slope at a brisk canter. Brushing at his eyes, Rollo scrabbled around for an insult, an accusation, mockery. Anything but an admittance the insufferable lord was right. Anything to pierce this man's impenetrable armour.

And then, he recalled the heat in those smouldering, polished mahogany eyes as Rollo's hand had lingered at the fall of his trousers. The something indefinable in that glance from the same playbook as the come-hither one Ralph Hart and Rollo had exchanged outside the barn, what seemed a lifetime ago now. Rollo selected the only weapon certain to wound.

"You can't even summon the courage to admit what you really are, can you, Fitz?" Angrily, he brushed at his face, wet with self-pitying tears. God, he felt a long way from home. "I might be young, and foolish with it. But at least I have that. I'll always have that."

For a second, the lord's pace faltered, then picked up even faster than before as if Rollo had never spoken.

Chapter Ten

My dearest Willoughby. I've made an absolute ass of myself. Not unusual per se, except that my poor form was called out by Lord bloody Lyndon of all people. The indignity of it.

Papa. The summer dance was truly an adventure! I'm still recovering!

A NEW DAWN did not improve things.

Quill in hand, Rollo stared out at the never-changing view from his bedchamber. Another bleaching-hot day beckoned, suffocating and airless, the harsh sunlight throwing cruel shade on the tawdriness of the night before. What had he been thinking? He knew the rules. Wherever he travelled and in whatever company, Rollo represented his father and Rossingley. Whether he wanted to or not. And it took a man who had forgotten that vital lesson in relation to his own esteemed family's honour to call him out.

Just as he was contemplating a stomp around the garden, and perhaps farther afield — Rollo's need to escape Goule Hall for a few hours
stronger than ever — a bleary-eyed Lucy appeared to tidy his bed clothes
and do whatever else housemaids did in the mornings.

Rollo attempted a weary smile. "Not halfway to Gretna Green?"

Lucy blushed. "We had the last dance, then Jack saw me home
safe and sound. We're officially courting."

"Are you now," Rollo teased, though his heart wasn't in it. "And
does Cook approve of this courtship?"

Lucy rolled her eyes. "Her and Mr Berridge's cart was two yards
behind us all the way back. Never took her bleeding eyes off us."

"It's amazing what one can get up to under the cover of a lap blanket and darkness though," Rollo observed. "Don't you find?"

Lucy giggled. "You've a naughty mind, sir." Opening the window
and shaking her duster out of it, she carried on.

"There was a right rumpus late on. After you and his lordship left.
Our Ralph, living over at Beccles, got himself a blooded nose from
somewhere. Don't know who gave it to him, but he was in a right temper about it. Started throwing things, swore this place was a shithole —
'scuse my French — and that he was gonna leave the wife and bairns and
clear off to Norwich. Ape-drunk, he was, and then he made the mistake
of picking a fight with two of the big farmer lads from out on the Yar-
mouth Road. He'll have himself a sore head and a matching shiner this
morning."

Rollo's pulse raced. Thank God he'd not divulged his name, or
Ralph Hart might have drunkenly bandied that about too. Nonetheless,
Rollo felt a twinge of sympathy for him, even if he did stray from his
wife when the opportunity arose.

"I don't think I came across the gentleman," he answered cautiously. "Do you think he'll carry it out?"

"Nah," Lucy prattled on. "That was the ale talking. He's me da's cousin; that lot are all talk and no trousers. He's thick as a barn door too. Couldn't find his way out of a privy without a candle, let alone the road out of Norwich. Got a mean streak in him though. I pity the man who bloodied his cork when he does track him down. They like their revenge, the Hart's do. Even gabsters like our Ralph."

Rollo relaxed a little. Mr Hart would come up against a brick wall taking on Lord Lyndon. Only a prize idiot would even try. One fell out with the local lord at one's peril.

"He was probably too foxed to remember," he suggested. "It was that sort of dance, wasn't it?"

"Always is. Always some drama." And with that, Lucy gabbled on about several folks with whom Rollo wasn't acquainted, thus very little was required of him except for an occasional nod.

Chapter Eleven

YOU BELONG TO me? What the devil had he been thinking? For a moment, Lyndon had almost given himself away. Cursing under his breath, then again, louder, he plucked a couple of weeds from around the Elliot's grave marker and flung them aside in frustration. Poppycock. He *had* given himself away. Even when called out, the boy was as slippery as quicksilver, his taunt skewering Lyndon like the tip of a bayonet. *You can't even summon the courage to admit what you really are, can you, Fitz?*

Honest concern had driven him to trail the pup out of the barn. Nothing more, nothing less. God knew why he should have cared, except that Benedict and bloody Rossingley would never forgive him if an accident befell the idiot. Young Duchamps-Avery didn't know a pond from a peat bog; the land around Goule at night was a snake pit for the unwary.

But laying his hands, in anger, on a local countryman? Guilty of nothing but the same desires stirring in Lyndon's own loins? Nothing but jealousy had driven that. Born from hostile self-pity, that Ralph bloody Hart had the ballocks to satisfy his cravings, whereas Lyndon did not.

His daily visit to the Elliot graves was short. Most days, it was nothing more than a nod hello on his way to spend time with Will. Lyndon was not a fanciful man. The dead were dead. He did not believe for a second that the essence of his friend's family lingered in that dismal spot any more than the ghost of the person Lyndon used to be lay there next to them. No, the worms had long since enjoyed their fill, the substance of the dead ploughed back into the ground. Something drew him there, but it wasn't a search for solace. More that he kept the marker tidy out of respect for Will, no longer able.

"He persuaded you to go to the dance," slurred his well-informed friend. "You're a soft touch after all, Lyn."

"Yes. And I should have stayed at home. I behaved like an addle-headed fool." He threw Will a wry smile. "And before you say it, even more than usual."

Will accepted his customary kisses, eyeing the cold cuts of meat Lyndon laid down next to him. "Over the Duchamps-Avery boy," he surmised.

With a dry laugh, Lyndon ruffled his hair. "Aye. You know the mixed-up corners of my soul even better than I."

Lyndon paced the floor of the small parlour as Will ate. "The damned pup unravels me like a ball of string, and that's the truth of it."

You belong to me. Bloody idiot. Discovering the boy in the unworthy arms of another, Lyndon had half a mind to punch Duchamps-Avery in the mouth. But with his own. And softly. He'd been awake most of the night imagining it.

"Ralph Hart took a shine to him," he groused. "Didn't take him long, and he was half-cut. Very nearly made a spectacle of them both. I had no choice but intervene."

"Jealous," pronounced Will around a mouthful of ham.

"Yes, yes, yes. Obviously."

"Obvious to the boy too?"

Lyndon glared at him, not that Will took notice. The man knew him so well it was like wrangling with his own mind. "In many ways, Duchamps-Avery reminds me of you. Not least in having scant regard for my sensitivities."

The boy's dishevelled and leaf-strewn body crawling from the undergrowth flashed through his mind, his pale face pink from his exertions with another man. The torture of picturing him succumbing to Ralph bloody Hart's grubby hands speared Lyndon anew.

"He is not like you in manners or his looks," Lyndon continued. "I believe he is unique in that regard." He drummed on the tabletop. "He's acidic as vinegar and has this…this curious inquisitiveness. He does not let the slightest comment slide without some sort of opinion on it. And he fidgets. Incessantly. Darts about like a bumblebee from buddleia to catmint to lavender and back again. Although do not make mention of lavender. The boy has a weakness for it."

Massage it in deep after an overenthusiastic, hard ride? The damned pup had been toying with him even then.

"And for yellow fabric too," Lyndon explained. "He wears a…a banyan thing. Two, actually. One is a plain mulberry, the other soft, yellow silk. A frivolous garment, one should throw it out for the beggars, though goodness knows it wouldn't warm them on even the mildest of nights. Too bloody thin and silky. Too bloody —"

A guttural noise interrupted him. He raced to Will's side and slapped him hard between the shoulder blades. His friend was choking. No, he was laughing. Or a combination of both. Tears ran down Will's uneven cheeks as he heaved for breath. Lyndon's second sharp slap sent a gobbet of ham flying across the room, which had the effect of making Will laugh even harder. And choke more. Lyndon slapped him again.

And then knelt at Will's feet as his precious friend recovered, hugging him hard against his chest—slobber, snot, ham, and all.

"My dearest Will." His throat felt full, his eyes sprang sudden hot tears. "If not for you, I would have despaired of myself many years back."

"You have fallen hard, Lyn," Will spluttered. "For the son of a man you despise. Only you!"

"I have not." Lyndon dabbed roughly at Will's chin and nose, his denial only serving to fuel his friend's mirth. "He's…a distraction. An annoyance. An extra mouth to feed. An unnecessary hindrance."

"He's a breath of fresh air. Just admit it. And that you want him."
You belong to me.

As Will's coughing subsided, Lyndon rose to his feet. "Enough. You have the remainder of your lunch to eat without suffocating on it." He began rolling up his sleeves. "And I have mangel-wurzels to weed."

Will grinned his twisted lopsided smile. "Weed your head while you're at it."

As Lyndon was half out the door, Will called again. "A lad like that won't stay here forever, Lyn. And you should think about leaving too. We're not both tied to this chair. Perhaps it's time you stopped behaving like we are."

"As you are not tied to this cottage," Lyndon retorted. Of course, Duchamps-Avery would leave as soon as he was able. Lyndon wasn't an idiot. And then things would settle back to how they were. Ordered. Uneventful. "I am more than willing to take you places," he added. "In great comfort too. And yet you always refuse."

He lingered, his hand on the door, watching his friend clumsily tear at the ham. One day, he promised himself, he'd coax Will to come up to London. He'd show him the back streets and alleyways so beloved of his gothic novels.

Sensing his eyes on him, Will looked up. "Aye." He nodded.

"Perhaps we both need to muster some courage."

*

MULLING WILL'S WORDS, Lyndon strolled back towards home, skirting the lake. Some days, he was bold enough to walk along the edge, even though it brought everything flooding back, especially on days he spent time with Will. Though, sometimes, with Will serving as a constant reminder, he wondered if it had ever gone away.

The sun beat down, suffusing his land with a drowsy warmth. After his work with the hoe, Lyndon felt as if the day's heat lived inside him, despite his light linens. He'd have swum in the lake if not for its sad history. Imagining stripping off his shirt and plunging in the cool water only made him even hotter. Reluctantly, he took a last lingering look at the tranquil, inviting pool before turning and taking the path through the woods.

A splash of colour caught his eye as he turned, a dancing shard of turquoise dipping between the trees, a dazzling stripe against the brown of the trunks. He squinted and, like a heavy branch falling upon him without warning, there came a rush of fear.

"No!" He broke into a run. His bellows carried through the still air as if fired from a musket. "No!"

Panting heavily, he crashed through the brush, emerging from the thicket at the exact point where Duchamps-Avery sat on the bank of the lake. His trousers were neatly rolled back to his knees; his two milky feet dangled in the cool water. Serene and still and safe. As quickly as it came upon him, Lyndon's terror leeched away, leaving him feeling a tad foolish.

"Lord Lyndon, I presume," Duchamps-Avery said without looking up. "It's either you or a rangale of frightened deer. Have you come to check up on me?" He spread his arms. "As you can see, I am quite alone. Not a married countryman within miles." He did lift his head then, regarding Lyndon coldly. "To what do I owe the pleasure of your company?"

Lyndon flattened his hair, composing himself. "I was not seeking yours, I assure you. I thought that…that… Am I not permitted to walk my own grounds?"

"The servants tell me you rarely come this way. Seems they are misinformed."

For once, Lyndon did not bite. Though full of his usual acerbity, Duchamps-Avery's appearance gave him a twinge of alarm. The skin covering his fine bones was impossibly pale, as if the day's bright sun shone through him.

"Are you ill?" Lyndon demanded.

"Should you care if I was?" The boy turned properly, and with a wash of relief, Lyndon saw fire in those pale eyes, still burning bright.

"Of course not," he snapped. "Though your father might, thus I am obliged to enquire."

Duchamps-Avery smiled humourlessly. "Fear not. There is little to report other than a severe dose of humiliation. And, though painful, it is a condition from which one generally recovers."

Lyndon knew that immediate sting all too well. "You should be grateful there was only me to bear witness."

His own humiliation, two years gone and at the hand of this boy's father, had been much more public, though Lyndon had long ceased to feel the acute pain of it. Indeed, as he stood before this troubled youth with a peculiar and unfamiliar desire to comfort, it occurred to him how much he had grown since then. Perhaps, in the long run, his disgrace had served him well.

"Use it for the good," he barked. "Learn from it." Deciding he'd provided ample sympathy for one day, he added, "And for God's sake, stay out of this lake."

"Why?" asked the boy, his pale eyes turning curious. "The heat is so relentless; I have a mind to swim across it. Willoughby and I bathe often in the lake at Rossingley."

"Well, you can't. Mine is out of bounds. I won't allow it."

The boy huffed, kicking his feet. Ripples spread across the still water. "You won't allow it? Will you wrestle me back if I'm tempted to disobey?"

The panicky feeling returned to Lyndon's chest. Even the slippery pondweed, swirling around Duchamps-Avery's slim feet, clinging to them like clawing fingers, unnerved him.

"Please." His voice cracked. He licked his dry lips. "Do not."

Duchamps-Avery threw him a strange look.

"A…a friend almost drowned here," Lyndon bit out. "Several years ago now. He is much changed since. I…I treasure the memory of how he was before."

Treasure, lament, pine — any verb would do. But mostly, Lyndon missed him. He missed the old Will's companionship, his constancy, how he would run with Lyndon through the marshes on light, agile feet. Knowing he had a person who loved him just because he could. *Aye*, and his sweet kisses.

"Do you store this memory in a glass jar on your desk?" Duchamps-Avery's chilly, harsh tone cut through Lyndon's drifting thoughts, the tone of a terribly upset person wishing to hide it. "Perhaps alongside a jar containing your own. Do you boast a collection?"

"No, but if you continue in that vein, my friend, I may well be tempted to start one."

The boy fiddled with his cuffs, then plucked at blades of grass. Wiggled his toes, examined them, this way and that, as though checking they were still perfect. Always so damned restless. As if impatiently waiting for something to happen, for his deus ex machina to shatter the tranquillity of Goule. See? Lyndon was a Latin scholar after all and, perhaps after his conversation with Will, able to recall how it felt to be young, wretched, and bored. And how hard it was to examine one's actions and find them wanting. Even when one wasn't so young.

"I have not been the most welcoming of hosts," Lyndon offered, surprising himself. "I would like to extend an apology. You have...have surmised that I am not the happiest of souls, and you are correct. I was hoping my prolonged, self-imposed exile here at Goule might...ameliorate that. Sadly, it has not."

"Thank you."

The boy was such a chatterbox Lyndon assumed he'd say more, but nothing else was forthcoming. At least it appeared he'd taken Lyndon's first-ever attempt at an apology in the spirit with which he offered it. But damned if Lyndon didn't need to be certain.

"You may wish to dine with me tonight. In the...um...dining room." He winced; a corpse would have sounded less stiff. "Jugged hare," he added. "Followed by jam and custard."

Duchamps-Avery seemed to consider. Lyndon half hoped his suggestion would be turned down.

"I thank you for the kind offer, my lord. But if I may, I think I will dine alone. Perhaps I have much soul-searching of my own to accomplish."

Chapter Twelve

FOR THE NEXT couple of days, Duchamps-Avery stewed in his own company. Lyndon told himself he was glad; the air had been cleared, and they could avoid any further awkward conversations. He also reassured himself he was glad not to have anyone barging into the study or the drawing room and cutting up his peace. Berridge had been informed by Greaves who had been assured by Cook and Lucy that his young guest had not again strayed close to the lake.

At this time of year, the morning light impregnated everything it touched with a white cleanness, as if yesterday, the land, a bloated and grubby drunkard, had today, rinsed sober. As Lyndon climbed the narrow back stairs to the old nursery and set about preparing his easel in front of the biggest window, his whimsical musings stayed with him.

By far the brightest room in the house, daylight poured through both the north and south aspects of it, elbowing its way into every corner. More capricious cogitations. Lyndon permitted himself a smile of acknowledgement and took up his brushes. Finally, he had the time and space to think in a straight line again.

He lost himself for at least an hour before light, echoing footsteps along the corridor signalled imminent company. Lyndon deemed them too sure of themselves to belong to Lucy, bearing refreshments, and far too bouncy for Berridge. More the approaching tread of someone who had never learned where the telltale creaks hid. Or simply didn't care.

Testiness at the interruption accounted for the fluttering in Lyndon's belly, or so he told himself at any rate. For the abrupt dryness of his mouth too. Furthermore, he comforted himself with the knowledge that his sense of relief on noting Duchamps-Avery had lost some of his paleness had nothing to do with *caring*, but everything to do with not being obliged to report his sickliness to the boy's sharp-witted father.

Be that as it may, even when slightly wan, Duchamps-Avery still walked like a poem, a ridiculous, overly long, dramatic Byronic one, all unnecessary flounces and trills.

"Oh! I say. What a rather splendid room. And isn't it peaceful up here?"

"It was," said Lyndon sourly. "*Was* peaceful."

"Yes, well, I…"

For possibly the first time in his short, secure existence, Duchamps-Avery appeared unsure of himself. "I have been doing some soul-searching, my lord. I would like to apologise for behaving in a cretinous fashion down by the lake, for being indiscreet and careless up on the ridge with that chap, and…um…being a self-centred and self-pitying prick pretty much everywhere else.

"And I'd also like to say that, whatever you are, my lord, whatever you believe regarding men such as myself and Ralph Hart, it is none of my business. And that, in fact, though your behaviour on occasion has suggested the contrary, I accept that you are nothing at all like me and Mr Hart, and I should not have insinuated as such. Indeed, my very flesh burns with the shame of it. I must stress that your inclinations — again, though none of my business — are as far from mine and Mr Hart's as it is possible to be. That, for absolute clarity, you harbour no desires to insert your member anywhere near the vicinity of another man's arse, and that to even begin to compose your desires and my desires and Mr Hart's desires in the same sentence, let alone paragraph, would be foolish, inappropriate, untimely, libellous, scandalous, and unworthy of a member of my dear papa's esteemed, distinguished bloodline and household."

He paused and sucked in a much-needed breath. "Or, indeed, a foolish, temporary, and unwelcome member of the Goule household."

Lyndon's shoulders shook. A laugh made its way up his chest. An insane, gurgle of one. It took him a moment to recognise the peculiar sensation, though it became impossible to suppress, almost as if the sunlight streaming through the window streamed through Lyndon too. Or perhaps that was the boy, laughing with him, albeit with a discombobulated expression on his pretty, pretty features. As if he wasn't quite sure what to make of the odd noise emanating from his taciturn host.

"Apology accepted," Lyndon managed at last. "If indeed that was one. To be honest, Duchamps-Avery, I lost interest halfway through."

The boy laughed again with delight and relief. "Damned shame, I spent hours honing that masterpiece. Even pinched a line from one of Willoughby's ghastly odes for emphasis. 'My very flesh burns with the shame of it', in case you were wondering."

"Really?" Lyndon found himself smiling at the pup. "If you'd asked me to guess, I would have taken a wild stab in the dark at 'insert your member anywhere near the vicinity of another man's arse'. Romantic flummery at its most divine."

"'A wild stab in the dark indeed'." The boy laughed again, free and pure.

At risk of joining in, Lyndon turned back to his easel. Duchamps-Avery was too distracting by half, especially when referring to Lyndon's member, which, at that point in time, was quite swollen and didn't need attention drawn to it.

"And I will take this opportunity," Lyndon replied, his gaze once more inexplicably drawn to the boy, "to acknowledge, again, that I have been a less than generous host." He nodded, signalling the end of the matter. "Now, if you'll excuse me."

Duchamps-Avery performed that wrinkle of his brow, the one he likely imagined to be a frown but, to Lyndon's eyes, simply made him even more edible. "Excuse you to do what?"

Lyndon groaned. Unless he tossed the canvas through the open window, he had nowhere to hide the large, square oil painting he'd begun that morning.

The pup bounded over. "Gadzooks! You're an artist, Lord Lyndon."

"Hardly."

Duchamps-Avery peered a little closer, and the stupidly smooth, insipid skin between his stupidly brilliant blue eyes wrinkled a tiny bit more. Even more appetising. "It's…ah…my goodness." His eyes darted from the painting up to meet Lyndon's. "I say. It's very…you, isn't it?"

"Afraid so."

It was possibly the most forthright analysis Lyndon had ever received. Even Will used to be a little more circumspect. Benedict, of course, kind soul that he was, had never heaped upon him anything but praise.

Side by side, Lyndon and Duchamps-Avery studied the mess of angry dark lines and swirls of colour daubed across the canvas.

"May I…um…enquire as to what it depicts, my lord?"

"That beech tree." Lyndon pointed with the tip of his brush into the garden beyond the window. "Next to the wall."

"Of course it does."

"I'm toying with naming it *Forlorn Hope*."

"Ah. Yes…um…fitting. Am I to presume that you are the…um…artist behind some of the other equally…um…interesting works I've spied around the house?"

"I am. Yes."

A tense pause ensued, during which his houseguest peered out at the tree, then more closely at the canvas, and then across to the tree again. Shielding his eyes against the sunlight, he tilted his head to one side like an exotic bird.

"It's dreadful," Lyndon pre-empted him. His pencil sketches were passable, his oils a perennial work in progress. "Isn't it?"

"Not…ah…*dreadful* as such." The youth cocked his pretty head to the other side. "More that it shows…ah…depths of immense passion." His lips shaped themselves into a pout as he further perused the monstrosity, a pout which Lyndon told himself he did not find attractive in the slightest and most definitely did not wish to plug with his own mouth. "Yes, that's it. Passion."

Duchamps-Avery nodded several times. The pout twisted into an even more problematically charming smirk. "I do believe, my lord, that with this artistic interpretation of one of Mother Nature's finest arboreal specimens, you have cleverly…ah…captured the void signifying precisely the nonbeing of what it represents. *Forlorn Hope*. Indeed."

A beat passed, and then he let out a booming guffaw, the likes of which Lyndon's little oasis of calm here in the nursery at Goule had not heard since…well, since many years earlier, before Lyndon's world had become a more hostile place in general. Even more alarmingly, Lyndon found himself briefly joining in again with that awkward, braying, unpractised sound of his own.

"Your critique of art holds as much wisdom as the chattering of a beggar's teeth," he growled, trying to sound firm but failing terribly if the delighted grin spread across his companion's face was any yard-stick. "I've never heard anything as nonsensical."

"It's jolly good, isn't it?" Duchamps-Avery was not put out in the slightest. "It's a variation of my papa's routine response whenever he's asked his opinion of the overrated artistic merits of others. One can adapt it to suit a painting, blank verse, or a dirge plunked on a harpsi-chord." He smiled naughtily. "Most members of the *ton* are too proud to admit his utterings don't make the foggiest bit of sense, in case they themselves appear foolish."

His candid gaze left the canvas to rest on Lyndon's, giving Lyndon the uncomfortable impression that he was reading every one of his impure thoughts. "You, my lord, by calling me out on it, have not fallen into the trap. And I expected nothing less from a gentleman as discerning as yourself."

Lyndon did not seek this boy's praise, nor did he need it. Neither did he require this boy's admiration, his mirth, his pale gaze, nor his endearing, retroussé nose. Regardless, his soul drank deep from all those things anyway, and for a moment, the nursery light shone even brighter. Even his woeful painting seemed a little less woeful.

Naturally, it would not do at all to give the boy a sniff of that.

"Be that as it may, it still remains a desperate representation of the damned tree," Lyndon muttered and added another splodge of paint as if to prove his point.

"But it has been painted with good intentions," countered Duchamps-Avery. "So, who cares? Willoughby pens some brutal verse. Only yesterday, he sent me his latest, where gratingly, he rhymes 're-morse' with 'worse'."

Duchamps-Avery laughed delightedly again, and Lyndon expe-rienced his own unwanted rush of pleasure at the sound of it.

"Papa adores Willoughby's verse, of course. He's the stoutest of his defenders. He says we're all simply failing to see the beauty in it, that's all. And he frequently remarks that it's a darned sight better than anything he or I could attempt." Duchamps-Avery pointed a slim finger to the canvas. "Just as *Forlorn Hope* is by far superior to any of my infantile daubs. So, bravo, Lord Lyndon. Bravo!"

Lyndon expected the boy to retreat after that. Instead, he drew up a chair and stayed put.

"You mention your twin frequently," Lyndon observed as he considered his palette. "Granted, not as frequently as dear Papa."

"I do. I miss him terribly. Until I came to Goule, we have scarcely been parted."

"You are identical?"

"In looks, yes." He lowered his voice. "Though I am far better endowed."

Lyndon rolled his eyes. "And more childish."

"Quite possibly."

They traded amused glances.

"He writes almost as often as you do," Lyndon commented. "Between the pair of you, I could kindle every hearth in Goule village for a winter."

Duchamps-Avery smiled. "And make better use of the foolscap. His letters contain far more intimate details regarding his courtship of a certain luscious lady than even a close twin cares to be privy. Being here at Goule, my…ah…*tempering* influence on him is woefully absent."

Lyndon poised his brush over the canvas as he contemplated darkening the chapel ridge. "You don't approve of his courtship?"

Duchamps-Avery shrugged. "Miss Lavinia is comely enough and blessed with a cheerful disposition. Moreover, I enjoy her company—we have known each other nearly all of our lives."

"But?"

"But…" Duchamps-Avery sighed. "Her mother demands Willoughby's presence up at the house all too often. Which, on the face of things, is perfectly fine. And...and I'm not denying that lounging around on a chaise politely listening to ladies tinkling on harpsichords in well-appointed drawing rooms has an important place in a young gentleman's schooling. Of course. Absolutely. But thrice weekly?"

He raised his eyebrows in exasperation. "Willoughby is as polite and respectful as any other well-bred young gentleman. But he's also no different; he'd much prefer to ride, or play billiards, or at least do *something* more interesting than watch a lady as she embroiders fluffy kittens on a cushion. Yet he's too damned polite to say so. All in all, Lavinia's dear mama makes many, many unnecessary demands on his time."

Lyndon chuckled. Duchamps-Avery's tale was all too familiar. "I'd wager she does."

"You are acquainted with the family?"

"Almost certainly." He glanced up at his companion. "I'm the brother of a duke and of marriageable age. Most members of the *ton* with eligible daughters have endeavoured to make my acquaintance at some point. *Before* I became persona non grata, at least. What's this chit's name again?"

"Miss Lavinia Higgins."

"Ah." *Higgins.* It made perfect sense. "Of the Stapleton Higgins's?" he confirmed. "Her father is Charles Higgins? Lord Stapleton? A weaselly chap, pigeon-toed, and with an unfortunate overbite?"

"The very same." Duchamps-Avery beamed. "Stapleton is but four miles north of Rossingley. On a fast, straight road. He is a friend of yours?"

Lyndon huffed. "Higgins is a friend of any man whom he thinks might be daft enough or foxed enough to lend him a few shillings. Not only can he not hold his drink, but he's of the unfounded belief that if he plays baccarat at White's often enough, the tables will turn." He threw Duchamps-Avery a wry smile. "They never do. As I, too, discovered the hard way."

Duchamps-Avery emitted a heavy sigh. "How funny. I don't believe Lavinia, nor her mother, has ever mentioned that. Can't imagine why."

"It's quite conceivable they have no idea. Fortunately for Higgins, his sister is married to a salt merchant with exceedingly deep pockets. The depth of his patience, however, is another matter altogether."

Duchamps-Avery's clear blue eyes studied him thoughtfully. "Lavinia marrying Willoughby would be a weight off Lord Stapleton's mind is what you're implying. Poor thing. She probably has no idea she's being used as a pawn to lighten his load."

"And to lighten Willoughby's pockets too. Don't forget that. Higgins won't be backwards in asking him to clear his debts."

"Precisely." Thin lipped, Duchamps-Avery nodded. "My dear brother is far too sweet-natured for his own good. He wouldn't spot a snake in the grass if it reared up and bit him."

Lyndon paused to regard his young companion. "Not entirely identical then, are you?"

"No." Duchamps-Avery smirked. "The downside of being the better endowed of us both is that it comes with a healthy cynicism and a tendency to speak one's mind."

They were both quiet for a while after that, Duchamps-Avery no doubt wondering how to impart Lyndon's information in a tactful manner to his infatuated twin, and Lyndon attempting to focus his attention back on his execrable painting. Damned challenging when the boy crossed and uncrossed his silly, willowy legs every couple of minutes immediately after reference to his manhood.

Chapter Thirteen

My dearest Willoughby. Lord Lyndon is a walking, talking mass of contradictions and, on occasion, I believe he struggles to keep them all afloat. He has a begrudging kindness, which he endeavours to hide, mixed with veritable self-loathing, as if, when regarding his reflection in a mirror, there is not one thing about himself of which he approves. A great pity. The man is a coppery beauty. On the outside, at least. The inside still requires attention, of course, but I do believe progress is being made. For instance, I have not been shot at for over a week.

I do hope you are widening your horizons in my absence. Fitz says there are always excellent exhibitions on at the Dulwich Picture Gallery, and Kit's sister and her friends are delightful company.

Papa. Lord Lyndon is a man of many, many talents. He paints! Unspeakably badly!

"YOU'RE HERE AGAIN."

"I am, my lord. Like a bad penny."

Under beetling brows, Lord Lyndon scowled at his canvas. "Why, may I ask?"

Rollo sauntered towards the open window, pausing on the way to peek around his lordship's broad shoulder at his latest oeuvre, *Pointless House of Worship*. He'd visited the nursery every day for a week, and his lordship's artistry hadn't improved. That Lord Lyndon cared not, was rather *winning*.

"You said I could have the run of the house," Rollo observed. "The air today is humid beyond all human endurance, and this double aspect room up here at the very top, with the breeze wafting through, is by far the coolest. My need for cold air surpasses even my fear of heights."

"Stupid thing to be scared of," sniped Lyndon.

Duchamps-Avery held aloft a slim novel. "Your concern is touching. But as long as I don't look down at the ground, I'm perfectly fine. I shall read this on the window seat. As noiselessly as a fieldmouse. You'll hardly know I'm here."

Fitzsimmons harrumphed as Rollo brought his legs up from the floor, crossed his ankles, and settled in. Finally, he'd discovered the newer section of Goule Hall library and found it to be stocked with a surprisingly sophisticated collection of barbarous gothic novels, which he was steadily devouring. His current volume took place in a remote Italian castle, whereupon a brooding aristocratic villain threatened a resourceful, trapped heroine with an unspeakable fate.

Putting a finger on the page to keep his place, Rollo flicked his eyes up to his own brooding aristocrat. Lord Lyndon's looks tended more towards villain than hero too. His lordship wasn't darkly handsome in the classical sense, unlike Papa's lover, Kit, for instance. Fitz's nose was too proudly hooked, his bottom lip too obstinate. His bearing was much less elegant than that of his twin brother, more...*threatening*.

Of course, no commentary on the man was complete without mention of that untamed coppery mane. Today, it fell freely to his shoulders, swirling like the violent shades of red in his painting, suggestive of all kinds of wicked fires burning beneath. Rollo pictured himself, Icarus-like, standing far too close to them, being gathered up, subsumed, and then spirited away to a high stone tower cresting an Italian hilltop, whereupon the dastardly lord flung him down onto a four-poster and —

"You're breathing," Lord Lyndon griped. "Through your mouth. Do stop. I'm trying to concentrate."

"It's because I've reached a terribly exciting chapter," Rollo lied. "The dishonourable Count Rodolfo is ravaging his young, naïve house-guest, whose whimpers for mercy are unheeded — there is no one within shouting distance. He is determined to have his wicked way over and over —

"Fantastical gothic tales are artificial literary structures combined with an unhealthy excess of blood and dusty cobwebs. Purposefully de-signed to contest upstanding Christian morals and to titillate feeble, sus-ceptible minds."

"From that precis, I can only surmise you've read all of them," Rollo deadpanned.

"I most certainly have not."

"The spine of this one was cracked." Rollo held it aloft. "And a couple of pages are turned down at the corners. Are you suggesting that old Berridge holds a secret *tendre* for our dastardly Count?"

The lord wiggled his fearsome brows in a way that made Rollo wanted to press his mouth against them. He wondered how they'd feel on his lips. Soft or coarse?

"Now be quiet, pup. Blending the perfect shade of ochre for the chapel roof requires the entirety of my focus."

"The chapel roof? I could have sworn you were painting the cows in the field yonder." Rollo shrugged. "My mistake."

Chortling, Rollo resumed the twin pleasures of Count Rodolfo's lustful pursuits and casting frequent glances in Lord Lyndon's direction. As was the nature of a window seat, he was positioned directly inside the window bay. Thus, by necessity, Lord Lyndon also had to glance in Rollo's direction in order to paint the distant chapel roof.

"You can't even read quietly," he muttered after ten minutes of Rollo returning each of his glances with a sweet smile and Lord Lyndon baring his teeth in exchange. "Each page turn sounds like a slap to my cheek."

Rollo produced an extra sugary smile. "If that is something you favour, my lord, then I'm sure it could be arranged."

A low rumbling sounded from within the lord's chest. A splash of blue paint had found its way onto his nose, to which Rollo had no intention of drawing his notice. Instead, he studied the room.

"You must have had some marvellous playtimes up here," he remarked. "If, that is, you spent much time at this house as a child? Or indeed, were ever a child?"

"Huh," the lord responded, which Rollo took as confirmation. "Every summer," he then offered, unbidden. "My grandfather and father liked to come here to fish. Bream and pike, mostly. Some trout."

Goodness, the man had volunteered information! Only dull fishing information, but still. With heavy-booted optimism, Rollo probed deeper.

"And whilst he was occupied fishing, you, the future Duke of Ashington, and your youngest brother, Lord Francis, ran riot up here?"

Lord Lyndon shot him a withering look. "Francis was too small to play games with. And Benedict has never been inclined to run riot anywhere." He prodded at his palette. "No. I played with a chum, mostly. One of the local farmer's sons. His family used to farm the Ashington land around Goule."

Rollo noted the past tense. "But not now?"

"No," answered Fitzsimmons, his lips thinning. "Not now."

Rollo had the distinct impression a story hid behind that firmly closed mouth. He hesitated, unsure whether to push further. "This chum, was…was it Will Elliot?"

Fitzsimmons's brush briefly froze. "Yes."

Something in his tone told Rollo it was time to leave well alone, despite wanting to keep his lordship talking. Gazing around for conversational inspiration, his eyes landed on a wooden rocking horse, partially covered by a dust sheet.

"Did you and your friend play on that?" he asked, pointing.

Lord Lyndon shook his head, relaxing a fraction. "No. That was Francis's pride and joy, and before that, Benedict's. Naturally, he wasn't permitted to drag his ponies into the house with him, so old Dobbin was the next best thing. Will and I preferred…more rambunctious games. Especially as older schoolboys. Pirates, highwaymen, you know. Clashing swords and the like."

Rollo smirked. "Clashing swords, eh? What fun."

"That sweet, innocent face of yours hides a commonplace mind," his lordship reprimanded. "You know exactly what I was implying — blunted, wooden swords, beloved of boys everywhere." He frowned. "Berridge carved them for us. They're probably still lying around here somewhere."

"In that old toy chest under the bookcase, I'll be bound," cried Rollo, leaping up. He adored toy boxes. Riffling through them generally stirred up all kinds of memories, and one never knew what old treasures hid inside. This one was huge. The clasp fell apart easily enough, but the lid was heavy and stuck as though it hadn't been opened in years. Legs apart, he braced himself to try again.

"That doesn't look very much like reading," Lord Lyndon observed. "You are very much a fidget."

Over his shoulder, Rollo shot him a quick grin. Fitzsimmons's hand holding the paint brush had paused halfway to the canvas as though forgotten. His dark eyes stared at Rollo intently, though not at his face.

"And you seem to be admiring my derrière bent over this treasure chest." Rollo gave it a little wiggle. "A much more favourable subject than the roof of a boring old chapel. Wouldn't you agree, Lord Lyndon?"

Chapter Fourteen

"I'M SIMPLY INTERESTED in the contents of the chest," Lyndon insisted.

On twiggy legs, Duchamps-Avery had danced over to the battered wooden chest and propped the lid open before Lyndon could fabricate a more credible defence. Furious at being caught, Lyndon couldn't decide which was the more exquisite torture, the view of those spindly legs stretched out on his window seat, trying not to imagine what treasure lay at the meeting of them, or the shapely back view, as Duchamps-Avery bent low at the waist, rummaging.

"Ahoy, Cap'n! Hoist the mainsail!"

The boy straightened and twirled around, brandishing a large wooden sword. Jammed on his head was Lyndon's old leather three-cornered hat. A yellow silk sash swirled at his neck, lighting up his joyful grin like the sunrise lit up the seven seas. A deep ache in Lyndon's ballocks, vaguely present since Duchamps-Avery had arranged himself on the window seat, intensified.

Conflicting urges to demand he stop at once and to bend him like a willow twig over the toy chest surged in equal measure. Hell and damnation. What had Will said? *Be braver with your life.* Not all treasure was silver and gold.

Nonetheless, not even Lyndon would stoop to seduce a man dressed up as a pirate.

"You are absurd," he chuntered, which only made the pup grin even more. "And you're not even wearing that hat properly. It's crooked. The pointy bit goes at the front."

"What, I should wear it like this you mean?"

Before Lyndon could flap him away, Duchamps-Avery plucked the hat from his own fair head, reached up, and plonked it upon Lyndon's. His pale eyes sparkled as he admired his handiwork, close enough that Lyndon could stoop and kiss him if he were truly that way inclined. Or at least shove him aside. He did neither, simply glared instead.

"Gadzooks, yes! Piratical indeed, especially with that snarl." Duchamps-Avery pushed the sword into Lyndon's hand then spun back to the chest. "A hat made for your head and your head alone! I'd wager swaggering, fearsome Captain Fitzsimmons steered the good ship Goule across the globe on many a happy occasion. Leaving a lovelorn damsel in every port!"

Another sword appeared from the depths of the toy chest, lighter than the first. Duchamps-Avery examined it briefly. "This isn't the weapon of a fearsome sea captain." He tossed it to one side. "The trinket belonging to a mere landlubber, perhaps. Too small by far."

He threw Lyndon a quick sunbeam over his shoulder, pointing to the first sword that he'd handed him. Obligingly, Lyndon gave it a little flourish.

"Yes. I believe this one did belong to me," he admitted, hefting it in his hand.

"The weapon of a wicked pirate king," Duchamps-Avery declared. "As soon as I laid eyes on it, I knew it was yours. Why am I not surprised that you wielded the largest, most impressive of swords, my lord?"

Defeated by Duchamps-Avery's ebullient humour, Lyndon sank into the nearest armchair, his grumbles about peace and quiet and solitude and childishness landing on deaf ears. The way the boy bandied around *sword*, making no attempt to sound anything but vulgar was, well, having an effect on Lyndon's personal, private sword that did not bear thinking about.

A pair of colourful pantaloons joined the second, smaller sword on the floor, along with the epauletted, long-skirted coat of a French infantry soldier and a bejewelled reticule once owned by Lyndon's grandmother. He hoped the baubles were made from paste but, from the lustre, had a dreadful feeling they weren't.

"Ah!" The boy pounced on another long bolt of heavy material, heaving it out and sending a cloud of dust spiralling into the air. "What do we have here, my hearties?"

Lyndon covered his mouth and nose as Duchamps-Avery vigorously coughed, bringing tears to his eyes. Flapping one of his silly, dainty hands in front of his face, he shook out the ruby silk garment, awash with a bold yellow floral brocade as if a meadow of dandelions were growing out from the fabric.

"Even the moths daren't attack this." Duchamps-Avery flattened it against himself, clearing dust from his throat and counting the layers. "Good lord, how many petticoats does one dress need? And look at all this puffery! I could lose both my arms forever down one of these sleeves!"

"My grandmother was a robust lady," Lyndon observed. "And you are not."

He expected a witty retort, but none was forthcoming because

Duchamps-Avery was too busy fiddling at the fall of his trousers and —

"What in heavens name are you doing, boy?" Lyndon spluttered. "This isn't a bath house!"

"Trying the thing on, of course!" Duchamps-Avery flung his trousers aside, caring not where they landed. On the wooden horse, as it happened. "One can't play pirates and damsels without a proper costume, can one? And I'm under no illusion you'll be content to take the role of damsel."

Thank all that was holy that the boy had taken up the vulgar fashion of wearing silken drawers. Lyndon had no intention of adopting modern ways; he was perfectly content wrapping his undercarriage in his shirttails, thank you very much. But then he also had no desire to strip down to his unmentionables in the bloody nursery. Blood heated his veins as Duchamps-Avery's shapely, milky, bare calves danced before his eyes. Calves sculpted by Satan himself for the singular purpose of wrapping around Lyndon's back.

"We're not playing damsels and pirates! I'm attempting to paint that bloody chapel roof, and you're supposed to be reading a disreputable work of literature. Quietly."

Lyndon might as well have been speaking to the damned three-cornered hat still wedged on his head. "And...what the blazes? For heaven's sake. Leave your undershirt on! Where's your sense of decorum, boy?"

"Oh, I don't know, hiding out there somewhere—" Duchamps-Avery flung a hand in the direction of the window. "—having kidnapped your sense of adventure and scarpered with it." By now, he was hopping about on one leg, the other caught up in the petticoats. "One can't wear a shirt under a dress like this." He laughed again. "For a start, it will spoil my decolletage!"

Never mind that, it was rapidly spoiling Lyndon's resolve to keep his hands to himself. To pretend he had a grip on things was an insult to grips and things. Briefly, he closed his eyes. Then prised them open again.

Hell and damnation. Those deft, delicate fingers had half the shirt already unfastened. And then the thing was off the pup's shoulders altogether. Not many seconds after that, time took on its own dimensions.

Lyndon stared. He couldn't help himself. Sometimes, beauty crept into your bones unnoticed in the warmth of a gaze, the generosity of a soul, the subtle swell of a breast. It seduced gradually with a sly glance here and a curvy hip swing there, until hooking one to be left dangling like a fish.

And then there was that other rare beauty. A beauty that screamed its name so loudly it made the hairs on one's arms stand up, such as when Duchamps-Avery stood near naked in the nursery, his modesty covered only by a flimsy pair of cream bloody silk drawers.

Mesmerised, Lyndon licked his lips. The portion of beauty allotted this man was undeserving—a beauty already tunnelling into Lyndon's core, into his very marrow, and stealing it away. And the devil was Duchamps-Avery bloody knew it. It was plain for Lyndon to see in the tips of his long fingers, idly smoothing a path along his flat belly, in the languorous, idle way he contemplated the dusty dress, in no hurry to cover himself with it.

"What ails you, Lord Lyndon?" The change in Duchamps-Avery's voice was unmissable, too, huskier, suggestive. "Have you never seen a man undress down to his drawers before? You have brothers, do you not? Surely you have boxed with other gentlemen at Jack's?"

Lyndon's blood burned. He wanted this youth like he wanted his next breath. Will's words floated back to him through the sun's rays. *Courage, my old friend.*

"None...none like you," he whispered. "None so fair."

Duchamps-Avery dropped his gaze, looking down at himself as if through Lyndon's carnal gaze. His long fingers teased at the ties of his drawers, and the corner of his soft mouth curved into a smile. "Why, thank you, my lord. Pretty looks aren't everything. But I like to think I have them anyway, just in case."

"Put on the damned dress," Lyndon barked. And then, because he could hide his desire no longer and knew that damned Duchamps-Avery had spied it, squeezed his cockstand through his breeches. "Before I am undone, damn you."

Even the most revered of French courtesans never made such a spectacle of covering themselves. Lyndon was torn between losing the miles of bare marbled flesh and yet gaining the most coquettish vixen he'd ever imagined existed. Having arranged his ruby decolletage to his liking, Duchamps-Avery sashayed towards him, picking up the small sword along the way. Flowing around his legs, the silk skirts whispered like a cool breeze.

"Now for the sword play, my lord." He trapped Lyndon in his glittery gaze. "Tell me, Fitz, when you played with your friend alone up here, did he ever wear this dress? Did he pretend to be a damsel in need of your strong, protective embrace?"

"Yes," Lyndon croaked. "Though never as well as you."

"You were of an age for swordplay?"

"He had eighteen years to my seventeen."

Duchamps-Avery nodded, fondling his wooden sword before encasing the blunted blade in the tunnel of his fist, performing a lewd action that could not be mistaken for anything else. That wicked smile played at his lips again.

"Did you chase your damsel first, as dastardly pirates are wont?"

"Yes," Lyndon breathed.

"And did you catch him?"

"Yes, but...but not without a fight."

With a grin, Duchamps-Avery offered his hand. "Then rise, Captain." He took up an elegant fencer's stance, one foot ahead of the other, his back ramrod straight. His short, blunted weapon pointed directly at Lyndon. "My family's honour is at stake!" he cried in a ridiculous high-pitched voice. "I must protect my virtue at all costs. En garde!"

Lyndon found himself grinning and holding up his own harmless sword. His brain insisted he'd never behaved sillier, that he must look an utter fool prancing around in his three-cornered hat, waving a wooden toy. He should cease immediately. His body, however, refused to pay attention as he easily parried Duchamps-Avery's cautious opening jab.

Duchamps-Avery was well-schooled, that much was evident. Nonetheless, the pup didn't stand a chance. Though rusty, Lyndon had the advantages of a longer reach and longer weapon, combined with an urgent need to catch his damsel and do *something* to relieve himself.

His opponent drove forward with a quick, forceful stab. Lyndon stopped it with a flick, lunging in a determined counterattack. He came down lightly onto Duchamps-Avery's shoulder, and the pup danced away, laughing delightedly.

"Your sword is thirsty for me tonight, Captain!" He feinted a high attack, then switched to a deft low strike. "You fight like a man in a hurry. Something more pressing on your mind?"

Lyndon smacked both assaults aside with a flourish, his face heating all the way to the tips of his hair. Duchamps-Avery retreated, stumbling over the hem of his oversized dress, giggling as he righted himself.

"And you fight like a dairy farmer, pup," Lyndon growled. "I shall lop your head from your shoulders."

Duchamps-Avery's next strike came from up high. Parrying it, Lyndon delivered a short thrust of his own, pushing him back another step. His blade glided down the layers of red silk covering Duchamps-Avery's arm. "Foiled again, pup."

Nimbly, Duchamps-Avery ducked, weaving around Lyndon's weapon. The dress slipped from one of his shoulders, exposing the jut of a pale collarbone, screaming to be licked. "It is nothing but a flesh wound, Captain. See? I am not so easily mastered."

Lyndon followed with a riposte, swift and precise. The boy was everywhere. On his skin and under it, crawling into his heart, menacing his soul, reeling him in with an infernal red dress and a child's damned toy. As Duchamps-Avery's blade harmlessly sliced through the air, Lyndon darted forward and pressed the rounded end of his own sword up against the pup's chin.

"Touché."

His opponent's weapon clattered to the floor. Chest heaving, Duchamps-Avery brought his hands up in surrender. His lips spread in a slow smile. "You have indeed slayed me, Captain. I am your prize. To do with as you wish."

As Lyndon nudged his chin a little higher with the sword, Duchamps-Avery glanced down to between Lyndon's legs. Then, quick as a flash, he ducked, catching the blade in his hand and putting the tip to his mouth. His pale gaze holding Lyndon's, he gave the end a lascivious lick, circling his tongue around and around the smooth wood.

"Do you have something like this in mind, Captain? As my punishment?" He gave it a final lick. "Shall I unsheathe you? Is that how games in the nursery with your friend used to end?"

"We were never so bold." Lyndon backed away until the backs of his trembling legs hit the chair. Gratefully, he sank into it. "Though sometimes he…he would kneel at my feet. Begging me for mercy."

"Did you offer it?"

Lyndon swore as Duchamps-Avery licked his lips. He might as well be licking Lyndon's member, the effect it had on it. "Never."

Flaunting the dress like a marauding king might a stolen crown, Duchamps-Avery stepped closer. Then, in a whisper of silk, he dropped to his knees. So confident and wanting. So comfortable in his seduction. This man bore no resemblance at all to his innocent William and his shy embraces, his tentative kisses. No resemblance whatsoever, yet the same hungry yearning Lyndon had never experienced since feasted on his bones. The same longing arms reached out to him, touching the same unnourished part of him, that same burning flame.

Lyndon loosened his breeches as, like a virginal supplicant, Duchamps-Avery settled between his parted legs. He caressed Lyndon's inner thighs, from his knees to the very tops, teasing him through the fabric. Lifting his head, he trapped Lyndon in his glittery, wicked gaze.

"Did your damsel please his lord in this fashion?"

"No...but...I wanted him to, I think."

Duchamps-Avery's mouth twisted naughtily. "How about like this?"

Lowering his head once more, he pressed his hot, damp lips against Lyndon's covered cock. Fire after fire after fire ignited along the length. Lyndon bit back a deep groan.

"No," he whimpered. "He...he...we...did not know how."

"But it would please you now, would it not?"

"God, yes. I have...I have been pleasured this way by true damsels, but never, never by one such...such...by a man such as you."

There, he'd admitted it, the weight of his secret gone in a trice and with no going back. A huff of laughter escaped his throat. Now he had confided it, Lyndon felt light enough to fly.

Duchamps-Avery mouthed at his swollen tip as his soft hands squeezed and stroked Lyndon's thighs. Lyndon's cock twitched and leaked; he clamped his hands around the arms of the chair.

"You have the grit of a man, yet you seduce with the tenderness of a woman, pup."

Duchamps-Avery's hot mouth paused in its torture. "Sometimes, I feel I am both man and woman within the same body, my lord. And it is nothing of which to be ashamed."

Pushing folds of linen aside, he took a moment to savour

Lyndon's cock, rising proudly from a halo of fiery red curls. Heat washed over Lyndon's skin as the pup's cool fist closed around the base. With a lick of greeting, he swabbed the tip. Then, stroking Lyndon's shaft, he guided him into the soft sheath of his mouth.

Duchamps-Avery had a mouth like a whore. Lyndon moaned with pleasure. His body thrummed as the pup squeezed and sucked and stroked, feasting on Lyndon's soul. As Duchamps-Avery's jaw worked, his extravagant eyelashes closed over his extraordinary eyes. His tongue laved; his throat swallowed; Lyndon's ballocks tightened. Never had the need to spend come upon him so fast or so strong.

He pushed a startled Duchamps-Avery aside. "I...you must..." Unstoppable, his release surged through him, rope after silvery rope of it. His numbed state vaguely registered Duchamps-Avery, with frantic jerks of his wrist, reaching the same conclusion beneath the folds of the rustling dress. Something Lyndon would like to see properly, if he weren't quite so jellified. As the entirety of his rational consciousness absconded through his cock, he decided that was a treat he'd savour for next time.

*

WHEN LYNDON ROUSED, Duchamps-Avery was once more ensconced on the window seat, trousered legs neatly crossed and book in hand. In a crumpled puddle at his feet lay the red dress. He smiled at Lyndon, though Lyndon didn't think it quite reached his eyes.

"You..." began Lyndon and trailed off.

"Do not feel you have to speak of this, my lord," offered Duchamps-Avery pleasantly. "We could carry on much as before if that is your preference." He held up the novel. "I shall reacquaint myself with Count Rodolfo's misadventures, and you may attend to your *Pointless House Of Worship*. I could ring Lucy for refreshments, and we could eat them whilst marvelling at how the light lands so beautifully on the stones of the north wall."

"I..." Lyndon was lost, a bewildered mess in the face of this boy's composure. Should he congratulate the pup on his excellent technique? How well the dress had suited him? How the vision of his red lips, stretched tight around Lyndon's cock, had been the most singular, spectacular, filthy thing he'd witnessed in the entirety of his fairly extensive sexual explorations? That the sound of the pup's melodic tenor, still hoarse, already had his cock stiffening again? Which of the hundreds of sensations pulling at his mind did he indulge first? Or did he explain that the yellowing limestone of the north wall was well known for its visual trickery at around this time of day, and that several had tried to capture its iridescence on canvas but miserably failed. Including himself.

Duchamps-Avery had given him a means of escape, and coward that he was, he gratefully seized it. "I...yes. It does rather, doesn't it? I shall ring for Lucy."

Chapter Fifteen

~~My dearest Willoughby. His lordship is as well hung as the innocent women at Pendle witch trials.~~

My dearest Willoughby. I find that his lordship is fast becoming Napoleon to my Josephine. Samson to my Delilah. Orsino to my Viola. He is wild and self-willed, and a desperate mass of inconsistencies, and I'm scandalously, hopelessly, one thousand degrees in love with him. And before you say it, yes, I know I've referred to him as an ogre, and I must confess that he has a darker side. But really, when one teases a tiger, shouldn't one learn to expect the odd scratch?

Papa. I must add another string to Lord Lyndon's already impressive bow: swordsmith extraordinaire!

"HIS LORDSHIP HAS requested your presence at luncheon, sir."

Greaves concealed his astonishment at this unusual turn of events by brushing imaginary lint from Rollo's topcoat. In contrast, Rollo's eyebrows rose to his hairline. "Mr Simpson and his daughters will also be in attendance," the footman elaborated.

Rollo could not deny a twinge of disappointment. For the shortest of seconds, he'd allowed himself to imagine Lord Lyndon as eager to be alone in Rollo's company as Rollo was to be in his.

He let out a heavy sigh. *Dear Heart, let's pretend yesterday never happened.* "I am to be a foil," he observed.

Greaves inclined his head slightly. "I believe there are to be some deeds drawn up finalising their charitable venture. His lordship and Mr Simpson are engaged in that currently. Naturally, the squire wishes to use the opportunity to encourage further *friendship* between his daughters and his lordship."

"Naturally," Rollo agreed. "Tell me, Greaves, has Lord Lyndon ever entertained the idea of marriage?"

Greaves considered for a moment. "I believe not, sir. There is talk he had his heart broken as a much younger man and never recovered from it."

Something in the footman's manner suggested he did not share that opinion.

"I understand he spent many idyllic summers here as a youth."

"He did." Greaves tidied Rollo's shaving things, seemingly determined not to meet Rollo's eye. "And this year, I believe he is finding certain aspects of his summer at Goule equally agreeable."

"Oh." Rollo's heart fluttered with hope. "Are you...are you suggesting that—"

"Shall you be requiring the charcoal stripe or the pale yellow today, sir?"

Greaves held up both cravats, his neutral gaze fixed somewhere over Rollo's left shoulder.

An idyllic summer. Rollo adored a challenge.

"Most definitely the yellow," he decided. It was the colour of endless possibilities. "And my navy waistcoat with the inlaid paisley." If Lord Lyndon requested his presence, then that was what he'd have. A shimmering, dazzling, unmissable bright spot of it.

*

HIS HOST'S EXPRESSION held nothing but polite acknowledgement when Rollo joined him in the dining room, not a flicker of what had passed between them. A less optimistic man than Rollo might have imagined he'd dreamed the whole thing.

Simpson and his daughters had already arrived, the man sipping at a thimble of dry sherry whilst his daughters had arranged themselves prettily on the chaise. From the way the ladies pounced on him, Rollo surmised Lord Lyndon's efforts at courteous chit-chat had been as feeble as he'd come to expect.

"Miss Eliza, Miss Nancy! Such an unexpected pleasure!"

Indeed it was, and not only because his gushing elicited one of Lord Lyndon's thunderous scowls.

"May I say, sir, your waistcoat is surely the most divine Goule has ever witnessed," Eliza trilled. "I covet those buttons."

"I shall fight you for them," declared Nancy.

"They were chosen with you two delightful ladies in mind," Rollo lied and swept a theatrical bow, making them giggle. "With your auburn hair, Miss Nancy, and your scarlet reticule, Miss Eliza, my navy complements you both to perfection."

Eliza's cheeks turned a delicate shade of pink. "And on a summery day such as this one, the shade of your cravat is also a joy to behold."

"You a shine as radiantly as a second sun, sir," added Nancy, rapidly fanning herself.

A faint groan sounded from Lord Lyndon's direction. It was a miracle he'd held back this long.

Pretending he hadn't heard, Rollo imparted his most charming smile on the sweet girls. "Then, with you and your sister in attendance, by my calculations, that brings the total number of suns up to four."

Lord Lyndon muttered something incomprehensible under his breath.

Rollo stifled his amusement. "Yet still, we cannot compete with this feast Lord Lyndon has bestowed on us today."

As the girls oohed and aahed, Rollo made a great performance of cooing his own admiration for their smart hats and pretty dresses. In truth, it was no hardship. If only his lordship would alight from his noble high horse, he'd discover it for himself. Both ladies were a credit to their father; the young beaux of the *ton* would welcome them with open arms — literally and metaphorically. Rollo would be more than happy to facilitate introductions.

Thoroughly enjoying his lordship's discomfiture, Rollo compounded it by unleashing his enthusiasm for an update on the vicar's lumbago. Much improved, it transpired. Lavender oil, on this occasion, had not been required.

"Such marvellous news, is it not, Lord Lyndon?"

"Rivalling, if not surpassing, this morning's headlines in the Norfolk Chronicle," Lord Lyndon responded in a tone drier than the parched lawns outside the window. "I'm quite giddy from it."

"Then that's twice you've experienced giddiness in a matter of days," said Rollo smoothly. "Perhaps it's the heat. Although, if memory serves me well, when you came over faint in the nursery, it was far cooler, and you were already seated, if I recall. You —"

"Lunch," Lord Lyndon declared. He marched over to the bell and gave it a furious jingle. "We need lunch. And something stronger than damned sherry."

*

SEATED BETWEEN THE girls and across from Lord Lyndon, Rollo batted his eyelashes in his host's direction every time the poor man looked up. It was set to be the most entertaining luncheon he'd had in years.

"I'm famished," Rollo declared, casting his gaze over the spread. At his shoulder, Greaves ladled steaming celery soup into his waiting bowl. "Cook has outdone herself again. Never have I been as well fed and watered as here at Goule." He shot another mischievous glance at Lord Lyndon. "Why, only yesterday, as I sought to escape this stifling heat by climbing the stairs up to the old nursery, did I quench my thirst on the most divine — ouch!"

His left foot found itself suddenly squashed between the hard parquet floor and a heavy boot.

"I need an update on the building progress, Simpson," barked Lord Lyndon so loudly the girls jumped. "If you would be so kind," he corrected more quietly.

"Certainly, my lord." Dabbing nervously at his mouth, Simpson launched into a complex, thorough, brick-by-brick account. Much of it flew straight over Rollo's head. Although, with his host's solid foot still grinding into his own, concentrating on anything except supping his consommé proved impossible. Thus, Rollo remained silent. As was the heavy foot's intention.

Listening attentively, Lord Lyndon ate in silence, too, though his strong, furrowed brows spoke eloquently on his behalf. Every now and again, he glanced up at Rollo, his dark eyes ruffled with thunder and, unless Rollo was mistaken, a promise of something else. How Rollo wished they were dining alone!

And that he could offer himself up as dinner.

He let his thoughts drift. What *was* the correct etiquette after unexpectedly fellating one's host? Should he follow his host's example, grimly tearing at a heel of bread as if it were Rollo's neck, whilst pretending absolutely nothing had passed between them? Or did one awkwardly join him and Simpson in a conversation about which he knew nothing, simply to remind his lordship of his existence?

Neither seemed satisfactory. Thankfully, at the end of the soup course, the dull discussion regarding building matters ran out of steam. Conversation lightened, and Eliza raised a rare glimmer of a smile from their host by expressing admiration for his lordship's gardening prowess. He began a description of how he'd pruned the bushes along his southern border. Should Rollo join in? Or would the temptation of double entendre prove too much? The topic of gardening was rife with them.

Or should he stay silent and use the time wisely to devise a strategy to seduce his lordship again, if only to convince himself the damned thing had actually happened?

Lord Lyndon's sensual mouth tilted in another half-smile at Simpson's appreciation of the hydrangeas clambering up his northern wall. Apparently deeming it safe, he removed his foot from atop Rollo's.

I'd like to clamber up his northern wall, thought Rollo. And his southern one. And also up his tree trunk legs and across his Herculean chest.

As he swallowed, Fitzsimmons's broad Adam's apple bobbed down to his impeccably tied charcoal cravat and then back up again. A desperate need to lean across the table and bite it assaulted Rollo, or at least nibble on it. He longed to mount the man's lap, to chew on the curve of that full bottom lip, to lick the wine from his tongue and —

"Hydrangea colours are so very susceptible to changes in the soil composition, are they not, my lord?" enquired Miss Nancy shyly.

Lord Lyndon nodded, delivering his third half-smile of the meal, not that Rollo was counting. His heart fluttered happily. *So beautiful.*

"It is my understanding that the shades produced in the flowers are related to the acidity of the soil," he explained. "In these parts, they naturally tend to blue, unless one meddles with the composition."

He took another sip, his damned Adam's apple teasing Rollo once more. Safely hidden under the table, he shifted uncomfortably. Twice now, Lord Lyndon had shot him glances loaded with intent. Once, Rollo was certain he'd foregone his napkin to deliberately swipe a drop of wine from his bottom lip with the pad of his thumb, regarding Rollo as he did so. Hydrangeas be damned. There was a limit to which restraint ceased to be a virtue.

Rollo sank a little in his seat, disguising the movement with a polite cough into his napkin. Then he stretched out a toe and lightly grazed Lord Lyndon's foot. The lord's hawkish nostrils flared.

"And do you think they grow best in an open bed?" Miss Nancy pressed.

Fitzsimmons toyed with his wine glass as Rollo ran the tip of his boot up his lordship's muscular inner calf, eliciting a brief unyielding stare from him, betraying every single one of his desires. None of them noble.

"Whilst they may crave a bed, Miss Nancy," Lord Lyndon stated calmly, "I find they also behave very well against a wall. Especially from a young age. It trains them."

"Is that so?" answered Nancy, her eyes widening with interest.

"Oh yes," he continued wolfishly. "I tend to pin the young ones against it. One must show who's in charge, don't you agree, Simpson?" Simpson gave a firm nod as the toe of Rollo's boot ascended higher.

"Even more so when they lack maturity," added Fitzsimmons.

By now, Rollo sported a cockstand fit to burst. Reaching the bend of Fitzsimmons's knees, he nudged them apart.

"Absolutely, my lord," agreed Simpson. "They require a firm hand; otherwise, they take liberties."

"Precisely." Lord Lyndon gave a satisfied harrumph. "I could not have phrased it better myself, Simpson. And when they climb too high, I snip them back down to size." His dark gaze fastened onto Rollo. "Believe me, I can be quite ruthless."

A small squeak slipped through Rollo's lips. Not trusting his own body, he retreated down his lordship's calf. As his foot touched the floor, a smirking Fitzsimmons once more trapped it under his own.

"Are you quite all right, Duchamps-Avery?" Fitzsimmons enquired, his face a picture of concern. "Have you bitten off more than you can chew?"

"Apologies," Rollo croaked, waving his hand in front of his face. "It is merely a tickle."

"I blame this awfully sticky weather," Eliza responded kindly. "So drying, I find." She turned her attention back to a surprisingly garrulous Lord Lyndon. "Does your personal taste favour a particular shade, my lord?"

Lord Lyndon tilted his head to one side as if considering it. His polished mahogany eyes continued to bore into Rollo, and the foot pressed harder. Rollo gulped. "I believe I run the gamut of all colours. I like to experiment. Here at the Hall, my tastes vary depending on my mood."

"And…how is your mood currently, my lord?" Rollo dared.

"Rather splendid, actually."

Chapter Sixteen

THEIR GUESTS DIDN'T depart for another three years. It seemed that way to Rollo, anyhow. When they did, Lord Lyndon suggested, in a tone brooking no disagreement, he and Rollo retire to the drawing room. Whereupon he dismissed Greaves, ordered Rollo to sit, locked the door behind them, and let out a prolonged, frustrated sigh.

"You vex me, pup," he declared, pacing from the door to the window, where he looked out, his hands clasped behind his back.

"You are not the first to make that observation, my lord. I believe that honour belongs to my father's valet."

Fitzsimmons made a huffing noise. "But perhaps my vexation is of a different nature. One which I am...at a loss as how to resolve."

Rollo could think of several ways, beginning with a renewed exploration between the man's legs.

His lordship cleared his throat, then addressed the garden. "I have bedded countless women. Too many to recall. I am not proud of it. I have not always treated them with the respect and common decency they deserved."

Rollo knew the rumours well, thanks to his father's gossip of a valet. Lord Lyndon Fitzsimmons—recklessly extravagant, a notorious rake. A man of insatiable appetites, housing a mistress in Brighton, a widow in Richmond, a married countess in Wessex.

"Only a good man would have the courage to acknowledge that," Rollo answered carefully. "So do not be too hard on yourself."

"Huh. That is a kind sentiment, sir, but misplaced. And I have committed many other, even more severe sins. Directed at people whom I love."

"But you are reformed, are you not? Since settling back in Goule?"

Rollo suddenly found it vital Lord Lyndon answer in the affirmative.

"Entertaining dull provincial folk at lunchtime and building somewhere to house the local poor and infirm are but feeble reparations. Five homes—ten homes—would be insufficient."

Abruptly, Lord Lyndon turned from the window and paced back again to take up a position in front of the mantel. He drummed his fingers on the cold marble, then raked them through his unruly hair. "But I have never swived a man."

This admission he directed towards a small oil painting of an ugly child clutching an even uglier black dog. Not one of his own. "Though I wanted to, once. And thanks to you and your persistent...*existence*, that *want* has reared its swollen head again."

Rollo bit back the smart witticism at the tip of tongue. *I'm maturing, at last.*

"You once held a *tendre* for your...ah...playroom friend," he hazarded instead. "But it was not reciprocated?"

"It most certainly was." Affronted, Lord Lyndon huffed and folded his arms. "Except it was not to be, and...and I request you question me no further on the matter. The subject is...well, it is painful."

"And now you have developed an inconvenient *tendre* for me. Am I correct?"

Fitzsimmons's gaze narrowed. "Damn your eyes, pup. And damn your insistence on that ridiculous word. There is nothing *tender* about this uninvited business of…of desire and affection. It is harsh and un-mannered and pricks like a thorn." Once more, he strode to the window. "In case I do not make myself clear, my *tendre* for you is an affliction to which I'd have rather not succumbed."

"You are implying I am irresistible?" Rollo teased.

"Like a shiny red apple laced with arsenic, yes."

Rollo found Fitzsimmons's petulant attempts to express his needs charming and his awkwardness seductive. Nonetheless, with burgeon-ing needs of his own, Rollo decided the time had come to help Fitz along a little. He dabbed at his forehead with his pocket square, then dug a finger under his collar.

"Miss Eliza was correct in her observations, my lord. It is awfully sticky today. If you have no objection now that the ladies have departed, I shall relieve myself of my coat."

The lord turned and, as Rollo rose to his feet, tramped back to the fireplace, his fists clenching and unclenching. Making more of a song and dance about things than strictly necessary, Rollo tugged ineffectu-ally at his cuffs.

"I do so adore the latest fashions, but goodness, these tight sleeves can be a devil. I'm of a mind to call for Greaves to assist."

"No!" Lord Lyndon strode to his side, mere inches away, close enough for Rollo to breathe in the warm woodsy, masculine musk of him. A flush spread across Fitzsimmons's cheeks. "No," he repeated more evenly. "My untrained service will suffice."

He removed the coat with surprising gentleness, easing out each arm before pushing the garment from Rollo's shoulders.

"And your cravat," the lord added, his voice rough as a saw edge. "You…remove that too."

His big hands fisted at his sides as if untrusting of them. "Tell me, pup. When men like you…like…like us…when they…what if they are not…not compatible? What if…" His eyes darted down Rollo's half-dressed frame. "What…dammit, what if they both desire the same thing from their…ah…liaison?"

"Then they simply take it in turns, my lord."

Fitzsimmons's jaw dropped, his expression aghast. "And do…do you…"

Cravat in hand, Rollo hid his smile behind it. Him flying to the moon was more likely. He drank in this big beast of a man, chest hard as whinstone, tying himself up in knots like an anxious virgin. The same man whose flinty gaze weakened Rollo's knees while stiffening his cock, a man capable of devouring Rollo's soul for breakfast. And then he spared a glance down at himself, at how his cinched waistcoat hugged his tiny, girlish middle, and at the sunny yellow cravat dangling from his fingers.

"Look at me, my lord."

Two dark eyes, blazing with need, lifted to his.

And Rollo continued. "One should never, ever assume a man's preferences. But look at me properly and then consider yourself. How you like things in bed. How it pleases you to pleasure a woman. And how I bent so readily at your feet and served you." He permitted himself a small smile. "I will hazard a guess that you enjoy playing the part of… the ship's captain. And I am very much accustomed to, and savour, the role of first mate."

Below the proud set of his jaw, his lordship swallowed, once, contemplating. Then nodded. "Understood."

His gaze slipped down to Rollo's slight chest. "Unfasten that waistcoat."

Two curt instructions later, Rollo was stripped of every item bar his drawers and his trousers, which both sagged at his knees, held there by his boots. Fitzsimmons's hand drifted to his jutting member, and he gave an audible swallow.

"Face the wall, pup. Put your palms like so."

Rollo shuffled around. A cool breeze drifted in from the open window, caressing his bare arse. Or perhaps that was Fitzsimmons's fingertip, mapping out his curves. Slowly, he lifted his arms and braced his palms either side of his head. "I'm to be pinned like a hydrangea."

Behind him, Fitzsimmons snorted. Then a firm hand gripped his hips. The other roamed over Rollo's buttocks as Fitz brought his mouth to Rollo's ear. "Perhaps. But they are the fairest blooms in my garden."

Rollo shivered. Again, a light fingertip traced down his crease. An impolite thigh shoved between his legs.

"I want these more apart," his lord demanded.

Rollo spread as much as his yoked knees permitted.

Fitzsimmons's hot breath gusted against his cheek in a long, hot sigh. "How eagerly you please me, *first mate*."

The finger stroked his crease relentlessly. Teasingly light, too much yet not enough. Every pass skimmed, not settling where Rollo craved it most. With a frustrated moan, he arched back into the touch. Fitzsimmons kneaded his bare buttocks.

"This..." He breathed harshly, cupping one of them. "This is carved from the finest marble." He groaned as, once more, he tracked the line of Rollo's crease down to his ballocks, this time cupping them from behind. He rolled one gently between a finger and thumb. "You are well sculpted, pup."

Rollo canted his hips, thrusting against nothing. His cock throbbed, seconds from spending, untouched. He followed orders, though his hands were not tied, merely held in position by that scorching breath against the back of his neck, praising him, promising him, *owning* him. And that damnable finger glided up and down his crease, tapping against his drawn-up ballocks, almost, but never touching, his quivering hole. Beads of perspiration trickled down his temple; moisture leaked from his swollen shaft.

"Fitz...I..."

For the briefest of seconds, Fitzsimmons stepped away, leaving Rollo on the edge of freefall. And then a sharp smack rang out, searing his arse with a flash of pain.

"That's for the devil inside of you," Fitzsimmons purred, but before Rollo's yelp of shock had chance to leave his mouth, a warm palm soothed his smarting cheek. Then smacked it again. "Your bottom infuriates me, pup," he crooned, smoothing away the pain again. Rollo melted into his hand, gasping with pleasure.

"The way it moves whenever you walk away from me." Fitzsimmons half laughed as if marvelling at his own foolishness. "Such a pretty shade of red you have turned. I am inclined to put the whole thing over my knee and give it another good, swift spank."

The devil inside Rollo wanted that too, and he pushed his arse out in search of the delightful sting. The devil inside Fitzsimmons didn't respond. Instead, he spat, rubbing the wetness into Rollo's crease. He hawked again, adding to it. Then, huge, hard, and wanting, Fitzsimmons bare cock slotted against the groove. Two large hands covered Rollo's, trapping them against the wall.

"I look at you, and I want so many things," Fitzsimmons groaned, thrusting hard. "You tempt me, pup, you tease out my every weakness. You make me so I can think of nothing but this."

Rollo whimpered, writhing with need. "Please," he begged. "Please, I need to —"

"Shhh." Fitzsimmons shoved two fingers into his mouth, stifling his moans. "You'll be entertaining the entire household, my precious. And I want you to myself."

His breath shuddered against Rollo's nape as Rollo clamped down on the fingers, and Fitzsimmons slickly pleasured himself between his cheeks, every brush against Rollo's hole an exquisite, unbearable torture. Wetness dribbled down Rollo's shaft, a single stroke of a fist and he'd reach his crisis. Yet he still kept his hands against the wall.

Fitzsimmons's thrusts turned more erratic, his breathing more ragged against Rollo's nape. Almost painfully, his fingers dug into Rollo's hip as every snap of his own brought him nearer to climax.

"Mine, mine, mine," he panted. "My precious, precious pup."

A guttural cry escaped his throat, and Rollo gasped as hot streaks of milky release, like the sharp welts of a whip, branded his tender backside. He felt Fitzsimmons smear it, and then a thick, slippery finger pressed inside Rollo. Fitz's other hand reached around to Rollo's cock and jerked it once, twice.

And Rollo shattered, neither Fitz's firm hand nor his intrusive finger relenting until Rollo cried out, squirming away from sensations so sharp, so delicious, so unbearable, that for a moment, he quite forgot to breathe. If not for Fitzsimmons's strong body, a veritable fortress of warmth and strength, then he might well have melted into a pool of jelly on the nursery floor.

*

"YOUR LEGS, DUCHAMPS-Avery, they're trembling."

Rollo gave a shaky laugh. "I fear my bones have dissolved too. And…Rollo, please. Your hands have been everywhere."

Taking his elbow, Fitzsimmons guided him to the settee. Naturally, the offer of using first names wasn't returned. Wordlessly, Fitzsimmons hitched Rollo's trousers back up to his waist, allowed him to collapse in an untidy sprawl, then took his usual seat across from him. For a long moment, they sat in silence. An overwhelming need for a snooze struck Rollo, and he'd have quite liked to indulge it in his lover's arms. Alas, that was not to be. Instead, Fitzsimmons picked up his bow and pressed his thumb against the string, examining the tension. Then, taking his time, he selected an arrow and nocked it. His expression had become blank and remote, almost as if the last few minutes had never happened.

My precious. Ah, well. Men uttered all kinds of claptrap when overcome with the force of release. This man was an utter enigma, which Rollo was too drained to ponder. As Fitzsimmons brought the bow up to take aim, Rollo allowed his eyes to drift closed. At least he was no longer a target. He smiled sleepily as a pewter soldier rattled to the floor.

"May I ask why you do that?"

Fitzsimmons let out a long, troubled sigh before selecting another arrow. "Does it offend you?"

Rollo thought for a moment. "Not especially. As long as I'm over here and the pointy end of the arrow is over there."

Another arrow thudded into another soldier. Just when Rollo thought Fitzsimmons might not answer, he began quietly speaking.

"Not so long ago, I had a terrible urge to kill myself. I planned to drown in the lake or succumb to an accident, a tumble from the roof or some such. Many times, I have climbed up there. Have even settled over the parapet, letting my legs dangle, contemplating the drop. Or agreed to let fate take its course. Would a puff of wind send me over the edge, or would I be spared? Would I trip on a loose slate?" He slotted another arrow. "I'd wonder if my death would be instant, or whether I'd survive the fall but spend the remainder of my days boxed up in a chair, sucking soup through a straw, and having my arse wiped by a woman paid a lot of coin to make a decent job of it."

He glanced sidelong at Rollo. "Naturally, I'd do whatever necessary to make it seem accidental to avoid disgracing Ashington. Though there would be enough evidence suggesting a temporary lack of sound mind." He smiled thinly. "My artistic endeavours, for instance."

Two soldiers fell in rapid succession, one toppling the adjacent. "Shooting at these soldiers began as a substitute for shooting at myself. And then became habit. It...it soothed my mind." He cut through the ensuing pause by adding, "That was not the answer you sought, I'd wager?"

Rollo's sleepiness dissipated, replaced with a pang of sorrow for the complicated individual to whom he was fast becoming attached. "It was not the answer I expected, that is true." But strangely, it did not surprise him. "May I ask why? Were you suffering from a deep melancholia?"

"No. I don't believe I was." Fitzsimmons made to select another arrow before apparently thinking better of it. "I simply realised I didn't care for myself very much. And that neither did anyone else."

"I'm sure His Grace and Lord Francis have always cared for you deeply."

"Hmm. Perhaps. I fear I have tested that care over the years. Certainly, my existence is not an essential ingredient for their happiness."

A yawning hush descended on the drawing room, disturbed only by a woodpigeon pottering about outside the window, cooing in a minor key. Rollo could easily have filled the void with barren platitudes, pointing out that so many at Goule were dependent on Lord Lyndon for their livelihoods, but he doubted it would have endeared him. So, he said nothing, whilst Fitzsimmons steadily worked his way through his miniature regiment.

"I am afflicted by a terrible jealous streak." Fitzsimmons's full lips pursed. "Along with a temper that flares like lit brandy. You witnessed the consequences when Ralph Hart placed his hands on you."

To think now that Rollo could ever have allowed another man to touch him when this one had been so close! "Your intervention was timely," he declared. "Though it didn't feel so at the time. I am grateful."

"Neither his damned hungry eyes nor mine strayed from you all evening. My jealousy would not allow it."

You belong to me. Perhaps the sentiments Fitzsimmons moaned at the peak of his crisis held a sliver of truth after all.

His lover let out a long sigh. "Benedict has borne the brunt. I have been jealous of my twin's birthright for as long as I can recall. It is astonishing, is it not, that two minutes, separating two babes in a bloodied maternal bed, can be of such profound consequence?"

"Amen to that," agreed Rollo. "My own mother bled out birthing myself and Willoughby."

"Ah. I was not aware," Fitzsimmons replied stiffly. "I'm so awfully sorry."

"You'll soon get over it." Rollo threw him a rueful smile. "But thank you for your kind sentiment. By all accounts, she was a marvellous woman, but one does not mourn that which one has never known. We have our dearest papa, and we have never lacked for love and affection. Neither have I ever been jealous of Willoughby and the weight of scrutiny he will bear in the future as Rossingley."

"No." Fitzsimmons regarded him thoughtfully. "As I have alluded, I have not always been terribly fond of myself. Growing up alongside Benedict, I was aware that I was stronger, possessed of greater intelligence. That my father favoured him in all ate into my soul." His dark gaze flicked up to Rollo. "I resented that my twin would one day become Ashington, and I tormented him. I drew Father's ire, which was never far from hand at the best of times. I was disruptive and grew to despise them both."

Rollo would need a far better understanding of the man to parse whether "my precious" and "you belong to me" were meaningless blandishments. But there was no mistaking Fitzsimmons's softly spoken words now as anything but brutal truths. They were all there, laid out in the crack of his voice, the white shine to his knuckles, the abrupt turn of his face towards the fireplace, away from Rollo. If they'd been seated closer, he'd have taken the other's hand in his own.

"Are you still envious?" Rollo asked. "As your brother learns to live with all the weight that being Ashington entails? I, for one, would not walk in Willoughby's shoes for every leaf of tea in China." Rollo pulled a face. "I'd have to force myself to marry and beget children, for one thing."

Fitzsimmons nodded acknowledgment. "History will remember Benedict as an excellent, dutiful duke in every aspect except that one."

Rollo's discreet papa had never alluded to the Duke of Ashington's preferences. Though Rollo had always suspected as much, and now Fitzsimmons had all but confirmed it.

"So it is down to you, my lord," Rollo replied lightly, "to keep the Fitzsimmons in heirs. After all, you are next in line."

Fitzsimmons gave a half-hearted shrug. "Yes, it is true that I am next. But who knows which of us will perish first? Francis, however, is far younger and already married. And has begat a son. I daresay more will follow."

He hesitated. "But in answer to your question, yes, I do still envy Benedict. It is a failure of my character. Though I no longer possess sufficient arrogance to believe I would perform the role better than he." Fitzsimmons sorrowful eyes shone with unspent tears. "He is kinder, generous, and…and a finer man in all respects. I know that now."

"Whatever you perceive to be your failings, your honesty is above reproach, my lord."

Fitzsimmons huffed a miserable laugh and picked up his bow. "It is hard won. At the cost of losing my dear twin brother's trust."

Rollo had heard enough. He rose to his feet. "Put down your bow and stand up," he ordered. "Lift your arms away from your sides, like so."

Demonstrating, he raised his own arms to shoulder height and walked over to the befuddled lord. Amid much grumbling, he hauled Fitzsimmons up.

"What the devil for?" Fitzsimmons demanded, though he complied, much to Rollo's astonishment.

"So that I may provide comfort." He encircled the lord's torso with his own arms. "Like this. For both of us."

Fitzsimmons froze. "I…what in God's…"

"Shush."

The great yew outside the window might have yielded more. As Rollo squeezed tighter, Fitzsimmons tensed. For a moment, it felt more like they were wrestling than embracing.

"What the dickens do you need comfort for?" Fitzsimmons groused. "You've only just had your ballocks emptied. Is that not enough?"

Rollo eyed him sternly. "I have been so unbelievably homesick these last few weeks. Rossingley is far, far away from this drawing room. My papa is a fair and reasonable dictator—our home is short on rules. One of them, however, is that when a person suffers distress, another seeks to comfort." He squeezed Fitzsimmons's middle again, for emphasis. "Like this. We both need this. You, because dwelling on the past saddens you, and me, for my homesickness, even though my family live forever in my heart and in my soul."

"I'm astonished there is room for them. Your heart is clearly jammed full of trite, romantic flummery."

Rollo grinned. The Fitzsimmons of whom he was growing awfully fond had returned. He turned his head to rest it against the soft white linen of the other's shirt. Woodsy cologne filled his nostrils, and a solid thump resounded in his ear. Rollo wished they were in a bed instead of the middle of the drawing room.

Still barely tolerating him, Fitzsimmons remained stiff as a tree trunk.

Rollo braced his feet. "Drop your shoulders, Fitz, and place your arms around me as I am doing to you."

"This is even more foolish than sword fighting," Fitzsimmons muttered. Nonetheless, two strong arms curled around Rollo's narrow back. For several minutes, they stood that way, one rigid as a pencil, the other trying his damnedest not to grind his fresh cockstand against a firm hip bone.

"Tell me," Rollo asked. "When were you last embraced?"

Fitzsimmons's low chuckle rumbled beneath Rollo's ear. "Is that what this is?"

"It's a facsimile of one, yes. More of a work in progress. Very much like your oils. We could call this one *A Study in Discomfiture*."

Another rolling chuckle reverberated beneath his ear. "I would cuff you for that." The lord's nose and mouth skimmed over the fine ends of Rollo's hair. "If I didn't think you'd enjoy it."

Rollo's urge to rub himself against the man's nether regions intensified. "My papa declares a warm embrace a cure for most ills."

"Sometimes, I feel as though your papa is in this room with us. Surely, he doesn't believe this...this thing we're attempting to be even more efficacious than oil of lavender?"

Rollo giggled. His lordship's posture had softened, now less a pencil or a tree, more a malleable but sturdy willow branch. Progress indeed. "That very much depends upon where one is applying the lavender oil, my lord."

Chapter Seventeen

THEY WERE STILL in a bloody hold. Or embracing, or whatever the damned pup called it. Five minutes later!

Just when Lyndon thought he'd have to suggest something devilishly uncomfortable along the lines of *shall we continue this on the settee*, Rollo tipped his head up from its nest on Lyndon's chest to regard him.

"The servants remember you as a lively child, but not a bad one," he said.

"How generous of them."

"You were always polite and charming. They say you suddenly changed."

"For better or worse?" Lyndon already knew the answer.

"Mmm. Worse, I'm afraid."

"I must sack them all immediately."

Rollo—Lyndon enjoyed testing his Christian name in his mind far too much—chuckled, locking his arms around Lyndon even more tightly. "They are very fond of you. And loyal. They fret for your happiness."

"Yes. I believe they do."

Lyndon leaned into the warm, slight body wrapped around his own. A body so insubstantial, Lyndon felt a sudden urge to pick Rollo up, sling him over his shoulder, and carry him up to bed.

Instead, as if they were a pair of starstruck lovers, he continued the damned foolish clinch. His defences against Rollo were as robust as a paper lantern. He had prised almost all of Lyndon's deepest regrets from him as easily as peeling a plum; a knife to the throat would have been less efficacious. And in Lyndon's bloody drawing room of all places, his refuge. He should draw the embrace to a close before any more truths and sorrows—the worst of him, in fact—bled from his soul.

Yet, a minute later, they were still entwined, thus ensuring even more words and confessions would pour from him as though Rollo had turned on a bloody tap.

"There was an incident," Lyndon admitted, "of which I do not wish to speak. When I was much your age. And, as a consequence, I became unwell. I quarrelled with my parents, incessantly. I drank too much. After reaching my majority, I spent several years as a scoundrel, a rake, a spendthrift. Our father died, but not before removing the bulk of my annual income. At the time, I could not see he did it in my best interests and in the best interests of Ashington. It felt like the cruellest blow and…and I sought revenge by hounding Benedict. I blamed him for everything. I behaved abominably and almost destroyed the Fitz-simmons name and my dear, kind brother's life."

"But you didn't."

"No."

Lyndon hated how his voice broke. How that single syllable could so easily have been a yes. And how much this extraordinary creature in his arms, on hearing that syllable, wanted to believe Lyndon to be a good man.

"Yet I would have done," he confessed. "Gladly. Except Benedict admitted his mounting concerns to your father, who intervened. Together, they taught me a most harsh lesson in a manner most brutal and humiliating and absolutely everything I deserved."

Rollo let out a long breath. "That is why you disliked me so."

"Yes." Lyndon laughed softly. "The arrival of the Earl of Rossingley's bantling did not improve my mood. Clearly, your father was of the opinion he hadn't punished me enough."

"I shall pretend I didn't hear that." Rollo's fine hair fluttered every time Lyndon exhaled. Even more so when Lyndon rested his chin on his head. Somehow, their feet had moved closer together too. They had become so interwoven that it was difficult to define where one had ended and the other began.

"Do you still feel the same?" Rollo enquired against Lyndon's chest. "Bearing in mind I am standing nearer to the poker than you."

Lyndon laughed again. "I have since found out that his unwelcome gift is a capricious sprite. And his torment is an excellent tonic for the blue devils."

"Heavens above. Better than lavender oil?"

"As I have absolutely no intention of ever putting my body anywhere near that most unmanly of potions, I shall never find out."

Lyndon embraced him even tighter, one last time, then stepped back a little. A smug smile crept across Rollo's face as if he knew exactly how much Lyndon had relished their intimacy. Lyndon could easily have kept it going another hour, though who knew where his garrulous tongue might have led him if he did. He attempted a severe look.

"Now it is time to leave me in peace. No doubt you have a dreadful novel to read and pages of foolscap to fill with inane drivel, and I certainly have a painting of the chapel roof to ruin. Otherwise, heaven forbid, you will think I'm soft."

*

"I SHALL TAKE my luncheon in the library today, Berridge," Lyndon announced, handing his hat to the waiting butler and continuing apace towards the stairs. "I'll wash first."

Having spent an hour reading to Will, then weeding his potato patch under a relentless hot sun and to a background of Will's running critique of his prowess with a hand fork, Lyndon was ravenous. "Simpson has sent over a mound of papers relating to the building accounts for me to wade through. I may as well get started."

"Um…" For once, Berridge appeared ill at ease. "Mr Duchamps-Avery has…ah…requested a picnic be made up."

Lyndon's long stride came to a juddering halt. "A *picnic?*"

"Yes, my lord. Cook advised him regarding your preferred meats and cheeses. He has food and drink in baskets. Rugs and a flagon too. Plates, and a cloth to cover the grass."

Pinching the bridge of his nose, Lyndon sighed. His routines and the running of his household used to be so straightforward. "I am abreast of the fundamentals of a picnic, Berridge. But I'm at a loss to explain how it pertains to me."

"You are to be his picnicking guest."

Lyndon sighed again. "I assume this is an outdoor picnic?"

"Yes, my lord. They…um…generally are."

The last time Lyndon had picnicked outside, he'd been in short trousers. "If I'd wanted ants crawling over my food, I'd have put in a request to Cook first thing. Could we not dine on the same lunch inside? Insect free?"

Berridge looked pained. "It…ah…it may be too late for that, my lord. My understanding is that Greaves and young Jack have already carted everything out onto the south lawn. They have set up under the beech trees overlooking Beccles Vale. Mr Duchamps-Avery has chosen a delightful spot, if I may say so. I believe he already awaits your presence in the gardens."

"I see."

"He particularly requested Cook prepare rout cakes, and I believe there is salmagundi."

Lyndon's mouth watered. Two of his absolute favourites. Since his extravagant display of verbosity two days earlier, he was no longer sure he had the nerve to look Rollo in the eye. He'd admitted he found the young man beguiling! And had poured out his woes, one by one. Even Will, privy to all of Lyndon's numerous failings, had never been subjected to the horror of hearing them enumerated so thoroughly.

Thus, Lyndon was ashamed to admit he'd been avoiding him. He'd found an excuse to spend the entirety of yesterday in Norwich, managing spurious financial affairs, rising early and returning late. But he couldn't avoid his house guest forever, and the trip had been rather less successful in relegating Rollo from his mind than he'd hoped. The warm leather of his carriage seat, for instance, had brought to mind the heat of Rollo's trim body crushed against his own. The squeak of a carriage wheel mimicked the cry of his release. The undulating curve of Bishop Bridge, taking Lyndon over the murky waters of the Wensum and into Norwich, had taken the shape of the supple arch of Rollo's back as Lyndon pleasured himself against him. Honestly, the damned pup was everywhere he bloody went.

So many years had passed since he'd ever come close to having a man. None but this young man and his dearest Will had ever given him cause to want to. But, by God, at this moment, how Lyndon wanted to.

"I've laid out your light charcoal linen topcoat, my lord, and linen trousers," prompted Berridge as if the damned picnic was a fait accompli. "Given that the day is so fine. And there is soap and hot water in your bedchamber."

"Huh." Lyndon resumed his path to the stairs. "Down by the beech trees, you say."

"Yes, my lord. It is an excellent day for it. Do have fun."

"You're a traitor, Berridge."

"Yes, my lord. Quite possibly." And on that note, Berridge became terribly busy polishing a silver candlestick.

*

FROM ACROSS THE expanse of lawn, Lyndon stood quietly for a few minutes, observing his young guest. Sprawled on a checked woollen rug, Rollo had made a pillow of another and read from a book propped on his chest, his neat bare feet crossed at the ankles. Lyndon had half hoped, in the intervening days, that Rollo's allure would have somehow lessened. Alas, watching him now, a bundle of silky, relaxed, elegant limbs laid out like a harvest feast, only fanned the flames of Lyndon's hunger.

He strode across the grass.

"You came!" Rollo exclaimed, turning with apparent delight at Lyndon's approach.

Lyndon stifled a grin. Give an inch and Duchamps-Avery would seize a yard. He'd have Lyndon making a crown out of daisies or hand feeding him stoned cherries. "The alternative was starvation, seeing as you have bewitched my servants and commandeered my lunch."

Indefatigable in the face of Lyndon's determination not to appear pleased, Rollo pressed a palm against his chest. "Your charm is unrivalled, my lord." He gestured to a small patch of rug next to him. "Look, there is space for both of us."

Resisting the urge to take Rollo's hand or, indeed, push him to the ground and mount him like a rutting stag, Lyndon distracted himself by plucking at blades of grass and watching his companion out of the corner of his eye as he poured them both modest glasses of wine. When he was done, Rollo lay back down and patted the rug behind where Lyndon stiffly sat.

"Lie here a moment. Rest yourself. Tell me about your trip to

Norwich. I have never visited."

"I thought the purpose of coming here was to eat. To endure a picnic."

Rollo laughed. Was there nothing Lyndon could say to pierce that excellent humour? "All in good time, Fitz. But let me warn you, I'm the picnic that talks back."

He lifted his head from his makeshift pillow to sip at his wine. Thanks to the awkward position, a few ruby drops dribbled down his chin. Eyes bright with amusement, Rollo wiped them with the back of his hand before his pink tongue darted out to lick them up.

Though shaded by trees, the picnic spot was still awfully close to the house. Too close for anything other than picnicking, and Lyndon's ballocks sensed a long, achy afternoon ahead. More so when the pup patted Lyndon's leg and then, as if checking his belongings were all present and correct, let his light fingers wander along it.

"Ravish me with your words, my lord," Rollo declared lazily. "This fine weather puts me in a romantic mood." He closed his eyes against the sun. "Undress me with your cleverness. Touch me with your soul. Seduce me, Fitz."

Reaching the end of their travels, the young man's long fingers took up thankfully modest residence on Lyndon's lower thigh. Perhaps his ballocks might get a reprieve after all.

"I'm not entirely convinced much seduction is required," Lyndon observed. "One, your hand is already touching my person. Two, you have invited me here, alone, to this sheltered spot, when we could so easily have eaten in the dining room in the presence of Greaves. Three, at your request, I am informed those baskets contain some of my favourite delicacies, and four, you are halfway down a glass of good wine." *Which has brought a rosy flush to your cheeks that I would like nothing more than to kiss away.* "Oh, and lest we forget—five, you have already seduced me. Twice."

"Oh, don't be such a curmudgeon. Do it anyway. Romance me, Fitz!"

"For heaven's sake. Must I?"

"Yes, you must. Otherwise, I shall keep all the pigeon pie to myself."

Lyndon adored Cook's pigeon pie. Gingerly, he lay down, but on his side and propped on an elbow so he could keep his eyes peeled for marauding ants and wasps. Most certainly not to admire the set of excessively fluffy eyelashes feathering his companion's cheeks. It was a wonder they didn't get tangled up in themselves each time the pup blinked.

The day's temperature had reached its peak, and a sliver of perspiration coated the youth's smooth upper lip. Dampness darkened the roots of his pointlessly showy blond hair. With his mere existence Rollo was successfully seducing Lyndon, laying bare Lyndon's own seductive inadequacies without even trying. What should he do? Romance and he were barely acquainted. Compliment his attire — again? Concoct an impromptu ode?

"I'm waiting," Rollo said in a sing-song voice. "There will be no pigeon pie."

Frowning, Lyndon tried to recall the romantic sonnets he'd been forced to learn by rote at school. Alas, only snatches of the most popular verses came back to him. Oh well, he'd improvise.

"'Shall I compare thee to a summer's day?'" he began.

Rollo clapped his hands with delight. "Do! Do! I am a mere swoon away from melting already."

"Fine." Lyndon grinned. "But be careful what you wish for."

Pursing his lips and straining at the edges of his memory, Lyndon adopted the grave baritone of his old English tutor. "'Shall I compare thee to a summer's day?' Thou art more sweaty and this heat is more hellish — rough winds today would be greeted with joyful abandon, and thou goest on and on interminably when more than anything, I'd like my lunch and then a peaceful postprandial snooze."

He clamped his mouth shut, at risk of producing an undignified giggle. "Art thou happy now?"

Rollo gave his thigh a well-deserved slap, then giggled himself, a sound warming Lyndon's bones better than the smoothest of French brandies. "You are a beast, Lord Lyndon, of the most delicious kind. And your grammar is atrocious. You and Willoughby would be splendid chums. You could concoct dreadful odes together."

Opening a pale, glittery eye, Rollo held up an admonishing finger. "Just one minor point, my lord: I do not sweat. I sparkle. My papa always says—"

"Oh, good. I wondered if your papa would be joining our picnic. When I'm finally allowed to have the blasted picnic. That's a strong hint, by the way."

Grumbling, Rollo sat up and began passing bread and cheese to Lyndon. "I was about to say my papa's a great fan of bastardising Shakespeare to suit his needs. He would have found your impromptu verse hilarious."

"Somehow, I doubt that."

Nothing Lyndon had ever done in his former existence as a rogue about town had ever met with the Earl of Rossingley's exacting approval. He had no reason to believe seducing his precious second son would either.

"You have the wrong impression of him entirely, Fitz. After all, he begat me, so he can't be all bad."

Lyndon should have argued that point on principle alone. But he was too hot and too sleepy. And Rollo was feeding him tasty morsels directly into his mouth as if his own hands had suddenly stopped working. Being so indulged was far too lovely to interrupt.

"My father wouldn't have sent me here if he didn't believe there was some good in you," the pup prattled between popping delightful slivers of pigeon pie between Lyndon's lips. "He cares too much for me to put me in the company of a poor influence."

As Rollo reached up to place a honeyed walnut on Lyndon's tongue, Lyndon took his wrist, his fingers easily wrapping around it.

"And if he knew of our sport in the nursery?" Lyndon asked. "And drawing room? What then?"

Rollo shrugged. "He is aware of my preference for men. He shares it himself."

Lyndon traced the path of a fragile blue vein with his thumb. "But a preference for me in particular?"

"He is, of course, unaware. But his opinions on the matter are not relevant. I may not have yet reached my majority, but I am still master of my own desires."

Lyndon chuckled. Lately, his own enslaved him. "You have mastered frustrating me and very little else."

With his belly full and his empty plate — a tasty lure for crawling insects — placed well clear of his person, Lyndon lay down again. As his eyelids drooped, he clasped his hands behind his head. Sun, wine, rich food, and a perpetual state of arousal tired him out.

Next to him, Rollo picked at the cold cuts, wittering on about how he enjoyed them with Cook's piccalilli, yet at bloody Rossingley, they also ate them with a ferment of fennel. Personally, Lyndon thought that sounded vile. Nonetheless, Rollo's light tenor, endlessly washing over him, was soothing. Lyndon would never admit that, of course. He'd already made a cake of himself admiring the pup's slender form. The compliment had slipped from him as Rollo topped up his wine before he'd had time to rein it back in. And then he'd pointed out that the slenderness extended to his fingers too — Lyndon had even held one up for closer inspection whilst rubbing his thumb along that bony little wrist, holding on to it for far longer than necessary. Bloody idiot. So, he decided to shut up for a bit.

"All this romantic twaffle is exhausting," he announced sleepily. "I need to recover. Which means silence, pup."

As the scarred old branches of the beech trees whispered to one another, Lyndon's mind drifted in that rare, comfortable twilight haze, which only the very best of afternoon naps reliably delivered. Not quite awake but not asleep either, he inhaled a few long deep breaths, letting the sweet scents of the wild Norfolk earth waft up his nose. Somewhere above his head, a lethargic orchestra of songbirds composed a few half-hearted sonnets, far sweeter than his own.

A drop of something warm and damp landed on his forehead. And then another, heavier this time, against his temple. Most odd. Lyndon didn't think he'd been snoozing for more than a few minutes and not a single cloud had marred the sky all day. Furthermore, the rest of him remained perfectly warm and dry. Begrudgingly, he prised opened one eye, expecting to see clouds gathering through the green canopy of beech leaves. Instead, Rollo loomed over him, his face awfully close and grinning like a court jester.

"What the devil are you doing?"

"What does it look like I'm doing. I'm kissing you. Or trying to."

As if to demonstrate, he bent closer and briefly pressed his lips to Lyndon's mouth. Soft and light as a feather. Then he pulled away. Lyndon frowned, dabbing a finger against where Duchamps-Avery had kissed him.

"Why?"

Rollo chortled. "My mouth has already tasted your cock, so I thought it was time I tasted your lips."

Lyndon's member thickened at the reminder. He glanced back towards the house. Alas, it had not moved farther away during his snooze. "Is that something sodomites do? Do they not simply fornicate in order to attain bodily release?"

Rollo's smile stretched even wider. "Do you not kiss your female lovers?"

Lyndon grimaced, remembering one particular experience which had felt akin to drowning, all too slowly, in a sea of ratafia and spit. "If I must. When one is not paying in coin, then they generally expect it."

Rollo rolled his eyes. "Your charm knows no bounds, Lord Lyndon. Did you kiss your boyhood friend?"

"Well, yes…but…we were mere…boys. And friends. Experimenting."

"Yes, but did you enjoy it?"

A flash of colour — the bright yellow walls of the nursery — seized Lyndon's mind. Two blunted swords and a wooden chest. Carefree laughter. His dearest Will in his worn breeches and thin cotton shirt, his long solemn face regarding Lyndon's as if the answers to the entire universe were contained within. But then the face changed, became fairer, the shirt crisper; loose linen trousers replaced ragged wool breeches.

"Yes. Very much."

Lyndon reached up to cup the narrow nape of Rollo's neck. He pulled him closer. "But I shall enjoy this more."

A fleeting second passed before their mouths met. A pause in time, during which Lyndon drank in the perfect bow of Rollo's upper lip and the sweeping curve of the lower, his delicate beauty, like grace itself, coming towards him.

Lyndon wanted to grasp it and claim it and never give it back.

Rollo kissed as prettily as he walked. Their first was long, slow, deep, and soft. Blissful, in fact. Yet terrifying, all at the same time. With a tight knot of want pooling in his belly, Lyndon rolled him onto his back, the better to devour his mouth. A few years had elapsed since Lyndon's own had been used for kissing. With relief, he discovered it still knew what to do.

When at last they parted, breathless and panting, Lyndon gently slid off him. He lay on his side, feasting his eyes on Rollo's flushed, bruised lips. "For a small, capricious sprite, you have an unnerving ability to unman me," he murmured.

Unable to resist, he slid a finger into the corner of Rollo's mouth and ran it across the swollen bottom lip. Against the fall of his trousers, his cockstand still throbbed uncomfortably. "If my servants weren't nearby, I'd strip you bare and take you right here."

His lover sucked the finger into the wet heat of his mouth in a manner leaving no room for misunderstanding. He might as well have been doing it to Lyndon's cock.

"It is only because your servants are nearby that you haven't already thrice had that pleasure, my lord. Though to be smothered all afternoon in your tender kisses is a more than adequate substitute."

Lyndon preened even as his skin pinked, the blush likely not escaping Rollo's pale, sharp gaze. As that same gaze cornered Lyndon's own, he folded one of Lyndon's big hands in his smaller one as if the hand was his to do with as he pleased.

"I have stirred up emotions you wished lay dormant," Rollo stated. "You believed yourself cured of attraction to another man." He smiled gently. "Your marvellous kisses suggest that you have concluded it is a tiresome condition for which there is no cure."

"Yes." Lyndon faltered at the candid summing up. A strand of unhappiness reminded him how undeserving he was of praise. "I…here…with you, I find I am the very thing I wielded against Benedict in a cruel attempt to bring him down. I used my knowledge of his predilections against him. Were it not for your father's intervention, Benedict's position as one of the most regarded dukes in the land would have tumbled. He would have been humiliated and shamed. And lost his well-deserved contentment forever."

Lyndon swallowed, that damned break in his voice returning with a vengeance. "But if our roles were reversed, he would never have done the same to me. Not for all the gold, tea, brandy, or damned to-bacco smuggled through the Thames docks. And still, the man has found it in his capacious heart to forgive me."

"You would like to make your peace with him, yes?"

"Yes," answered Lyndon carefully. "When I was *exiled* here —" He gave Rollo a wry look. "—I was still too angry, too proud to properly express my remorse." Blowing out a long breath, Lyndon examined their joined hands. "And perhaps too ashamed. But now, there is much I'd like to say to him."

Rollo nodded. "Excellent news," he declared softly.

"Is it?"

"Oh, yes."

Even before it spilled from Rollo's delectable lips, Lyndon sensed trouble brewing. The sly expression crossing his lover's face was too reminiscent of his damned *papa*. Sealing Lyndon's doom, Rollo brought Lyndon's hand up to his mouth and kissed each finger, one by one, be-fore his lips curved into an enticing smile. At that moment, Lyndon doubted there was nothing his companion could do or say that would meet with his disapproval.

Well, almost nothing.

"The day after tomorrow," Rollo said, "the Duke of Ashington ar-rives at his solicitor's office in Norwich on business. I have arranged that we, too, shall visit. A light lunch is planned, and then the duke is of a mind to tour your charitable venture."

Chapter Eighteen

My dearest Willoughby. I pray to God that you and Papa are right about the duke's forgiving nature. Fitz can't even form his name without tying himself in knots about the possible consequences of his impending visit.

Papa. Fitzsimmons is an ardent enthusiast of summer picnics. Especially when ants are involved. And his splendid garden is awash with hydrangeas; I could lie on a blanket for hours, under the shady beeches, admiring every single living thing in it.

Your Grace. Forgive me for speaking out of turn. But know that your brother has much to say, even when he does not say it.

ROLLO HAD EXPERIENCED various iterations of his lover since arriving at Goule. The dour, brooding lord taking pot shots at him was a memorable highlight, absent of late. A much friendlier fellow had since taken his place, someone still trying his hardest to be a crotchet, but his crabbiness diluted by a desire to kiss Rollo wherever and whenever they were alone. He proved so during another picnic the following day, when his thirsty tongue licked against Rollo's as if his life depended on it. And again, on the settee in the drawing room, with Rollo hauled into his lap. And also, against the encyclopaedia shelves in the library.

Even more extraordinary was his lordship's apparent contentment with kissing. He cherished Rollo's face between his warm palms, stroking his thumb tenderly across a cheek, catching his chin and lifting it as if he were made of porcelain. Pressing his lips against Rollo's nose, his eyelids, his temples, before seeking out his mouth.

It was almost as if he had acquired and was honing a brand new skill.

Notwithstanding, this panicked, anxious version of Fitz sharing a carriage with him was a newer one still. As his handsome pair of roans picked their way through the busy Norwich streets, he repeatedly straightened his cravat and fiddled with his gloves. Beginning to feel on edge himself, Rollo took over after first pressing a firm, quick kiss to his lips.

"You're meeting your beloved twin brother, not heading for the gallows."

"At present, swinging from the gibbet is looking more attractive."

Rollo tutted. "Now you're being ridiculous." He kissed him again briskly. "You have put off making your reparations for far too long. You said so yourself." Fitz's silk cravat slipped around his fingers. "Whilst avoidance is a highly commendable strategy and not without its advantages, on this occasion, you've allowed this rendezvous to build into something it's not."

Leaning back, he admired his handiwork. His father's son through and through, the cravat was geometrically flawless. "Most likely, His Grace will wave your apology away, tell you how much he's missed you, and within five minutes, you'll have moved on to other matters."

For the first time during the journey, Fitzsimmons smiled. "If I forget later, thank you for coming with me today. You have an old soul behind those young eyes, Rollo."

Rollo. If the carriage weren't slowing, Rollo would have kissed him again. *Rollo.* Spoken fondly, with deliberate, quiet intent.

As his heart skipped several beats, the carriage drew to a halt, and Rollo peered through the window. He found his lover's hand with his own and gave it a squeeze.

"Everything will be fine, you'll see. Just be yourself. Say something nice."

Fitz emitted an agonised noise. "Which? I can't do both."

Rollo chuckled, unnecessarily tweaking his own hat and gloves as the groom opened the carriage door. "Everything will be fine. I promise. Courage, dearest Fitz."

"I have all the courage I'll ever require," he grumbled, "if I die within the next minute."

Rollo didn't catch the solicitor's name. Clearly prewarned by His Grace as to his minimal role in the lunchtime proceedings, the man produced two or three obsequious bows, then, citing an urgent engagement elsewhere, left his most distinguished clients to get on with things.

Which neither of them did.

Despairingly, Rollo regarded them both. That the two men were brothers—twins even—was evident in their strong bearing and wary dark eyes. For his part, the Duke of Ashington was as diffident as he was handsome. His austere demeanour at complete odds to his charming nature, Rollo could only assume that a penchant for sombre clothing must run in the family. Fitz, of course, for all he was as beautifully, darkly clothed as his twin, hulked in the doorway like a cornered bear, hiding his nervousness behind a scowl.

"Your Grace," Rollo said smoothly, seeing as the brothers were both finding the worsted carpet of great interest. He tipped his hat. "How excellent it is to see you again."

"And the same to you. But dispense with this 'Your Grace' business. Ashington, please."

A second man, slim, elegant, and familiar, rose from a seat by the window.

"Tommeee!" squealed Rollo. In two leaps, he was across the room and hugging him tight. "Nobody told me you'd be here."

"Can't imagine why," muttered Fitz from somewhere behind him.

Rollo twisted in Tommy's embrace to see his lover glowering. "Fitz. This is Tommy Squire, one of Papa's oldest friends."

"We've met," Fitzsimmons replied sourly.

Ignoring him for the moment, Rollo disentangled himself. "What in heavens name are you doing here, Tommy?"

"Accompanying Benedict." Tommy cast his eyes over to the bemused duke. "I…ah…do that quite frequently."

Tommy and His Grace exchanged an indulgent look. The sort of look Rollo and Fitz had enjoyed over recent days.

"You…oh… Oh!" For once, Rollo was lost for words as the duke dropped his eyes to the floor.

"Good heavens," Rollo said finally, "Papa tells me nothing. Really?"

"Really." Tommy ruffled Rollo's hair. "We're *very* good friends. And, lest I forget, your papa sends his love. We dined together only last week." Turning to Rollo's lover, he offered the smallest of bows. "Lord Lyndon. Good afternoon."

Fitz inclined his head the minutest fraction.

"Of course. You are acquainted with each other through Squire's," said Rollo happily, referencing the most exclusive of Tommy's gaming hells.

"Alas, only the rear steps of Squire's," said Fitz in icy tones. "And more specifically, the stone cobbles at the bottom."

Rollo's eyes widened.

"His man once threw me out."

"Oh. My goodness." This meeting wasn't going according to plan at all. Rollo retreated to Fitz's side. Where he belonged. Whatever wrongs Fitz had committed.

Tommy took up a similar stance next to *his* man, eyeing them both curiously. Rollo had a dreadful feeling this whole venture might turn out to be a terrible mistake.

"Fitz has been so looking forward to showing off his charitable works," he said earnestly. "Haven't you, Fitz?"

Rollo's lover emitted a pained noise. Rollo elbowed him.

"Haven't you, Fitz?" he repeated.

"I'm very much looking forward to seeing them," offered the duke in his usual soft tone. His worried eyes reached his brother's. "Lyndon. It's been far too long. You appear well."

"I…thank you. As do you."

The moment grew in awkwardness. Fitz's suffering was almost palpable, the duke's not much better. No wonder they'd let discontent simmer between them for so long. If Rollo and Willoughby had been parted for nigh on two years, they'd have run at each other like charging bulls whatever the root of their separation.

The comparison hit Rollo with a sudden pang of longing, a craving to bask in the warm, open happiness of his own relations. This type of warring family quite flummoxed him, and for once, he'd run out of ideas.

Fortunately, the duke found his tongue.

"I have some estate matters I would like to discuss with my brother," he said. "Alone, if I may."

Ashington didn't much care for wielding ducal authority, as Rollo well knew, but something in his voice made his meaning quite clear.

"Then I shall take Rollo to the public ale house on the corner," declared Tommy. "And leave you both to it."

*

THE ALE SAT badly in Rollo's belly, for all it was decently brewed and supped in excellent company. And even though he'd visited very few public houses and felt decidedly out of place, that wasn't the reason either.

"You're one of the many people Fitz has wronged, aren't you?" he said to Tommy sadly. "He said there was a list, but I expected it to be composed of ruffians and chaps I'd never like very much anyhow. Not...someone like you."

"I am," Tommy confirmed. "He nobbled several horses, including a prize thoroughbred belonging to his own twin, and then placed heavy bets against them." He threw Rollo a wry smile. "My betting stands lost out. Not huge sums, compared to some, but sufficient to notice."

"Is that why you kicked him out of Squire's?"

"No." Tommy shook his head. "Though I would have done if I'd known at the time." He leaned forward, lowering his voice. "I booted him down the back steps because he was on the cusp of revealing his brother's preference for men in front of twenty distinguished members of the *ton*."

Tommy drained his mug. "I daresay some men in Benedict's lofty position wouldn't care. Except Benedict prefers his nature to remain private. Thus, for as long as there is breath in my body, and likely your father's, too, it will remain so." He shook his head as if remembering."

I doubt Lord Lyndon will attempt to besmirch him again."

"You can rest assured he won't."

Rollo had nothing much to say after that, so he took a few pulls of his own ale and stared at the worn tabletop. Fitz might not express his regret eloquently, but one only had to spend some time in his company, as Rollo had done, to know how much he wished he could turn back the clock.

"Fitz," observed Tommy. "That's…awfully familiar."

Rollo shrugged. Willoughby was privy to all, of course, but like his ducal twin, Fitz's private matters were his own to share as he chose. And as much as Rollo adored Tommy, given their past, he was probably one of the last people Fitz would select. "We have been thrown together," he said neutrally. "I wasn't especially happy at Goule when I first arrived. But I have since grown fond of him."

"He has a temper and a cruel streak," Tommy countered. "If your father hadn't believed you man enough to stand up to him, then I daresay he wouldn't have sent you." He signalled for another ale. "Have you refused to let him torment you?"

"He has not tried," lied Rollo, remembering his first few weeks at Goule and how entering that drawing room had taken every scrap of bravery he possessed. Just as Fitz was using all his resources now to beg his brother's forgiveness. "Whilst I was unhappy with Papa's decision to send me away, I believe he chose well. Fitz may be all that you say, but his life experiences have taught him quite a bit about making costly errors. He has passed some of that wisdom on to me."

Tommy laughed. "So you shan't be racing curricles up and down Pall Mall in the dead of night when you come up for your first season?"

Rollo laughed too. "I didn't say that. I've already bet Willoughby fifty pounds that I'll best him. And I expect on occasion that you'll want to throw me down the back steps of Squire's too." He paused. "But, thanks to Fitz's influence and cautionary tales, I shan't cheat, lie, be anything but charming to the ladies, or do whatever else might tarnish the good name of Duchamps-Avery."

"Pritchard will be disappointed," Tommy commented, smiling. "And when the season starts, will this pillar of wisdom be returning to London with you from his Norfolk exile?"

"Yes, that is my plan." Rollo had yet to share it with Fitz, but he remained an eternal idealist. "So, you must all be terrifically nice to him." He grimaced. "He's going to need all the allies he can get. I suspect a lot of folks would be delighted to see him fail."

"Your papa and Benedict have influence far and wide amongst important families in the *ton*, albeit they wield it with a quiet power. If Fitzsimmons is part of their group, then I assure you, Rollo, he will be cut by nobody."

Rollo checked his pocket watch as Tommy finished his drink. They'd left the brothers alone for over an hour. Plenty of time to patch the holes in their relationship and visit Fitz's poorhouse. Though an hour was also plenty long enough for Fitz to bugger it up.

Chapter Nineteen

LYNDON SLEPT FOR the first part the homewards journey, drained of everything he had, with his head resting on his young lover's shoulder and Rollo's hand warming in his lap. When he woke, two anxious blue eyes latched onto his.

"Did he accept your apology?"

Lyndon brought Rollo's hand to his dry lips. "Yes. Of course."

That Benedict would be gracious was never in question, no matter how clumsily Lyndon delivered his apology. And God knew it had been. His feet had shuffled as if he were kicking up dirt in the stable yard. His eyes had insisted upon counting every book on the shelves behind where Benedict sat, and his mouth had stumbled over the words as if stuffed with his pocket square.

And patiently, Benedict listened and then forgave him. His inherent kindliness would forgive Lyndon thrusting a dagger through his heart if it gave his twin peace of mind. Lyndon didn't believe he'd ever achieve or deserve that. But when Benedict's familiar arms wrapped around him, folding him back into the Fitzsimmons family, it had given his mind enough of something not too many steps removed. At the least, Lyndon liked himself a little more than he had yesterday.

"So it's over. Done."

"Yes," Lyndon repeated. And he'd managed to keep his chin held high and hold back his tears, though they threatened to breach the barrier now.

"You showed him your new venture?"

"Yes. He thought it was splendid. He agrees we should join forces and build several more in a similar style." And Lyndon had cringed at the praise. "He's a good man," he added, abstractedly toying with his lover's hand. "To think I once fancied myself as a better duke."

"You would be just as fine," insisted Rollo, making Lyndon smile. He didn't bother contradicting him. Not even Rollo's dogged determination to see the good in him would change the essence of Lyndon's nature. His jealousy would never leave him, nor would his orneriness and his penchant for brandy. Nothing and no one could rearrange the essential elements of his soul and transform him into a benevolent, thoughtful, God-fearing duke.

He could continue to strive to be a decent lord and lover though.

"Whilst you two were putting the world to rights, Tommy and I had a fine old time at that tavern. I had no idea he and your brother were so *close*. Tommy has a…um…chequered past."

"He does," agreed Lyndon. "And some brutish, chequered friends. I suggest you never find yourself on the wrong side of them."

"I can't believe he had you thrown down the back steps of Squire's. The brother of a respected duke."

"He told you why?"

"Yes."

Lyndon experienced a rush of shame. "At the time, I didn't understand why he was so…protective of Benedict."

"Well, now you do. And Tommy is an excellent chap. One of the best."

Lyndon laughed mirthlessly. "Apparently so. I don't expect we'll become bosom chums any time soon."

"Yes, you will," promised Rollo. "I shall work on you both."

"Your diplomacy skills may be required sooner rather than later. I've…um…invited Benedict to spend some time at Goule in the early autumn. I suggested we could try our hand at fishing, as we did with our father when we were boys."

Through gritted teeth, Lyndon had extended the invite to Squire. He wondered what Berridge would make of it, deciding he'd assign them the green and blue bedchambers in the east wing. The old butler hated climbing up that rickety staircase, and in any case, Benedict would bring his own retinue of staff.

Lyndon's reward for such generous behaviour was an open-mouthed, sloppy kiss, tasting of cheap ale and something indefinable that melted his insides and stopped the world from turning, if only for a minute or so. Such was Rollo's delight that Benedict and he had rebuilt their bridges that for the rest of the journey, Lyndon allowed himself to be petted and stroked like a rich widow's bloody lap dog. If there were finer ways to travel, he had yet to discover them.

Goule Hall came into view as the carriage rattled through the gates, low lamplight burning in several of the narrow windows. A peculiar place, Lyndon thought fondly. Shunned by most, it never looked quite at ease in its habitat. And as the forbidding front aspect loomed closer, it held an imposing stature and a questionable interior. Lyndon allowed himself a private smile. Not too dissimilar to himself.

In his arms, Rollo yawned widely, making no attempt to hide it.

"Count Rodolfo will have to fight his dastardly duels without me tonight," Rollo declared. "I'm fit for nothing but a hot bath and a warm bed. All this renewed brotherly affection is quite wearing."

"My bed," stated Lyndon, putting his woeful seductive skills to use. But the quickest distance between two points was a straight line, and he wasn't yet ready to release his lover. Just because Lyndon didn't look fragile, didn't mean the day hadn't broken parts of him. And Rollo Duchamps-Avery was the best repairer of souls he knew.

"What?" Rollo gathered his things as the carriage drew to a halt.

"My bed. With me."

Rollo hesitated. "Are you sure?"

Lyndon had never been surer of anything in his life. Especially tonight. "Yes. It has been a tiring day. Join me. I'd like another one of those silly, pointless hugging things."

*

HE CAME ON bare, silent feet, dressed in the playful yellow banyan and very little else. His hand hesitated on the door key as he looked to where Lyndon lay, already under the covers. God knew Rollo was no blushing virgin, but he seemed uncharacteristically nervous.

"Lock it if you wish. But we will not be disturbed. The servants only enter my bedchamber when I am not in it. And unless I request otherwise, I dress myself in the mornings."

Lyndon's intent was clear. That embrace, the kissing, the fellatio — aye, even the fellatio — were not enough. He wanted it all and more tonight. *All* night, and again in the morning.

Without fuss, Rollo slipped into the bed. His silk-covered arm immediately snaked around Lyndon's bare middle. A blond head tucked under his chin, and Lyndon pressed his lips against the top of it. Fine blond strands tickled his nose.

"Your hair is as aggravating as dandelion fluff. It makes me sneeze."

Rollo snorted. "*Shall I compare thee to pollen?* Your words have the allure of a siren, my lord."

"I fear I am a lost cause," Lyndon agreed and kissed him again. God, he smelled divine. "In the drawer next to this bed, you'll find a jar of almond oil. I do not intend to use it to aid my sleep."

Rollo snorted again. "I don't recall ever learning that sonnet." He tipped his head up, seemingly surprised. "How is it that you are familiar with the alternative uses for almond oil?"

"I said I'd never partaken in sodomy. I didn't say I'd never given it thought."

Lyndon wormed his hand under the banyan to run his fingers lightly down the smooth curve of Rollo's back. He continued lower, probing a little. Rollo gave an appreciative hum, the sound settling in Lyndon's groin like a caress. "You like me touching you there."

Shamelessly, Rollo hitched his thigh higher. He rolled his hips. "Like you wouldn't believe."

Almond oil was a marvellous invention, Lyndon discovered. Fingers weren't too terrible either, not when they elicited those sorts of breathless pleas and whimpers. When Lyndon pressed deeper, Rollo ground his hips, his cockstand already rubbing damply against Lyndon's hip. One finger became two; Rollo's breathy sighs muffled against Lyndon's neck. Lyndon's own erection ached for attention.

Slow seduction and pretty sonnets were overrated.

"Get on all fours, pup."

Rollo's head shot up, his dark pupils big and round, thinning the silver-blue of his eyes. "But this feels so good. I'm reluctant to move." His sultry gaze danced over Lyndon. "You might have to make me, my lord," he said in a whisper.

Fitz gave a throaty chuckle, pinching one of the delectable buttocks sharply. "I fully intend to. But, fair warning, you might moan a little."

Driven by instinct, as if born to know how to please his lover, Lyndon flipped Rollo over. He grinned at Rollo's feeble protest. "Up," he chided, lifting his lover's hips. "And spread your thighs wider." Roughly, he nudged them apart. "This skinny arse is mine to do with as I please."

"So bossy," gasped Rollo.

"Not bossy." Lyndon ran a firm hand down Rollo's smooth, oiled divide. Rollo arched up to meet him. How willingly he yielded under Lyndon's hands.

"You are so. And I love it." As Rollo twisted his head around for a kiss, Lyndon stroked himself — showing off his size and his desire.

"I simply know what I want," Lyndon stated.

"You want to be my captain," Rollo responded around Lyndon's mouth. "And I want that too."

When their lips parted, Rollo's eyes fixed on Lyndon's engorged member. He swallowed once, and then his words came out in a rush.

"I liked it when you smacked me. I...I have not experienced that before. It...I liked it. Please."

That *please*. Desperate, self-conscious. A little uncertain, a half question. Lyndon might not have invited a man to his bed before, he might not have a silken tongue, but he knew neediness when he saw it. "What? You mean like this?"

Before his pup had time to think, Lyndon delivered a sharp smack to his rump. And then another to the other cheek as Rollo yelped. And then a third when he begged for more. Then Lyndon soothed the red welts with his palm as his finger strayed back to Rollo's hole.

"You want me inside you now, my precious?"

Rollo pushed up against his fingering, sucking him in farther, writhing on him, unashamedly pleasuring himself. "Please, my lord," he whimpered and looked back, his pupils blown wide. "Please."

Lyndon's cock nestled between Rollo's buttocks as if coming home. The swollen head teased at the gaping hole. Rollo shuddered into him with a whimpering sigh. So soft and pliant like this, when he was at Lyndon's mercy. So capricious and scratchy when he wasn't.

"Perhaps I'll rest myself here awhile first," Lyndon tormented. False bravado. The 1st Royal Dragoons on his mantel, if they came to life, couldn't have held him back.

"Then I shall dissolve in a lake of agony all over these fine sheets," panted Rollo. "Inside. This second!"

For all he wanted to tease, for all he wanted to take back control, Lyndon couldn't stop himself. Inch by inch, he sank into his lover, sensing when to push forward from Rollo's needy cries and gasps, and then sensing when to still. When to kiss him, when to whisper the foolish type of sentiments one only ever felt moved to whisper in the heat of the damned thing, yet carried on the tip of one's tongue for most of the day.

And then, as heat and want and urgency flooded him, it became simply two desperate bodies pressed against each other, united as one, cock's surging and hearts thumping. Doing that silly, undignified, indecorous thing that bodies were made to do, that after a certain point they did instinctively, of their own accord. And Lyndon held Rollo's hands tightly in his through all of it. He left gentle caresses on Rollo's skin. He buried his nose into the warm column of Rollo's neck, breathing in his biscuity smell. And Lyndon's heart ached with how he was so maddeningly, undeniably falling in love.

Afterwards, they snoozed where they fell, messily tangled and too wrecked to move. When Lyndon eventually hauled himself away, it was to bring Rollo a washcloth. Sleepily, Rollo allowed him to wipe it across his belly and between his lax, open thighs.

"You are a kinder man than you allow others to see, Lord Lyndon."

"You are alone in that opinion, pup."

"No." He shook his head. "Your servants here would disagree. And so will your old London acquaintances, given time. You are changed. Whilst we cannot help others judging us by our past, it should not dictate our futures."

"Huh." Lyndon's brain wasn't quite ready for a philosophical discussion regarding the past. Nor a future. Especially one pertaining to himself. But then, if not in the dark stillness of a bedchamber with one's lover as a shield, then when?

He climbed back into bed. Fearful Rollo might return to his own bedchamber, he made it challenging for him by wrapping him up in his arms and, to be certain, resting his solid leg across both of Rollo's. Then he took a deep breath. "You once asked me why I became a changed man. I did not give you a fully honest answer."

In the curve of Lyndon's arm, Rollo lay very still. "Do not feel obliged to do so now," he answered softly. "That you are changed is enough. It relates to your friend, does it not?"

"Yes," Lyndon exhaled. "Will Elliot. The son of Henry Elliot, a tenant farmer. His mother was Mary Elliot, she worked in the kitchens alongside Cook. They were good, honest folk."

"I have seen their grave markers at the chapel. That they were well-loved, and remain so, is clear."

"I keep them tidy," admitted Lyndon, "because Will cannot."

He stared up at the ceiling, unseeing, letting his reminiscences wash through him. "When he was small, Will used to come to the house with his mother and play with Benedict and myself as she worked. We are of an age. And then, as we became older, he would come to the house alone and play private games with me."

"You had a great *tendre* for each other."

Lyndon huffed a small laugh, giving his bed mate a sharp poke. "We did. I believed it to be nothing but a youthful folly, but have since come to realise that I have an...an attraction to both the male and the female sex. Alas, for Will, I always suspected it was nothing but a passing infatuation."

He rubbed his nose against the top of the Rollo's fair head, breathing in his sweet warm scent. "Will was a virile, unworldly youth with a preference for women. But there were very few comely and unmarried ones within ten miles of Goule. If things had been different, I daresay he would have soon found one and consigned me to the playroom along with dusty old swords and dresses." He chuffed again. "And for my part, it's hard to believe, but I was far more winsome than I am now and, of course, possessed the intrigue of being the son of a duke living in this fine house."

He smiled at the memory before an unpleasant thought struck him. Rollo was not much older now than Will had been then. What if… "You are not that way yourself? Awaiting a time when you can more readily seek out female company?"

Rollo snuffled a laugh against his chest. "Do I act like a man created to please a woman? I should sooner sprout wings and fly."

Lyndon let out a relieved sigh. "Over the last few weeks, I have wondered if you were created solely for the conflicting purposes of annoying and pleasing me." His jealous streak flickered to life. "And no one but me."

Rollo giggled. "Then I shall delight in my endeavours to succeed in both."

Kissing distracted them for a few minutes. Lyndon might have let that and more distract him for a good while longer, except Rollo pulled away.

"And?" he said. "That is not the end of the story, I feel."

Lyndon shut his eyes briefly. Nothing dampened one's ardour like a terribly sad tale, but today had been a day for unburdening. He'd never related this one, not even to Benedict, though all his family knew the bones of it.

"Will and I had spent the early afternoon down by the lake on a summer's day much like today. We swam to stay cool and then lay on the bank in the sun to dry off." He pressed his lips against Rollo's forehead as if to remind himself he could. "And to do a little of what we're doing now."

The memory of what came next turned Lyndon's belly sour. Goose bumps prickled the hairs on his arm, and he squeezed Rollo tighter. "Cousins of ours were coming to stay. I had promised Mama I would not be late for tea. When I heard their carriage wheels spitting up gravel, I said my goodbyes to Will and left him there, waiting for his own mother to finish working in our kitchen. They often walked home across the fields together; he helped carry whatever linens she took home to press or mend."

He swallowed, his mouth suddenly dry. "And I heard nothing more. I *thought* nothing more until dinner that evening. There were twelve of us at the table. The meal dragged out, my cousins were dull, and they had interrupted my afternoon of lovemaking. And then…and then, without warning during the fish course, Mama told everyone that the body of Mrs Elliot, the farmer's wife, had been dragged from the lake not two hours earlier. And her son, Will, alongside her. And that the rhubarb was forced this year and more woody than last. And that Cook should be commended for the excellent turbot."

Hot tears pricked at his eyes. He tried in vain to blink them away. "And that was that. As if it didn't matter, as if an ordinary young woman who laundered your drawers whilst you sipped champagne and dined on excellent turbot, was expendable. And that her death was as noteworthy as a poor rhubarb crop but certainly no more."

Lyndon dashed the heel of his hand across his eyes. God knew he wasn't perfect, but he cared for those who loyally served him with a great deal more compassion than that.

"But Will lived," confirmed Rollo.

"Barely." Lyndon shook his head. "I despised my mother from that day forward, though she never knew. Whilst my resentment of my father had already festered for years, that he allowed that horrific event to pass in such a callous fashion strengthened it into a hatred which began to consume me. And swept along in its path, a bitterness grew towards Benedict, whose birthright was no more his fault than my own."

Dampness trickled into his hairline unchecked. Unblinking, Lyndon stared up at the ceiling, waiting for his eyes to dry and the dull ache in his chest to subside. He'd read somewhere that grief was as individual as snowflakes; his manifest itself in a cold, dark anger, which he'd never quite resolved.

Rollo remained silent, and for a long minute or so, there was only the sound of their breathing.

"What do you believe happened at the lake?" Rollo's fingers tangled with the coarse hair covering Lyndon's chest, his nails scratching at the skin.

Lyndon gave a small shrug. "No one is sure. On account of our guests, Mrs Elliot had worked later than usual. Will might have taken another swim to cool down. Or she may have slipped, walking along the lake's edge, and Will tried to save her, or the other way around. The pond weed is virulent on the shaded side down by the woods, and the bank easily crumbles when the weather is dry. Will has no memory of any of it, so we shall never know."

He sighed. "In a way, it matters not. Because that is not the end. Will's father perished six months later. He'd been left with a much beloved young wife in a wicker casket and a son more like a waxwork effigy than the boy he loved. Though he took to drink, the local folks say he died of despair and a broken heart. I cannot find it in my own heart to disagree."

"And a vital piece of you perished too," whispered Rollo. He hugged Lyndon close, every bit of him clinging, as if he would crawl inside if he could.

Lyndon huffed a humourless laugh. "Or lies at the bottom of that damned lake. And I have spent the last decade searching for something to fill the hole it left."

Perhaps, in this funny, wise, sweet young man, he'd found it. He stroked Rollo's hair, planting kisses to the top of his head, his forehead, his eyelids, working his way down until he sought out Rollo's slack, pliant mouth. Rolling him onto his back, Lyndon blanketed his lithe body with his own, captured by a sudden need to touch his lips to every living, breathing part of him. Raw, carnal, lust took over as his mouth trailed a path down Rollo's soft belly. All thoughts of the past fled. There would be no ghosts in this bed. Not tonight. No "what could have beens," no "if onlys." Just two men, together as one. And for the first time in a long while, that was enough.

Chapter Twenty

Dear Fitzsimmons, I hope this finds you well. I must express in words my thanks for making my darling son, Rollo, so splendidly at home at Goule. Tommy Squire also reports that he is in fine fettle. Rollo's numerous and voluminous missives home have overspilled with examples of your kind spirit and generosity.

It would be no exaggeration to acknowledge that you and I have not always seen eye to eye. Nonetheless, I feel I owe you an apology. From Rollo's singular praise, you are a much better man than I have given you credit for. Whatever aberrations occurred when you last stayed in London, you have clearly put all that behind you. I am determined to do the same. In his turn, and thanks to your guidance, it appears that Rollo, also, has turned over a new leaf.

Willoughby and I miss him dreadfully. To that end, we shall burden you with his company no longer. Though he has only been with you for half the time we agreed, he is now free to leave Goule and return to Rossingley, whereupon, thanks to you, I daresay he shall continue shaping up to become an excellent young man. A carriage will be leaving Rossingley forthwith.

Yours etc, Rossingley.

His missives home have overspilled with examples of your kind spirit and generosity.

THE PUP HAD been true to his word. How easily he could have carped on about Lyndon's peculiar ways and unfriendly manner and begged his papa to retrieve him. Instead, he'd chosen courage over his own comfort. He'd painted Lyndon as a beacon of respectability and good sense, because when Rollo had insisted that a man's business under his roof was no one's but his own, he had meant every word. Not knowing that, one day, his father would play his exact words back to Lyndon.

Never had Lyndon's heart felt so full yet so empty. The thought blindsided him.

"I'm in love," he informed the letter he grasped in his hand. He said it out loud again, testing the veracity of it, those three simple words sounding even more sure of themselves the second time. "I'm in love," he declared. "I love him."

He stared at the foolscap. For a moment, Rossingley's looped, elegant hand and brute reasoning stared back at him. Then Lyndon crunched up the letter and hurled it across the room.

"Damn your eyes, Rossingley. You can't have him return yet.

"It's unfair," he added, then felt a little foolish. Young boys railed at the unfairness of life; grown men did not.

*

IT WASN'T WRONG to feel sorry for oneself. Just like it wasn't wrong to shoot miniature arrows at miniature regiments whilst marinating in far from miniature glasses of French brandy. But neither pursuit was especially productive, unless one relished fixing all the divots in the mantel the following day with a head like a burst mattress. So, Lyndon stomped to Will's cottage to pour out his woes to a sympathetic ear.

"As far as I see it, the earl has simply sped things up a little. Your young man was always going to depart sooner or later."

"Huh." Slumped in the chair opposite, Lyndon scowled.

"What?" Will unsubtly nudged his empty teacup across the table in Lyndon's direction. "Do you disagree? Did you imagine you would use the last month of his stay to persuade him to remain, long after his summer here ended?"

Lyndon glared at him. Will calmly glared in return.

"No," he lied. "Of course not."

Making excellent use of one of the few parts of his anatomy that still functioned correctly, Will raised his left eyebrow.

"All right. Yes," Lyndon bit out. "What I mean is, I don't know."

A year and some had elapsed since he'd contemplated ending his life. Things might not have always seemed to be any easier since — he was still himself — but love rang like bells through his ears, and he'd be damned if he'd let it slip through his fingers. "Possibly," he concluded.

"Glad you've cleared that up," Will remarked. "Tea, please."

With a lot of unnecessary clashing, Lyndon filled the small kettle then hung it over the hearth to heat. Returning to his chair, he hacked an apple into ragged chunks. He fed a cube, none too gently, into Will's mouth.

"I have considered not showing him his father's letter," Lyndon said. "Or pretending it was somehow delayed or lost. To buy myself some more time."

Will chewed carefully, swallowed, then waited for Lyndon to feed him another cube.

"But you have decided against it," he said finally.

"Yes." Lyndon dabbed at Will's mouth then popped more apple in it. "See? He's made a better person of me already."

"Will you insist he stay longer?"

"Insist?" Lyndon huffed. "You've clearly not met Rollo. He's not a tame tabby cat, and I'm not in a position to insist on anything."

"Ask him nicely, then?"

"No." Lyndon shook his head. Of that he was certain. Rollo was homesick, though he put a brave face on it. And because Lyndon loved him, he would set him free. He would send his beloved back to his loving father and adored brother. "If he stays, then it must be his choice."

*

THE AFTERNOON TURNED into yet another of those late August hazes, when the sun shone hot, and the still air smelled of blackberry wine. Rollo suggested they venture down to the lake. Seeing as he appeared to have Lyndon on a bridle, Lyndon agreed. He discovered that because Rollo's hand slipped into his, the placid stretch of water didn't instil any of the terror in him that it usually did. Not taking any chances, however, they laid the blanket on a patch of grass a good way clear of it.

Rollo nestled in his arms. "I received a letter from Papa this morning. He is sending Dobson and a carriage."

Whether it was good news or bad, Lyndon couldn't interpret, though he was thankful he hadn't tried to conceal the existence of his own correspondence. "Yes. I am aware. I expect they will arrive any day."

Unsure what to add, he kissed Rollo ardently for at least five minutes. And then Rollo fell uncharacteristically quiet as if waiting for

Lyndon to express his opinion further, which he knew he should but wasn't entirely certain how. A great craggy boulder seemed to stand in the middle of the path joining his feelings to his tongue. Yet, if he didn't say something, it might be too late, as this Dobson person was already en route, and Rollo's things were already packed.

"It is a pity our friendship must come to an end sooner than anticipated," Lyndon ventured at last, which wasn't what he'd intended to say at all.

"Must it?" The smooth skin of Rollo's forehead bunched in a puzzled frown. It was absurdly endearing. Was Lyndon really going to let Rollo escape his clutches? Was his heart really too frozen to shape the words consuming his every waking hour?

"You are returning to Rossingley," Lyndon pointed out uselessly. "It is at least a three-day ride from here."

"Yes," Rollo conceded. "Though it feels like double that distance when one only has Dobson for company. But...the thing is, Fitz, I wasn't aware it was a one-way ticket. Unless..." He frowned again. "...you prefer it that way?"

"I...ah..." Lyndon's mouth had dried. "No." He wetted his lips. "I...um...I will be rather...um...disappointed to see our friendship terminated."

"Disappointed?" Rollo's face fell.

"Uh. Tremendously." *Stricken. Bereft. Heartbroken.* "Yes. Tremendously."

"But you are prepared to let me sail off willy-nilly into the sunset anyhow?"

"Yes, but—"

Rollo sat up, exhaling audibly. His nostrils flared, and there was an obstinate jut to his chin Lyndon had not seen before. And even though Lyndon knew he was in for a jolly good shoeing, he found that absurdly endearing too. It occurred to him that he'd miss it dreadfully, along with the lecture and scolding it undoubtedly heralded.

Rollo threw his hands up despairingly. "Why must the English upper classes always be so damned constipated when it comes to saying what they really mean? Why is this bred in us so ruthlessly, as though civilised democracy would crumble if we dared for one second to lay bare our emotions?"

Sensing these questions to be largely rhetorical, Lyndon kept his counsel. If pressed, the status quo of English nobility suppressing their every sentiment suited him admirably.

"Viking warriors," Rollo continued, launching into his stride, "were as quick to soak their thick Viking beards with tears as gouge out a man's entrails. And were not ashamed of it one tiny bit. Fancy that! Yet buttoned-up English chaps with their hearts full to bursting, like ours are, seem to have developed a foolish compulsion to conceal their every desire. Are you going to pat me on the shoulder and wish me a jolly safe trip?"

Lyndon squirmed. When had the workings of his mind become so transparent? "Um...possibly."

Rollo made a harrumphing, I-knew-it sort of noise. "Well, bless your delusional soul for making up that unsatisfactory conclusion to us." He grabbed Lyndon's hand and squeezed it tight. "Just in case I haven't made myself absolutely clear, you fabulous idiot of a clogged-up lord, I am besotted with you." He gave Lyndon's hand a tug. "I love you, Fitz. I don't know why, how, or even when it happened. Only that it did. And you love me too." He crashed his mouth against Lyndon's so firmly, his teeth rattled. "We're a tribe, you and me. A tribe. And tribesmen love each other hard."

I love you. Rollo's impassioned declaration settled around Lyndon's heart, melting there like dazzling flakes of snow. *I love you.* It had been a good many years since he'd received a declaration of love. He remembered prising one once from Will, though probably at sword point, and Benedict must have said it too. But none so fervently. Or to be fair, referencing jammed up bowels.

He committed his lover's heartfelt sentiment to the walls of his memory, hanging it amongst his most treasured possessions to savour later when his lover departed.

"This is the moment when you tell me my love is returned, by the way," Rollo prodded. He smiled at him tentatively. "Otherwise, I've made a complete clot of myself."

Lyndon huffed a soft laugh and ran his fingers through Rollo's fine hair. "This picnic blanket is far too small for two complete clots."

He shook his head wonderingly. How hard he'd tried and failed to make sense of things over the last decade. He'd searched for it in a bottle, at the card tables, the racetrack, in the beds of bawds. And after all that, he'd found the answer here at Goule, in the shape of a beautiful young man, who, bizarrely and against all the odds, wanted and loved him.

"Your love is returned," he replied, the words slipping from him easily. So easily, he wanted to repeat them, over and over, even as a tiny corner of his happiness whispered the conversation wasn't truly finished.

And so, he did, in between hauling Rollo into his lap, grabbing his face, and kissing him as if his entire existence depended on the success of it.

"I'm not your only tribe though. Am I?" He cupped Rollo's chin, needing the truth. "You have people waiting for you at Rossingley who miss you very much."

"I do, and I shall return to them gladly."

Lyndon nodded as if he expected as much, ice already snaking through his veins despite the heat of the day. But he would not stoop to begging. He would keep his self-respect intact. In front of Rollo, at least.

"Except then, I shall come back here."

Lyndon's heart thieved a beat. "You will?" God, he sounded desperate.

"Of course! I shall return to Rossingley, ensure Willoughby breaks off whatever is brewing between himself and Miss Lavinia Higgins, give everyone a hug, then inform my father I'm passionately in love with you, and return here."

"When you put it like that, you make it sound very straightforward."

Lyndon remained unconvinced. There were many a slip twixt cup and lip. In Lyndon's mind, Rossingley had taken on mythical proportions, like a palace from a children's fable. And the way Rollo told it, his family were enthroned there in a perpetual state of nirvana. How on earth could Lyndon, with his gloomy old hall, his jealousies, and his crosspatch tendencies, ever measure up to that? Why on earth would his pup ever trek back to dull, dreary Goule?

"It is," Rollo exclaimed. "Three weeks' work at the most. I shall join you here in plenty of time to prepare for the duke's visit in the autumn, and afterwards we shall all travel up to London together."

"We shall?" said Lyndon faintly. This part of the plan sounded even less likely. It assumed Benedict would overlook Lyndon's less favourable traits, for a start, and invite Lyndon to lodge in his London home, seeing as Lyndon no longer owned one.

"Of course." Rollo wormed his way in closer. "I mean, obviously, only for the season. Papa says nobody with any sense stays in town longer than that. And we would have to be terribly discreet, although Papa and Kit always seem to manage things. But I'd like to..." He coloured a little. "I've never done the full season. All the routs and soirées and all that nonsense. Willoughby and I were too young until now. Would you come with me?"

I'd ride to the ends of the earth for you.

"An association with me would not bode well for your social

currency," Lyndon felt obligated to point out. And as for Rossingley's opinion on the liaison, he shuddered to imagine.

"Absolute tosh, Fitz. You are Ashington's twin brother. And would be a part of Ashington and Rossingley's intimate circle. No one who cared about their own social currency would dare cut you. You shall accompany me to every ball, whereupon I shall dance and flirt with every eligible daughter and make you insanely jealous."

"You can't, and you won't," Lyndon growled, "because you belong to me." He pushed Rollo onto his back, and with his other hand, Lyndon wrenched loose the fall of his own breeches. To hell with the servants and whoever else chose that moment to wander past his lake.

Rollo's laughing eyes gazed up at him as Lyndon tugged down his trousers, cursing as the voluminous folds of their shirts impeded his progress.

"I can and I shall." Rollo lifted himself for up a kiss as Lyndon found his prize, and his cock found bare flesh. "But I shall only have eyes for you. The pain of our farewell will be but a scratch, you'll see. I shall be back before you even notice I've gone."

*

AS WAS THE warp and weft of things, the moment of Rollo's departure the next morning dragged on for far too long, yet was over in a flash. And still, Lyndon succeeded in making an utter hash of it.

Even though he had sworn not to, he woke in an enormous, childish sulk. Made a million times worse because he'd woken alone. With Dobson already loading his valises, Rollo had crept from Lyndon's bed at first light, which had given him far too much time alone, prior to his own toilette, to contemplate and to brood and to doubt.

How easily he was swept away on a tide of love and desire with Rollo in his arms! How readily he believed in Rollo's promises of a rosy future, how the troubled waters of his mind stilled. How peacefully his demons slumbered. And all because a youth of nineteen years, with no more knowledge of the workings of the world than the old beech tree outside his window, said so.

As young bucks, Lyndon and Will had also once believed in their own invincibility, and look how that had turned out. Lyndon had always taken Benedict's constancy as his divine right, too, not to mention the bottomless wealth. Then he'd had it all pulled from under him in the blink of an eye. What did Rollo know of the harsh realities of life, cocooned at bloody Rossingley all these years?

By the time he'd completed his half-baked toilette, Lyndon had worked himself into a foul temper. He scowled at himself in the glass, at his fiery coppery locks. Who cared that his hair looked as if a dangerous winter animal nested in it? It wasn't as if anyone would be running their silly, dainty little hands through it any time soon. As he slammed his bedchamber door behind him, Lyndon all but concluded that his destiny was to be alone. Heartfelt declarations of love whilst wrestling on a soft woollen blanket under a limpid blue sky did not change that.

His sulking intensified throughout breakfast. Instead of indulging Rollo's excited chatter with his usual snippy witticisms, Lyndon treated him to a series of grunts until, eventually, his lover gave up and fell quiet. Undaunted, Lyndon directed his smouldering, barely suppressed misery at Cook's excellent beef sausages.

"These are undercooked," he declared.

"Mine are fried to perfection," answered Rollo coolly.

"And my poached eggs have sat too long in water. The yolks are as hard as yesterday's bread."

"And yet you have eaten three." Rollo threw him an amused smile over the rim of his coffee cup. "Is the coffee too bitter, also?"

Lyndon nodded. "As a matter of fact, it is. I drank the second cup just to be sure."

With a long-suffering sigh, Rollo put his own cup down. "Care to tell me what's really the trouble?"

"You leaving me is the trouble." Lyndon balled his napkin in his fist. His fingers itched for his bow. "My bed's going to be lonely tonight. And cold."

"Three weeks, Fitz," Rollo answered in a voice suggesting Lyndon was testing his patience. Already dressed in his travelling clothes, he had chosen a place setting halfway along the dining table. If he wasn't leaving, he'd have been in Lyndon's lap, feeding Lyndon tasty slivers of crisp bacon from his long, greasy fingers. And peppering his mouth with greasy kisses. Another reason to be sulky.

"Longer," grunted Lyndon. "You'll be so happy at your perfect, flawless Rossingley, with your perfect, flawless papa, and perfect, flawless twin that you won't return."

"Don't tempt me," Rollo warned. "If you continue like this, then I shall regret that I'm not already there." His tone softened. "Fitz, darling, please don't spoil things. I wish Rossingley were closer to Norfolk, too, but it isn't. So that's that. We just need to be grown up about it."

Grinning, he selected a triangle of toast. "And you have more than a decade on me in that regard. So perhaps you should lead by example."

God, he looked young. Lyndon's heart ached as he watched Rollo slather his toast in butter, then take a healthy bite. How on earth he'd tricked himself into imagining this beguiling young man would be constant and faithful only to him, for the rest of his days, was an utter mystery.

"Having a decade on you is part of the problem. I should know — I've been as young as you are now. You say you love me, and I believe that you do. Currently. But you won't come back. Everybody gets fed up with me in the end."

Lyndon dropped his knife and fork with a clatter and pushed his chair back. He'd burst into tears if he stayed much longer, or worse, drop to his knees and plead. "If you'll excuse me, I shall sojourn to the drawing room."

"Wait! Is that it?" Rollo stood, too, a look of hurt on his face. "After making love all night, is this how we part? On a quarrel?"

Lyndon's throat tightened. What did he want? Tears? Entreaties?

"I'm not a man for showy goodbyes," Lyndon stated. "We said all we needed to last night in each other's arms. I...I..." His eyes filled. "Goodbye. Until we meet again."

*

ROLLO HAD BECOME a firm favourite amongst the servants. Despite the lashing rain (naturally, Rollo had packed the fine summer weather to take with him), they lined up on the drive, every single one of them, to wish him a pleasant journey. It would have been churlish of Lyndon to disallow it. Irritatingly, Berridge dragged him from the drawing room to join them, with Cook at his shoulder. It had been many years since she'd tanned his arse with her rolling pin, but the expression on her face suggested he wasn't too old for her to give it another go.

Thus, Lyndon was obliged to play lord of the manor. Which was how he ended up, under the cover of an umbrella, solemnly wishing his lover a safe, short trip. When really, he wanted to crush Rollo against him as he'd done all night, apologise for being such an ass at breakfast, then take a leaf out of Count Rodolfo's book and lock him in his bedchamber and throw away the key.

But it was far too late for that, and all his servants were watching him with curiosity. Before Lyndon knew it, in a cloud of spitting gravel, Rollo was gone.

Chapter Twenty-One

My dearest Fitz. I was greatly moved by your distress at my departure. Your dreadful attempts to cover it up with surliness at breakfast only make me love you even more.

PS You know how much I adore you when you growl.

DOBSON'S HALITOSIS HAD not improved during Rollo's absence. Thanks to the hazardous wet road conditions, he suffered it at close quarters for an extra day.

Yet it mattered not, as Rollo believed himself the most fortunate man alive. He had Rossingley, his papa, his adored Willoughby, and now he had his fabulous Fitz too. Even if Fitz had woken with a thick head and pouted like a spoiled child whose nursemaid had refused him a twist of barley sugar. The stupid thing was, Rollo didn't care. In fact, he positively relished Fitz's mercurial moods. As both a savage and a gentleman, Lyndon aroused Rollo on a deep, visceral level he didn't fully comprehend. But, by God, every single inch of him missed his lover already. What were roughly three weeks apart when they had a whole lifetime to enjoy? Rollo had already written to him thrice, and he hadn't even reached home!

The only problem with nestling in the bosom of such a loving family was that Rollo never knew whose arms to fling himself into first. It all ended up being a bit of a jumble, with him throwing himself at Willoughby and squeezing until he could hardly draw breath, Kit swinging him around in a mad waltz, and finally, Papa enfolding him inside his familiar, warm embrace and hugging him tight, near suffocating him in swathes of slippery silk. His homecoming would have been absolutely perfect if only he hadn't had to leave Fitz behind.

"I'm so sorry, darling, for sending you away for such a long time," crooned Papa. "Kit can confirm. I have been drenched in guilt from the moment you left."

He stepped back, but only for half a second, so his glittery eyes could examine Rollo from head to toe as if checking he was, indeed, returned and in one piece. Then Papa clutched him to his chest once more. "Was Fitzsimmons so terribly beastly?"

Over Papa's shoulder, Willoughby smirked and made an obscene gesture. Rollo suppressed a snigger. Goodness, how marvellous it was to be home.

"Terribly," Rollo confirmed, winking at his twin. "On many occasions, the man was a veritable animal." He pulled away from his father in order to expand his lungs. "But I have learned my lesson, Papa. I am returned healthy, older, and wiser."

Letting out an enormous sigh, Papa fondled his pearls, beaming at Rollo as if he'd just laid a golden egg. Another suffocating embrace was brewing, Rollo could feel it. "Oh, my darling. Such a brave boy. And on your own all that time too."

Willoughby snorted. "He's nineteen, Papa. Even our Rolly can survive a few weeks being fed, watered, and entertained in an aristocrat's Norfolk manor house. And surely, he wasn't alone all the time, were you, Rolly?" He threw Rollo a leery look. "Surely Lord Lyndon gave you *some* of his attention."

"Oh, you know. Dribs and drabs."

Rollo attempted to look hard done by as Papa swept him up again. If he played his hand well, he could milk this for several days. Or at least until he plucked up the courage to admit to his father the extent of his relationship with the dastardly lord. "He has a large library and gardens. And a particularly fine and airy nursery. It wasn't so terrible."

*

DRESSED IN HIS oldest, comfiest nightshirt, Rollo sprawled across Willoughby's bed with a happy sigh. As much as he adored Papa and Kit and their undivided attention, the evening had seemed interminable. He'd regaled them with tales of the dance, the Simpsons, a vivid description of his host's beautiful gardens and a less complimentary description of the murky Norfolk Broads. His love for Fitz and his imminent return to Goule he kept to himself. He would wait for a few days, carefully erect the scaffolding of a man much changed from the feckless ogre Papa once knew, and then pick the perfect moment.

He could bore Willoughby with his heart's desires though. That was what a twin brother was for, was it not?

"I'm so in love, Willoughby. I feel as if I'm a star shooting across the heavens and forever falling, falling, falling. Faster and faster. With no end to it!"

Willoughby rolled over to clutch his hand. "Then I am a star too, and we shall gladly cartwheel through the firmament together."

Rollo raised an eyebrow. "Three is a crowd, Willoughby. As much as I adore you, if I'm to perform acrobatics through space at breakneck speed, then I'm somersaulting with Fitz."

"Four of us shall plummet to earth," Willoughby contradicted.

"Not three. In fact, I've a mind to compose a poem about it first thing in the morning. I visited Stapleton again today, my second visit this week. My sweet Lavinia receives my courtship warmly and matches my affections with her own. I am of the opinion that Lord Stapleton is very much in favour."

"How marvellous," responded Rollo neutrally. *I'd wager they are.* Fitz's blunt appraisal of his twin's situation played in Rollo's ears. Shrewd observation or weary cynicism? Regardless, simply recalling his own lover's lazy, deep baritone set his heart thumping.

"And does Papa approve of this match?"

For the first time since his return, Willoughby's face fell. "Oh, he's being awfully tedious about the whole thing. He says I'm too young, of course, to know my own heart. Naturally, I pointed out that he and Mama were betrothed at a similar age, yet he was having none of it."

"But that was not a love match," interjected Rollo. "They hardly knew each other. Neither had a lot of say in the matter, though Papa strove to be a good husband."

"Well, Lavinia and I have been pals for yonks. Since we were infants, with never a cross word! We get on splendidly."

"'Getting on splendidly' is hardly the same thing as a love match," Rollo felt obliged to point out. "I get on splendidly with the old chap who delivers the coal."

An occasional spat, such as the one he'd been embroiled in with Fitz prior to his departure, was a healthy sign of love, in Rollo's opinion. Almost as health-affirming as the intimate reconciliation he planned on his return.

"A shared history of making perfume out of ground-up rose petals and toddling around the nursery together is not a formula for a love match either," he pressed. "It's a form of love, certainly. But is it a love that sends you wheeling with the stars, your soul broken loose, galloping like a wild horse on the breeze?"

Willoughby eyed him suspiciously. "You sound as if you've be-gun penning a few love poems of your own, Rolly. Anyhow," he con-tinued, "I informed Papa that I am of a mind to make an offer for her soon, and he did his darndest to put me off. He says I should bide my time and have a season first, that there are many a tempting armful waiting for me in the *ton*."

Willoughby fixed his blue gaze on Rollo, beseeching him. "What is your opinion on the matter?"

Rollo's opinion was that Fitz and his father perhaps weren't so very different after all, although his father seemed better versed in the art of diplomacy and approached the thorny problem from a different angle. A vague unease settled in his stomach. The downfall of being a kind-hearted, generous chap such as Willoughby was that he assumed everyone else's motives to be as pure as his own. If what Fitz said about Lavinia's spendthrift father was true, then whatever calf love his brother and Lavinia believed they entertained was not a recipe for a long, happy marriage.

"Willoughby," he began carefully. "Answer me this: do your in-sides tremble when you picture Lavinia? Or when you visit her?"

Willoughby gave a shout of laughter. "Of course not, why on earth would they? She's a girl, not an earthquake! And I don't need to ever picture her. I've known her for so long I could draw her in my sleep."

"But do you feel as if you could not live through another day with-out her by your side?" Every hour without Fitz felt like something lost that could never be remade.

"Hmm." Willoughby thought for a second before a slow smile crept across his face. "I certainly don't want to live through another *night* without her."

Ah. *Now* Rollo was getting to the meat of it. In more ways than one.

"Do thoughts of her consume your every waking hour?" he queried. "Or just your lonely, night-time ones?"

Willoughby snorted. "Some of them. Except when I'm out riding with Kit or writing a poem. Oh, and playing whist, of course. Then, I concentrate hard, or Kit and Papa will fleece me for every sou."

"I see." Rollo gave a solemn nod. "Let me get this straight. You and Lavinia are great chums. You think of her mostly when you are alone, especially at night. But you don't particularly miss her during the daytime when she is not by your side. In fact, might I suggest that hours can go by when you don't think of her at all?"

"Yes, but"—Willoughby looked crestfallen—"now you are in love, too, you must understand. She is from an excellent family and has a sensible head upon her. She will make an excellent match."

Rollo frowned. He didn't recognise this picture of love his brother painted at all. His dearest Fitz was difficult, blunt, exacting, and an absolute bloody curmudgeon when the mood struck him. Yet he was the most certain thing Rollo had ever known. Whereas Willoughby was describing an undoubtedly pretty, fun young woman with whom he could rub along. And he was desperate to swive someone. Which wasn't the same thing.

He composed his features into a stern expression. "Listen to me, Willoughby. According to Fitz, Lord Stapleton is not all he seems."

"Your Fitz hasn't always been all he seems either," Willoughby retorted.

"No, but he's a changed man, I swear. And when you meet him, you will see that too. Lavinia's father and he were well acquainted with each other in the gambling hells—Stapleton is notoriously bad at baccarat. His wealthy brother-in-law is widely known in those circles for covering his debts, but for how long? Maybe until his daughter marries a rich man who can take over the burden."

"That would explain why Papa seems so…unenthusiastic, I

suppose," Willoughby accepted. "Are you sure about Stapleton?"

"Fitz has no reason to lie. And as far as Papa goes, I suspect he's hoping that when you have a season, your affection for Miss Lavinia will wane as you'll be having far too much fun. Much more subtle than downright refusing the match."

Willoughby nodded unhappily. "That sounds very much like our papa."

"Will Lavinia be heartbroken if you were to cool things?"

Willoughby shot him a wry smile. "Truthfully? Yes. But only for about five minutes. Personally, I always thought she held a candle for James Rothby, the Marquess of Fording's second son, and he for her."

"So did I."

"She certainly mentions him a lot more than I'd wager she ever mentions me."

"The two families have always been awfully close," agreed Rollo. Willoughby was taking the news far better than he could have hoped. "Although—and it is unfortunate for poor Lavinia—the Marquess of Fording is not renowned for his especially deep pockets. Unlike our papa."

"So that's that, then," said Willoughby, running his fingers through his hair. "I've been a ninny of the highest order, haven't I?"

"Naïve, that's all." Rollo gave his glum twin's shoulder a squeeze. "And in possession of a soul far too trusting."

"Unlike you and Papa."

"That's why we work so well together."

Thank goodness his brother was being reasonable. And thank goodness Rollo had come home in time to talk some sense into him.

"I have every faith that Lavinia is as delightful as she always has been," Rollo assured, "and is unaware of her father's machinations. But even if he wasn't in debt, what you are describing does not sound like love. It sounds more like—" He searched for the right word. "—

convenience. And believe me, as much as finally bedding a woman would be convenient for you, it would be thrice as convenient for a cleaned-out Lord Stapleton if that woman happened to be his comely daughter. You know I'm right."

"I do." Willoughby thumped the bed hard, making an anguished, frustrated sound. "Stapleton is but the first of many, isn't he? How will I ever know if a girl wants me simply for me or whether she simply has an impoverished father desperate to palm her off? I shall be Rossingley one day. One of the richest men in England!"

"You'll know," Rollo promised, "because you are surrounded by people who won't ever let you fall into that trap. Papa and Kit, for instance. Even bloody Pritchard — that valet has an ear on every street corner in the *ton*. And me, of course."

"But you won't be with me," Willoughby wailed. "You'll be with Fitz in some godforsaken gloomy manor house in gloomy Norfolk. I'm going to need you, Rolly. I'm not going to be very good at this earldom thingy."

"Absolute tosh. You'll be amazing." Crisis averted, Rollo smiled at him. "And you know it. And who says I'll be spending all my time in Norfolk? We shall do the seasons together, and afterwards, I'll bring Fitz to stay here."

"Papa will be thrilled, I'm sure." Willoughby huffed a sigh. "Dammit, Rolly, swiving someone would be the most convenient thing there is. I'm so desperate for it; I can barely think of anything else."

"Can we both agree that is not a sound basis for marrying the girl next door? There are some excellent and very discreet bawdy houses in London and some wonderfully competent ladies housed within. I think it high time Father introduced you to one."

*

NEXT MORNING, IN a much happier frame of mind, Willoughby suggested a ride. Given the amount of rain that had fallen and continued to threaten (if the ceiling of black clouds overhead had any say in it), Rollo had been of a mind to stay indoors with a good book. But he could deny Willoughby very little, especially when he was still a tad bruised from Rollo's candid appraisal of his marriage intentions. Reluctantly, he trudged after his brother down to the stable block.

"I shall inform Papa of my imminent return to Goule after dinner tonight," Rollo declared, tightening Sapphire's chin strap. "After outlining all of Fitz's marvellous good works. And then I shall suggest he accompany us to London for the season."

He swung himself smoothly into the saddle. He hadn't ridden once at Goule as Fitz's small stable comprised only his matched pair and an immense chestnut stallion named Fury. Any time Rollo strolled within six feet of the stable block, the horse had stamped his hoof and breathed fire. Typically, Fitz adored him.

"You really are besotted, aren't you? One doesn't wish to grumble, but you have made mention of your beau at least fifteen times since breakfast."

"And you have mentioned Lavinia nought. Perhaps picturing yourself with a high-class wanton dressed in a scrap of lace and not much else has assisted?"

Willoughby giggled. "Yes, yes, yes, you've made your point. I shall ask Papa to introduce me to some discreet ladies forthwith."

In truth, Rollo hadn't missed riding very much. Willoughby lived for it. Like their papa, he'd been blessed with an excellent seat. In contrast, despite growing up around horseflesh and developing a certain degree of competence, Rollo had always felt a bit of an imposter. He pretended comfort astride a horse, mostly to keep Willoughby company, but more often than not, his fear of heights reared its ugly head. He'd find himself staring at the packed brown earth and worriedly calculating the distance down — seven, maybe eight feet?

At least there was a break in the rain. They set off companionably, trotting side by side, hooves splashing through mud and puddles, and the lush, rolling hills of Rossingley stretched before them in every direction. About to remark how different it was to Goule's flat, brooding landscape, Rollo bit his tongue. He'd managed not to mention Fitz for at least ten minutes.

"Let's head up and around Langford's farm," suggested Willoughby, and at the click of his tongue, an obedient Bunty turned left.

With less enthusiasm (and less command of his horse) Rollo followed, glancing up at the leaden sky. A few spots of rain pattered on his riding coat. "Summer has departed with a vengeance and autumn has arrived with a bang."

"Quite literally," agreed Willoughby as a roll of thunder burbled in the distance. "Come on. I'll race you to the top."

Willoughby won, of course; he always did. Rollo didn't mind. He preferred finishing a ride with his body in one piece, thank you very much. The rain fell more heavily now, his coat's padded shoulders gradually becoming sodden with it. He cursed as a trickle ran down the back of his neck. Though not yet cold, he was most definitely wet.

"Time to turn back?" he suggested, and Willoughby nodded, pointing towards a narrow track through a dense copse.

"That way's quicker. I know it's tight, and there's a hedge to jump at the end. But it's a very low hedge, and you'll be in a hot bath within the hour."

"Looks a lot muddier though," observed Rollo, but he couldn't deny the bath sounded tempting. "I still think we should retrace our steps. My bath can wait an extra half hour." He pointed back the way they'd come. "We know the track isn't flooded as we've ridden that way already, and the section past Langford's is much wider. And there are no hedges to jump at all."

Willoughby tutted. "Oh, where's your sense of adventure, Rolly. Have you been spending so much time with your ancient lover that you've become an old man yourself?"

"He's not ancient. He's mature, like a fine wine." Rollo smiled at the memory of Fitz's copper-gold chest, thick with curls. Rollo's own was yet to sprout a single hair. "Older lovers have a lot to commend themselves, Willoughby. As you will soon find out on our return to London. They know how to pleasure a man, for a start. Thoroughly. And, for your information, Fitz's and my love for each other transcends all boundaries, including age."

Willoughby made retching noises, justly deserved. "Then follow me down through the copse and prove to me he hasn't fucked all of your bravado out of you, lover boy."

Sapphire's every sure step reminded Rollo he was no child or novice rider. Nonetheless, as the jump loomed closer, his unease soared. If their father ever found out what they were up to, he'd wring their necks. Even the birds had fallen into a reproving silence, the only sounds echoing through his ears were the squelch of Sapphire's and Bunty's hooves ploughing through slippery mud, the percussion of heavy rain on his shoulders, and a little voice inside his head telling him this was a really, really dreadful idea.

But it was too late to turn around; the horses would have a devil of a job climbing back up the hill. Shaking his head, Rollo blinked away the rivulets of water streaming into his eyes and tried to ignore the fear slithering in his belly. Ahead of him, straight backed and sitting proud in the saddle, Willoughby picked his way down the hill, making quick work of it. Parched of moisture for so long, the contours of the thin dirt track snaking through the copse had already disappeared below a fast-flowing torrent of rainwater. With every step she took, Sapphire's fetlocks slipped below the surface. Rollo gripped the reins even tighter, wishing with all his might he'd insisted they take the safer route.

"The hedge is coming up," Willoughby shouted over his shoulder. "You go first. Loosen the reins, get up into two-point early. Keep her at a steady canter. Stay in control."

"Easy for you to say!"

A fork of lightning split the sky. Oh Christ, that was all he needed. Sapphire let out a panicked whinny, tossing her head. Rollo patted his mount's bedraggled mane, crooning reassuring, soothing babble. His heart thumped.

"You'll be fine, Rolly. You've done jumps bigger than this on a rocking horse. Picture that hot bath. With your bloody Fitz naked in it!"

Rollo took the jump, squealing with terror. He was not ashamed to admit to it. Nor that he prayed, eyes screwed shut, to every god he could think of, including Poseidon and a few other false idols he made up on the spot. For an agonising second, as all four of Sapphire's hooves left the ground, Rollo was suspended weightless in mid-air, holding his breath and with his stomach plunged into his riding boots.

And then all four hooves were down with a lurch, which nearly unseated him. He was safely over. Sapphire resumed her miserable plod through the mire, and his belly climbed back to its rightful place. With his feeble thighs quivering and his heart pumping out of his chest, Rollo brought his mount to a halt. Still gasping, he twisted to watch his twin demonstrate how a true horseman navigated such a trifling little hedge.

At a brisk canter, Willoughby set off down the last part of the slope. Rollo couldn't hear his shout of joy over the thrumming of the rain. But he could see his grin, even from this distance, brilliant white, glinting like freshly driven snow in the morning sunshine. High out of the saddle, Willoughby approached the jump at a gallop, his slight frame hunched over Bunty's flying mane. Even a zig-zagging flash of lightning directly above their heads didn't faze either the charging horse or rider one bit. A few strides before take-off, Willoughby sank low, sending Bunty soaring into the air. Rollo shook his head at the beauty of it. Forget penning love odes, his twin should write verse about himself. Willoughby and that prized horse of his were veritable poetry in motion.

A crack of thunder rent the still air, clashing like a mighty gong. For a second, the whole copse seemed to vibrate with it. Startled, Bunty's front hooves slammed into the mire. Her back ones followed, sending Willoughby reeling forward in the saddle and scrabbling at her mane. At a second almighty, bowel-shaking crash, Bunty's head whipped up, and in blind panic, she bucked her rear end, kicking Willoughby out of the saddle altogether. Abruptly, he was airborne and somersaulting violently over the horse's lashing head. Time froze as he hung there, neither attached to his horse nor attached to the ground. And then, like an angry Zeus himself had ordained it, Rollo's twin's fragile, precious body came hurtling back down to earth. With a different sort of sickening sharp crack.

And then everything went deathly quiet.

Chapter Twenty-Two

My darling Fitz. How I wish that you were with me now, more than ever. Goule is so far that when we gaze up at the sky, can we even see the same clouds?

An accident has occurred here at Rossingley. One so terrible that, as I pen this, my ink mingles with my tears. Dearest Willoughby, the most exquisite brother a man could ever wish for, has been thrown from his horse. He lives, praise God, though he is black and blue all over and hardly wakes. His thigh bone pierced his flesh and is broken in two places. The finest surgeon money can buy has set it straight and put him in a traction device. He is being attended daily by the most distinguished physician in the land. Everything has been done. Now we wait and hope and pray that infection is not also set within.

I will travel to Goule as soon as I am able – we have a lifetime of love ahead of us! But even for you, my dearest lover, I cannot leave Willoughby in his hour of need. I would never forgive myself.

It will be several weeks until he is out of the woods. I shall write daily. I carry our precious love in my heart, my darling, until we meet again.

Your faithful pup, Rollo.

SEVEN DAYS AND seven nights later, Rollo still heard that blood-curdling whip crack of snapping bone in a door slam, a serving dish set down heavily, the sudden spit of a log in the hearth.

He hardly left Willoughby's side, dozing fitfully in a chair next to his bed. Servants attended to him, of course, a rolling roster of house-maids, and all of them kindly. But it was Rollo who mopped his fevered brow, who coaxed willow bark through his parched lips, who fed him laudanum when his screams woke him from his opium-addled dreams. The surgeon visited daily, sweeping in and out of the bedchamber with the sole purpose, in Rollo's opinion, of self-congratulation. Most days the puffed-up physician accompanied him, and they prodded and poked poor Willoughby as if he were a tailor's mannequin.

Even darker hours came and went. Hours when Rollo knelt on the hard floor next to the bed, clasped his hand in Willoughby's, and bent his head in silent prayer. Hours when the next world lusted for his twin's thin broken body like a lovelorn youth lusting for his first kiss. Nearly snared him too. Dank, yellow pus seeped from the wound, and many a night, Rollo clung to Papa, counting each and every one of his brother's tortured, shallow breaths. Yet Willoughby held on.

"There is no room for doubt, Rollo," asserted Papa when he tear-fully voiced his fears. "Not in this bedchamber. I shan't allow it." He'd barely left the bedside either, his long, bony fingers twisted around his pearls, his striking features tense and drawn. "Willoughby will be fine.

He is strong. The doctors say he will recover."

"I should never have let him jump. I knew it was too dangerous. Should have insisted harder."

"He's a daredevil on horseback. There's no stopping him." Papa's pearls twisted into a tighter knot. "And he will be again. You'll see."

And so it went on, whilst outside the sick chamber, the rains came down, the wind blew, and the storms mocked them, reminding them of their infinite power. More than anything, Rollo wished he had Fitz by his side.

*

"FRIGHTFUL WEATHER WE'RE having," commented Kit from behind his newspaper.

Papa had coaxed Rollo to join them for breakfast with a promise that Pritchard would not move from Willoughby's side until Rollo returned. Miserably, he pushed the food around his plate as Papa and Kit attempted a semblance of normality.

"The water-logged roads between here and Winchester are treacherous," Kit continued. He tapped on a page, shaking his head. "Impassable for over a week. It says here that a mail coach driver has been seriously injured and one of the horses succumbed."

"Gosh, somebody must have penned some truly atrocious missives," Rollo's father murmured. "Even Willoughby's poems don't directly kill."

Kit lowered the newspaper, his lips twitching. "The rear axle broke going over the flooded bridge at Hempton. The chap took a blow to the head when the horses bolted. The remnants of the coach and its contents were last seen floating towards Guildford. Terrible business."

"Quite," agreed Papa, nibbling on a slice of buttered toast. "Reminding us we should count our blessings, however meagre they may feel at the moment."

White-faced, Rollo pushed his coddled eggs to one side. Willoughby's fever had broken in the early hours. For the first time in over a sennight, he'd seemed lucid when he briefly woke and asked for a glass of cold water.

"May I be excused, Papa?" Rollo asked. "Cook has made a mild chicken broth, and I would like to feed it to Willoughby myself if he is able to stomach it."

"As long as you let me hug you first, my darling." Dabbing his mouth, Papa gave him a weary smile. Tiredness etched his usually flawless skin. Willoughby's near-death experience had taken its toll on all of them. As Rollo sank into him, for the millionth time he tried not to cry.

"He's going to live, my darling, and everything will return to normal. You'll see. I will not allow it any other way."

*

"WHAT DAY IS it, Rolly?"

"Tuesday, my love," answered Rollo. "And if you're very good and swallow five more mouthfuls, I'll even tell you which month."

Attempting to shift in the bed, Willoughby groaned. "It hurts so much, Rolly. Everywhere. I want to close my eyes again and do nothing but sleep until I feel better."

"You've been employing that strategy remarkably well."

Obediently, Willoughby opened his mouth for the spoon. "I've been out of it quite some time, haven't I?"

"A sennight," Rollo agreed. "Give or take."

"My last memory is grass, bramble, stars, and then blackness." Willoughby huffed a dry laugh, then winced. "I was an idiot, wasn't I?"

"Yes, but you weren't to know that the loudest thunderclap the heavens have ever cobbled together would choose to unleash its demonic powers over Rossingley at the precise moment you took your jump."

"Is Papa dreadfully cross?"

"Dreadfully," teased Rollo. "As soon as you are well enough, he will have you writing out one hundred times: *I must not lead my trusting and impressionable younger twin into trouble. I must not lead my trusting and impressionable younger twin into trouble.*"

"That was the first time in our entire history," scoffed Willoughby. "And you know it."

Rollo adjusted the pillows behind his back. "Of course he's not cross. He's hardly slept with worry about you. None of us have."

"You do look awful," his brother remarked.

"Thank you, you are too kind. But a damned sight better than you. For a moment there, I was in line to be the next earl, and frankly, I don't have the time or the patience for it."

He kissed Willoughby's forehead. "Ugh. Your poor skin is terribly dry. I must find a salve."

Willoughby rolled his eyes. Rollo fed him more broth. "How is Bunty? She hasn't been punished, has she?" His eyes darkened. "Or injured?"

"Don't be ridiculous. She's tough as iron. And being treated like the pampered queen she is. Though she's missing your ministrations. Kit and I are poor substitutes."

"You have to kiss her nose twice every evening and treat her to half a carrot chopped into batons, otherwise she won't settle. And if that doesn't work, you must stroke the soft tufty bit between her ears and sing her a lullaby."

"Do I look like the sort of chap who'd sing *lullay, mine liking, my dear heart, mine sweeting* to a damned nag?"

Rollo had finally got his hands on his papa's chartreuse banyan, and he wore it today, paired with a delicate lace neckerchief. Willoughby regarded him solemnly.

"Don't answer that, Willoughby."

*

WILLOUGHBY'S CONDITION IMPROVED in leaps and bounds over the next two weeks. As did his ability to direct orders from his sickbed, a sure sign he was on the mend. Kinglike, he demanded his pillows be plumped, then flattened, lowered then raised. Broth was too hot or too cold, the window too draughty when open, the air too close when shut. If Rollo wasn't such a sweetheart and so relieved his brother was still sufficiently alive to bark orders, he might have snapped a few of his own in return.

"Rolly?" his twin asked weakly after Rollo's attempts to comb and tame his brother's knotted locks had almost resulted in fisticuffs, "Why are you still here?"

"That's a jolly good question," he answered sourly. For the third time that hour, he refreshed Willoughby's water, too warm the first two times, apparently. "Would you like Pritchard in my stead? Or Dobson?"

"God, no. It's…it's…" Willoughby's brows knitted together. "But don't you have a decrepit old lover to visit?"

"If you're referring to my darling virile Fitz, then yes. And I miss him dreadfully. But I also have a sick brother. Fitz will understand — we have the remainder of our lives together."

"Do you?" Willoughby sounded incredulous. "It might be churlish of me to point this out, but as I'm ill, I can be excused anything. So I'll go ahead and say it anyhow."

He sipped at his water. "You and Papa both encouraged me not to pledge my troth to Lavinia. Mostly because her father is an inveterate gambler, but also on the grounds that I was too young to throw in my lot with the first chit to catch my eye. Does that argument not apply to you too?"

"Fitz is not my first, as you damn well know."

"Yes, but cricket masters and stable boys aside, Fitz is the first for whom you have declared a *tendre*. Do you want to be tied to a…another person when we go up for the season? Or, indeed, for several years to come?"

"We shall hardly be parading our amour arm-in-arm at one of Lady Butterworth's soirées, Willoughby. I'm afraid that for chaps like me, discretion is a hard and fast rule."

"That isn't really the answer to my question, is it? Surely, you've had your fun with him, but perhaps you, too, could move on. There are plenty of other chaps like you, aren't there?" Willoughby hesitated. "What's so special about this one? You could find someone younger perhaps. And more…straightforward?"

"Dull, you mean?" For a moment, Rollo pictured himself sitting beside the fireplace, drinking tea with a faceless but impeccably dressed chap opposite, discussing the politics of the day. Not a toy soldier or brandy decanter in sight. "No thanks."

Nonetheless, his brother did have a point. Willoughby's illness had afforded Rollo many hours to ponder the nature of love and loss. Life in general, in fact. And whilst Fitz's absence had taught Rollo that they could live apart perfectly well, it had also taught him he didn't want to.

"Papa says that sometimes in life, one feels as if one is in freefall," Rollo began. "As if one has misstepped and hurtled off a ledge. He was referring to some of the unexpected, unavoidable griefs we all face, often without warning. Your terrible accident, for instance."

"And our poor mama's demise," agreed Willoughby, his face sombre. "I have heard him say it."

"Yes. He was horribly lonely afterwards, I believe, until he found Charles. And then he fell in love with Kit. But even when one finds a person that one is prepared to love for years and years, as I intend to love Fitz — as Papa loves Kit — these dreadful events will still occur. Such as your accident."

"Tragedy, illness, and other various horrors are simply the

unavoidable consequences of being alive," observed Willoughby grimly. "Even if one is never idiotic enough to jump a hedge in a raging thunderstorm."

"Yes," Rollo agreed. "But with Fitz, I imagine I shall survive them all. We shall fall from the ledge hand in hand. And that's all there is to it, really."

Chapter Twenty-Three

ROLLO WOULD CHIDE him for moping about, so Lyndon threw himself into fruitfully filling his days. With Benedict's visit planned for later in the year, some of his rarely used rooms required attention. To keep himself occupied, he oversaw his small household's every task. Lyndon might never fully convince his brother he was a decent man, but at least he could demonstrate he ran a tight ship.

When he ran out of chores at home, he made a nuisance of himself at Will's. He harvested mangel-wurzels and, under Will's exacting supervision, pickled his haricots in brine before the moisture set in and ruined them all. Lyndon restocked his library. He instructed a picture framer to do something with his ghastly attempts at landscapes, strewn all over the nursery. He visited the poorhouse with Mr Simpson and then dined with him afterward and even expressed interest in the vicar's latest ailment without a grumble.

But, most of all, Lyndon pretended he was not anxiously awaiting news of his beloved. He pretended not to notice that not a single letter arrived. He pretended not to notice the emptiness of his days. After all, how could they be empty? They were no different from before Rollo Duchamps-Avery had opened his box of old toys and donned a dusty red dress. Lyndon told himself that his stupid sulk and their subsequent quarrel, the last time they breakfasted together, was nothing more than a lover's tiff. He reassured himself he'd been less of an ass than he imagined.

"You could always pen a letter yourself," Will suggested one afternoon, not unreasonably. Four weeks had trudged by without either the crunch of carriage wheels or fresh news.

"No." Lyndon daubed a streak of mud-brown paint across his current effort. *Broken Plough in Autumnal Gloom.* For a change, he'd had the stable boy bring Will up to the house so that Lyndon wouldn't be absent should Rollo arrive. In fact, he hadn't left Goule for over a week, one half of his mind still determinedly kidding the other that one of Rossingley's fine carriages would parade along the gravel at any moment.

"Dare I ask why not?"

"No, you may not."

For the next minute, Lyndon concentrated on mixing up another equally miserable shade of brown, aware of Will's sharp gaze trained on him.

"I'm not gifted in penning letters," Lyndon blurted. "And I have too much self-respect."

Will made a scornful, snuffling sound. "Ah. That's what we're calling it, are we?"

"That's what it is," retorted Lyndon. "Rollo was warned of this before he left. I've never been a chap moved to pen *mooning* love letters, and I'm not about to start. Especially when he's going to roll up at the front door any day now."

"Your self-respect flirts far too easily on the edge of pride," Will remarked. "And pride, after four weeks of staring out of the window waiting for him or news of him, is a luxury you can ill afford. In my opinion."

"Then it's jolly fortunate I didn't ask your opinion, isn't it?" snapped Lyndon irritably.

"True," Will agreed. "But as I'm stuck here until Jack appears to take me back, you're getting it anyhow. At least if you wrote to the boy, you would have peace of mind."

"He will come," insisted Lyndon obstinately. "He is a man true to his word."

Chapter Twenty-Four

NEVER HAD THE rain inspired so much fear. Never had thunder-clouds felt so ominous. The marshes were awash; it was relentless. It felt like the end of the world.

And Rollo Duchamps-Avery, second son of the eleventh earl, did not come.

Chapter Twenty-Five

BERRIDGE ORDERED GREAVES, who delegated to Jack, to send for Will.

Will duly appeared. "It has been more than six weeks, Lyndon. He promised he'd be here after three. You've heard nothing. He might be ill! Or dead! Or he could be absolutely fine and have a perfectly reasonable explanation for his absence. It could be something as simple as a letter going astray. At least if you attempted some form of communication yourself, then you'd know."

A stray arrow pinged off the mantel. "Buggeration," Lyndon slurred, awash with brandy. "These arrows haven't been carved straight."

"Just swallow your pride and bloody write to him!"

"No." Lyndon let another arrow loose. It landed perilously close to Will's chair. Will swore.

"Right. I've had enough. Ring for Jack to take me home, please. I'm not wasting another afternoon like this."

"You've only just got here!"

"And I'm ready to go home!"

"Everybody strives to leave me in the end," Lyndon garbled. "Even you." He laughed mirthlessly. "And you can scarcely bloody move."

"Don't be so daft. I'm going two hundred yards down the road. But if you continue to make heartless comments like that, you'll find two hundred yards change into a veritable ocean."

"I am heartless," Lyndon growled. "That damned boy has cut it out and taken it for himself."

"And if you weren't so stubborn, you could strive to win it back. Instead, you're wallowing in brandy, His Majesty's 1st Dragoons, and execrable art."

"Go away."

"I shall, don't worry. And I shan't return until Jack brings word that you've pulled yourself together. Actually, don't expect me to return any time soon, whether you have come to your senses or not."

Lyndon jerked his head up. Losing Will as well was too much. If only he wasn't so foxed, he'd dredge up his manners and have a crack at apologising.

"Buggeration," Lyndon announced, instead, firing off an arrow. "Buggeration to all of you. Don't bother returning at all. Ever."

Well-versed in Lyndon's flashes of poor temper, Will merely tutted. "Calm yourself, old friend. You aren't getting rid of me that easily. My second cousin, Lucinda, is taking me to visit a dying aunt in Norwich. Which will be far more entertaining than watching you fall apart at the seams."

"I'm not."

"You most certainly are."

Lyndon fired another arrow, not caring where it landed. "You're right. I am."

He was. Lyndon was unravelling like that old red dress, his whole being loosening and fraying at the seams. Soon, he'd be nothing but a messy ball of yarn rolling around the dusty nursery floorboards, watched over by a heap of ugly paintings and stinking of brandy. And there was nothing he could do to halt it.

"He's not coming back," he pronounced. "Is he?"

Will sighed. "It is certainly looking that way. And I'm sorry about that. Youth is a fickle flame, God knows we've both learned that lesson. But you…you deserved something. An explanation at the very least."

Lyndon stared into the dying embers of an afternoon fire. "I'm a clogged up, constipated lord." He shook his head. "That's what the pup had the gall to call me. Teased me rotten whenever I became too crabby. Then he cheered me, turned me into something better. *Someone* better. But…" He blew out a long weary breath. "But on our last morning together, I behaved abominably."

"Nothing but a tiff," scoffed Will. "You've said so yourself. You were upset he was leaving. He understood that because he understood you."

"What if I was simply showing him how it would be? A glimpse of the future? How unpleasant a life companion I would make? I believe that's the reason he's not returned."

Will let out a frustrated noise because they'd had this unsatisfactory conversation several times now. "If only there was a way to communicate with him and find out for sure."

Treating that sarcasm with the disdain it deserved, Lyndon returned to firing arrows and drinking brandy. Tomorrow afternoon, he would occupy himself doing the same. And the afternoon after that.

"Why are you visiting your aunt, anyway?" he grumbled. *I don't want you to go.*

"It is an important trip. One I should have taken weeks ago."

"It all sounds very spur of the moment. You never do anything on the spur of the moment. And you haven't mentioned your cousin

Lucinda in eons. Or that you have a dying aunt."

"That's because we only ever talk about you and your woes."

"Not true," Lyndon retorted crossly. "Why, only yesterday we talked about your mangel-wurzels."

Will huffed. "You're a bloody mangel-wurzel. A clogged up, constipated one. Your Rollo had a way with words, I'll give him that."

They were speaking in the past tense about him, depressingly.

"And why are you going away for so long?" Lyndon barked. "Norwich is but half a day. You never travel anywhere overnight."

"No, but perhaps it's time I began. We can't both idle our lives away in this godforsaken corner of the country. I daresay I'll come back."

Chapter Twenty-Six

DECLARING HIMSELF WEARY of the unchanging view from his bedchamber, Willoughby decamped to the drawing room, whereupon he regally dictated proceedings from an ornate recliner, which their father had always grandly referred to as the *gondola chaise*. When they were small, Rollo and Willoughby would dress up as sailors and pretend to paddle it.

Willoughby had grown weary of being a patient, too, and though he'd never admit, Rollo had wearied of pandering to his every whim. With his brother's strength returning by the day, he'd become less a nursemaid and more a punchbag for every one of his brother's understandable frustrations. Yesterday, with the aid of a crutch and some colourful language worthy of a sailor, Willoughby had walked five paces. The effort had exhausted him, though afterwards, he ate like a soldier returned from battle. Moreover, he'd beaten Rollo twice at dominoes already this morning, as sure a sign as any that he was thoroughly on the mend.

"Tonight, at dinner, I'm going to announce my amour for Fitz," Rollo confided as he shuffled the dominoes face down. "And that I would like to return to Goule, if you are able to manage without me. I've already sent a letter proclaiming the good news to my darling man this morning."

"I suppose I shall do my very best to cope," answered Willoughby magnanimously. "Though you must write daily. Stuck here, limping about, I shall be living vicariously through you." He frowned. "Why haven't you heard from him? Do they not have quill and ink out in the wilds of Norfolk?"

"He's an artist, not a writer," Rollo informed him. "If one can call it art. And Fitz's feelings towards me are too…fulsome…to put to paper."

"Too vulgar, more like," huffed Willoughby.

With a smirk, Rollo served them each seven dominoes. Just imagining running into Fitz's open arms warmed his nether regions. He'd drag the man to bed and not let him leave for a week. "When I write to you, I shall be sure to include every detail."

"Please don't," Willoughby said hastily. "A rough outline will be fine, thank you. I've been very ill, you know."

Smiling, Willoughby examined the tiles in his hand and cursed. "I suppose I should be grateful that at least one of us will have some…intimacy to look forward to. How the devil am I going to seduce a blasted girl in the *ton* this season if I'm hobbling around on a crutch?"

Rollo heaved a sigh as Willoughby placed a double, and Rollo picked up from the stock. "Listen to me, Willoughby. You are Lord Cavendish, heir to Rossingley. You will be shaking them off. And as for, you know, the rest of it—" He pointedly flicked his gaze down to the fall of his brother's trousers and then back up again. "'To him that will, ways are not wanting'."

Willoughby snorted. "Why are you quoting ancient poetry at me?

What does it mean? How can I swive a woman when I can scarcely move one of my wretched limbs?"

An image of himself sitting tall and proud and naked above Fitz, pleasuring both himself and his lover, flashed through Rollo's head. *Soon, my love*, he silently promised them both. *Soon.*

"It means," Rollo said, "that there is more than one method of satisfying a man's needs if one is determined to try. Flat on your back and thinking of England, whilst a chit does all the hard work, would be a jolly good place to start." He grinned at his exasperated, innocent treasure of a brother. "Though I suspect with your increasing desperation, her work wouldn't be very taxing at all. And I imagine the view looking up is delightful, if one is of that persuasion."

His unworldly twin blushed adorably. Teasing Willoughby was one of Rollo's favourite ways to pass the time.

"Frankly, I don't understand how a chap could be of any other. Hidden under those demure layers of taffeta, Lavinia has a bosom I'd give my inheritance to get my hands on."

"You very nearly did, you clot. And I don't know whether it has escaped your notice, but dear Lavinia and her divine bosom haven't paid you a single call since you nearly died. And how come you have had the double-six in your hand every single game?"

Willoughby placed his final winning domino then clasped his hands together with satisfaction. "Because I'm not as beastly as you."

"Master Rollo?" Inglis, the head butler, appeared. They'd been bickering so happily neither heard him approach. "You have unexpected callers. Two gentlemen and a lady."

Inglis's contemptuous tone conveyed his belief that Rollo's visitors were neither. "I informed them of the need to make an appointment, but one of the gentlemen is adamant that his message is urgent."

Rollo and Willoughby exchanged puzzled looks.

"I took the liberty of putting them in the tradesmen's parlour.

I...ah...decided they weren't suitable for the library." Waspishly, Inglis wrung his gloved hands. "The *gentleman* making demands is...ah...confined to a Bath chair. It is my impression that the other two are assisting him."

"I am not acquainted with anybody needing a Bath chair," Rollo stated.

"Aside from me," groused Willoughby.

"Precisely," said Inglis with a bow of his head. "But they were insistent, and they appear to have travelled some distance."

"Did you take the gentleman's name?"

"A Mr William Elliot," Inglis said sniffily.

Rollo pursed his lips. He knew that name. Elliot. *Elliot*. Elm trees. Mossy grass. The tiny chapel at Goule. William Elliot. *Will!*

His blood ran cold. "Inglis? Bring them in here at once."

"Master Rollo, I am not entirely sure your brother's sick bed is a place for—"

"Willoughby is fine. I'd like you to do it, please, Inglis. Now." He pushed himself away from the card table, not caring that Inglis would go telling tales on him to Papa within the minute. Sometimes in the household pecking order, he had the impression he ranked several rungs below his father's senior servants.

"There must be something wrong with Fitz," he gasped after Inglis flounced out. "Oh God." A surge of panic threatened to overcome him. He clapped a hand over his mouth. "William Elliot is Fitz's childhood best friend. He's...he's...he nearly drowned. Years ago. He never fully recovered. I believed him to be incapacitated, feeble in the mind. Perhaps he is, but—" He clutched at his hair. "He's here, Willoughby, and I have heard nothing for weeks, and so there must be something wrong with F—"

"Shush, Rolly. Calm yourself. Only minutes ago, you explained Fitz wouldn't write. You didn't expect to hear news. Why don't we find out what this Elliot man wants before we jump to conclusions? Perchance he's simply on route somewhere else and decided to pay a call? He might be passing on a message from Fitz. Or a gift."

The drawing room door opened, and Papa wafted in as serene and impeccably attired as ever, with a bemused Kit in tow. Rollo was hardly surprised. Nothing occurred at Rossingley that Papa didn't already know about.

"I hear we have a deputation arrived from Goule." He composed himself elegantly in the most prominent seat in the room and then threw Rollo a searching look. "Inglis informs me one of them is a woman. A young housemaid in the employ of Lord Lyndon. Am I about to receive an unwanted surprise?"

Rollo's heart stalled. Lucy. It must be. Will Elliot and Lucy. It could only herald awful news.

"Of the womanly variety?" he managed to croak. "I think you know me better than that, Papa."

"Marvellous. Then this impromptu visit will be no cause for concern, will it?" He offered Rollo a dangerous smile. Papa did not appreciate being the last to know something, especially where his sons were concerned.

Inglis ushered the three guests into the drawing room, introducing them almost as reluctantly as if they were three beggars hauled in from the street.

If his father wouldn't deem it improper, Rollo would have grabbed Lucy, hugged her, then demanded to know what the hell was wrong with Fitz. As it was, he anxiously stood next to his papa's chair as the earl accepted her shy curtsey and Jack's awkward bow. Twisting his hands together and his face red as a beetroot, the stableboy looked as if he'd rather be anywhere else.

William Elliot was nothing like Rollo had imagined. Even with his face cruelly slackened down one side, it was easy to see how he'd once been handsome. Rollo had assumed him feeble-minded, but the man's eyes were as sharp and clear as two bright sapphires. And, though ordinarily dressed and at a lower height by virtue of being hunched in a Bath chair, he somehow managed to rival even Papa's command of the room. A feat Rollo doubted Willoughby or himself could ever achieve. If this lame son of a tenant farmer felt over-awed by the grandeur of his surroundings or, indeed, the slight but imposing figure of the Earl of Rossingley himself, he didn't show it. But then, Rollo recalled, he'd been managing Fitz and his varying moods for nigh on a quarter century. The man was due a sainthood.

"My lord," Mr Elliot began, his enunciation slow and slurred. "I am an old friend of Lord Lyndon. I come on his behalf, though he is not aware of it." He paused whilst Lucy darted forward to mop at his mouth. "Forgive the intrusion."

"Forgiven," responded Rollo's papa, clearly intrigued. "I only hope your trip proves worthwhile."

"I am r-requesting that Mr D-Duchamps-Avery" — he stumbled over the longer words, his lower lip struggling to mould the shapes — "consider returning to Goule. Lord L-Lyndon needs him."

"Oh God." Rollo clapped a hand over his mouth.

The earl frowned. "Whatever for?"

At this, Will Elliot craned his neck up to Rollo. "He needs him," he repeated. "He's not right."

Rollo could stand it no longer. "Please. What's the matter? Is Fitz injured? Is he ill? Is he…is he dying?"

Mr Elliot threw him a long look. "Only of incurable stubbornness." He shook his head. "But it's making him ill. He's stopped doing…everything. Eating. Sleeping. Masquerading as an honest upright member of the noble classes. You need to come back. Or at least explain to him why you haven't come back. You owe him that."

Lucy darted forward again. "He's painting a canvas he's called

Hopeless Last Dawn, sir. Fills half a wall, it does. He's at it for hours. Can't get him down from the nursery, sir. It's…it's…"

"Hopeless?" Rollo supplied, his belly plummeting. He could well imagine it.

"Bloody awful, 'scuse my French. Cook says it needs putting on the bonfire. Even worse than *Bloated Dead Salmon Floating Down the River*."

"That doesn't sound possible," murmured Kit. He exchanged a glance with the earl. "I have a suspicion I know where all this is heading, don't you, Lando?"

"I wouldn't wager against it, darling."

"And Berridge says his lordship has annihilated the Third Corps," supplied Jack. "Marshal Davout is beyond repair. The wooden mantel too. The Fifth Corps is on its knees. Made a right mess of it."

Will Elliot nodded. "All true. He's spiralling fast, and I'm not sure I can do much to halt it."

"But I wrote to him! A dozen letters. With pressed pink petals from the hydrangeas in the walled garden here at Rossingley folded in the crease. Daubed with the scent of lavender oil." Rollo's eyes filled with tears. "I explained about Willoughby's dreadful fall and how he almost perished and how I must delay my return…and…and…how much we would enjoy our London season together and…how much I miss his silly little bow and his Count Rodolfo…and…and how I would gladly follow him through the annals of time!"

Hot, salty tears spilled down Rollo's cheeks. A deep and profound silence ensued, during which his father contemplated their unusual visitors before settling his steely gaze on his second son. Rollo tried not to wilt under the strength of it. Willoughby was mended. Lyndon needed him by his side. He needed to go. This minute. He'd walk to Norfolk if he had to. On bare feet, wearing only the banyan on his back for warmth and with thruppence in his pocket. He'd sleep in hay barns on beds of straw, drink from ice-cold bubbling streams, and scrounge kitchen scraps from—

A delicate dry cough interrupted his bleak travel arrangements. All eyes swivelled to the earl, who raised a beautifully arched brow in Lucy's direction at the same time as he rang a small silver bell. "Miss…"

"Lucy, Your Lordship." She bobbed again. "One of Lord Lyndon's maidservants. And this here is Jack, the stable boy."

"Naturally a stable boy would feature somewhere," Kit muttered.

"Quite," agreed the earl. "Thankfully, on this occasion, I don't believe he has a starring role." He eyed Jack severely. "You don't, I trust?"

"No, my lord. Only here to escort and assist Mr Elliot, my lord. Berridge's orders. Don't hold no truck with all this travelling abroad, myself. Never left Norfolk afore, never will again."

The earl breathed a sigh of relief. "Excellent."

As if pulled on casters, the butler materialised in the doorway.

"Inglis, dear," the earl instructed. "Miss Lucy and young Jack have journeyed an awfully long way. Take them to freshen up somewhere and make sure they are well fed." His pale gaze narrowed. "They are my valued guests."

As all three servants departed, and Rollo dabbed at his eyes, the earl pinched a thumb and forefinger to the bridge of his nose.

"Rollo, darling. Correct me if I'm misinterpreting things, though I believe I have the gist of it." His lips thinned. "It would appear that your lavish, lively correspondence from Goule, addressed to Kit and myself, may have omitted one or two tiny details? Lord Lyndon's *Count Rodolfo*, for instance?" He shuddered. "Four words I had never envisaged putting in a sentence when I breakfasted this morning. Or, indeed, ever. Though I am of the opinion that you've been putting his Count Rodolfo somewhere else entirely."

"Um…possibly." Rollo's wet cheeks heated. "Except we…um… don't call it that. Count Rodolfo is a character in a book and is really of no relevance here, Papa."

"But I can surmise that you and Lord Lyndon have been rather more intimate than you have led me to believe."

He impaled Rollo on his pale, glittery gaze.

"Yes. Um… quite intimate."

The earl digested that with a nod. "And through some postal mis-understanding, of which I am yet to reach the bottom, he is of the belief that you have discarded his suit and is making himself ill."

"Yes, Papa."

"Have you discarded his suit? Indeed, is it welcome?"

"Most welcome, Papa. More than welcome. As welcome as one could imagine."

Though Rollo had a million things to say on the matter, he bit his tongue and stared meekly at the carpet. At least he'd learned something since his last dressing down.

"I wrote the day after Willoughby was injured. And a thousand times since. I am at a loss to explain how he did not receive any of my correspondence."

Kit spoke up. "Just a thought, and I might have to check the date and the routes. But regarding that mail coach accident near Winchester, where the horse sadly perished and that poor driver was injured. There's a chance your letter regarding Willoughby's fall is languishing at the bottom of the River Test."

Rollo sucked in a deep breath. His poor, poor Fitz. "Kit might well have hit upon the reason for the first letter going astray, but that doesn't explain the others, does it?"

"No." The earl pursed his lips, his clever mind whirring. "You say Fitzsimmons has not received any of these missives?"

"Not one, my lord." confirmed Mr Elliot. "And they don't sound easy to overlook."

"No," Rollo's papa agreed thoughtfully, then switched his

attention back to Rollo. "You say Fitzsimmons is a changed man," he stated in a disbelieving tone.

"Yes, Papa. He is terribly hard on himself. All the pain and destruction and unhappiness he has caused in the past have hurt him deeply. And…and made him fragile, though he doesn't know it. Nor would he ever admit it."

The earl's pale eyes swivelled back to Will. "Is this the description of a man you recognise, Mr Elliot?"

"Always been a good one, my lord. He just forgot for a while. Events of the past got the better of him."

"And you are friends."

"Yes. Since we were but lads. I live in one of his cottages rent free, and he pays a village woman to tend to me. I'd like as not be in the poorhouse otherwise. Most days, he comes himself; he reads to me, helps me eat. Digs the vegetables."

The earl cocked his head on one side. "May I enquire as to why he is so attentive? Why he takes these tasks upon himself?"

"Because we were the best of friends growing up. And his father, the old duke, treated mine something terrible when my mother passed, and I had an accident, leaving me like this. You may ask any of the folks in Goule. They'll all tell you the same thing. He's a good man, and he doesn't leave anyone behind."

His expression turned mulish. "And that's why I'm here today. For what it's worth, I've never been out of Norfolk either." Clumsily, he patted the arm of his chair. "Didn't imagine I ever would, since being stuck in this thing. But I'm not leaving him behind. I'm not letting him ruin himself over your lad and a pile of lost letters. I'd never forgive myself, and nor would anyone else."

"He has also built a home for the infirm," Rollo added.

"Gosh, he is good with his hands." The earl and Kit exchanged a look.

"In more ways than one, by the sound of things," Kit murmured with the glimmer of a smile.

"He's not actually built it himself. What I mean to say is, he's used the Fitzsimmons name to persuade the church and the council to allow it. And he's provided half of the funds and overseen the build personally."

The earl rose from his seat and paced a few steps. "In his absence from society, it seems Lord Lyndon has become a model of morality. How one treats those who can do one absolutely no good is a true measure of a man."

"Samuel Johnson," slurred Mr Elliot.

Surprised, the earl looked up.

"Fitzsimmons reads a lot of books to me," Mr Elliot explained. "In truth, I prefer gothic horror, but as you can see for yourself, I'm a captive audience. Don't tell him I said so, but he even does the voices. Women too."

At this, Rollo's eyes sprang another leak. "His Count Rodolfo is masterful, Papa."

Willoughby made a choking sound. Rollo gave him a teary glare.

"He's terribly misunderstood," he continued. "But goodness shines through him, I promise you. He warned me about Lord Stapleton's gambling debts, for instance, so I could alert Willoughby to his machinations." Rollo scrabbled around for more examples, determined to impress on his father how desperate everything was.

"And he prevented me making an absolute cake of myself at a dance."

The earl paused in his pacing. "Do tell," he said coolly.

The truth would out sooner or later. Rollo might as well get in first as his father had an uncanny knack of conjuring it from thin air.

"A misdemeanour of the stable boy variety—not actually with a stable boy," Rollo added quickly. "And the misdemeanour wasn't…

completed, but only because Fitz put a stop to it. There was a local married man, a Mr Hart, who takes the mail from Goule and the surrounding villages up to Norwich. He scrabbles around with all sorts of jobs, actually, according to Fitz. Can't hold on to anything; he's a bit of a rogue. I didn't know any of this at the dance, just as I didn't know he was married with a family, of course. Fitz gave us both a thorough dressing down, ordered the man to not bring shame on his poor wife, and sent him packing with a flea in his ear."

"I'm warming to him," said the earl drily. "Dalliances with one's own sex are all well and good, but one should maintain discretion. And never more so than if one has a wife." His gaze narrowed. "And, unless one is paying for the pleasure, one should stay within one's class, darling. Understood?"

Rollo dabbed away his tears. "Yes, Papa."

"This chap with whom Fitzsimmons has had a contretemps," interrupted Kit. "Hart. He takes the local mail up to Norwich, you say?"

"He does," Will Elliot confirmed. His distorted face crinkled. "And Lyndon was right in saying that he's a wrong 'un. If you're sending anything of any value, then you send it yourself, if you catch my drift."

Kit's lip curled in a small smile. "And does this Hart fellow also bring mail back from Norwich?"

Mr Elliot nodded. "From the coaching inn where the horses are swapped over."

"In which case—" Kit and the earl exchanged guarded looks. "—the mystery of the missing letters has suddenly become less mysterious."

"Quite possibly," agreed Rollo's papa. "Either he was intrigued by the smart paper and hoping they contained something of value, or he was seeking revenge on Fitzsimmons by humiliating him. Spite and envy can often be found living side by side."

"What? You think Ralph Hart might have stolen my letters, preventing Fitz from knowing the extent of my love?"

"Prevented him having to read page after page of drivel, more like," interjected Willoughby.

"He's done far more than that," screeched Rollo, throwing his brother a foul look. "He's driven my poor, darling Fitz to despair. But…" He frowned, chewing his lip. "If that's the case, how did this Hart chap know that stealing my letters would be Fitz's undoing?"

Kit shrugged. "Perhaps he didn't. For all we know, he's pinched a whole bunch of correspondence, and your letters simply happened to be part of it. Though—" He hummed in thought. "—who can resist reading love letters? Once he'd smelled one and opened it up, he would have realised their importance. And enjoyed collecting them and seeing Lord Lyndon suffer. Goule's a small place, isn't it? Word will have got out that his lordship is plagued by poor health."

Oh goodness, the thing couldn't get any worse. How Rollo's chest ached. If he lifted his shirt, he'd swear he'd find his heart bleeding through his flesh.

The earl's attention returned to Mr Elliot. "You say the balance of Lord Lyndon's mind is disturbed." His voice softened. "My dear Rollo does have that effect on one."

"It is," agreed Elliot. "And I fear it will deteriorate further. I don't wish to be melodramatic, but to put it bluntly, the man's running out of reasons to give a damn. Coming here myself was my last hope."

"Hmm." The earl sighed. "Then there is only one thing for it."

"Is there?" Rollo held his breath. Whilst he was fully prepared to travel to Goule under his own steam, one of his father's well-sprung carriages, even with Dobson for company, would be far more comfortable.

"Of course. You must return to Goule at once and explain the events that have occurred." The earl paused. "And I must accompany you."

Swelling with joyous relief, Rollo's heart beat faster, then almost stopped in horror. "You...you..." Papa was coming? To stay with Fitz? The two had barely exchanged a civil word.

"Ooh. Good. Then I must come along too," announced a clear voice.

Everyone turned to stare at Willoughby, draped limply across the chaise like an exhausted gondolier after five tours of the Venetian canals.

"But..." Rollo felt suddenly dizzy. "But you are ill."

"No, I'm not, Rolly. I'm much better. I just can't walk very well, that's all. And I'm so bored of being bored, I could weep. If I hadn't tumbled from my damned horse, none of this would have happened. It's only fair that I meet this paragon of virtue with whom you have fallen headlong into love, so that I can apologise to him and then tease you mercilessly before writing godawful poetry about you both. Seeing as I've stopped writing about Lavinia."

"And Kit will come, too, obviously," continued the earl with a fond smile at his beloved. "Then there is Pritchard, of course. And two footmen — Dobson can be one of them as he's familiar with the route."

Once more, the earl rang for Inglis, his sharp mind already corralling his household. "We'll take the crested carriage, the larger barouche, and the landau, so that Willoughby may travel in utmost comfort. Three outriders should suffice. And the trunks shall follow behind with two grooms. From Goule, once this pesky mess is sorted out, I propose we travel onwards to London for the start of the season."

As Inglis appeared, the earl cast his gaze around the room. "Anything I've forgotten? No? Good. Then we shall leave at first light."

Chapter Twenty-Seven

ROLLO FIDGETED, FEELING restless and caged. Even sharing his father's most spacious and comfiest landau, with only Willoughby for company, the journey was interminable. His father, Kit, and Mr Elliot travelled together in the crested carriage, whilst Pritchard had the pleasure of Dobson's halitosis. If he hadn't been so damned anxious, Rollo would have savoured this fact a lot more.

"Something is very wrong, Willoughby." Since entering Norfolk County and its poorer roads, their progress slowed to a painful, bumpy walking pace. The dreary constancy of the landscape made Rollo feel as if he were travelling the same stretch over and over, as if the very earth under their horses' hooves conspired to keep him from his anguished beloved. "I feel it in my bowels."

"So do I," answered his brother, suppressing a yawn. He rubbed his belly. "I told you that beef pasty at the coaching inn tasted odd. But at least the blessed rain has stopped."

Rollo felt for his hand and squeezed it. "Cease teasing me, please.

I'm too overwrought. I mean, about Fitz. He's…he suffers from the blue devils. He denies it, of course. He's too proud. And he has a vicious temper which gets the better of him. I fear when he runs out of pewter regiments, he will wield it against himself."

Willoughby squeezed his hand back. "Then we must hope that old Bony and his Imperial Guard stand firm a little longer."

Their father and Kit joined them for the last few miles. Rollo was grateful for their presence.

"Goodness, it's squally out," the earl commented, wrapping his lap blanket tighter. "And such a flat, barren landscape."

"Yes," Kit agreed. "The winds must howl across it in winter."

As much as Rollo appreciated their attempts at small talk, it failed to distract from his heart beating faster and the tumult in his belly.

"Mr Elliot is a delightful fellow," continued the earl. "He holds your Lyndon in very high regard. I've heard all sorts of tales of his generosity of spirit. Did you know that Fitzsimmons engaged some of the finest physicians in Europe in an attempt to help him walk again?"

"I did not," answered Rollo, though he was not surprised. Nor was he surprised Fitz had been too modest to mention it.

"And even though they have been unsuccessful, he's forever trying to persuade Elliot to venture out more." The earl peered through the glass to admire a distant steeple. "It is ironic, don't you think, that the one time he does venture farther afield is without Fitzsimmons's knowledge?"

*

HIS FATHER AND Kit were still cataloguing Fitz's finer points when the carriage rattled through the gates of Goule Hall, though their conversation very quickly juddered to a halt. A trail of decapitated hydrangeas heralded the first sign that something was amiss, the pristine Goule lawns strewn with ragged pink and blue heads like the aftermath of a bloody battle. Even the big beech tree had not escaped the slaughter, with torn branches, like brittle bones, scattered at its foot.

It was as if a tornado had swept through the garden.

"I can appreciate that it's breezy today, but still…" commented Kit as he peered through the window. His handsome face took on a troubled expression. "This destruction looks very much as if done by hand."

"Oh, no," breathed Rollo. He swallowed drily at a looming sense of foreboding. "It's…it's Fitz. It must be."

"Then he is indeed a swordsmith," murmured Papa, his lips tight. "I fear Mr Elliot was right in his assessment."

Rollo clutched his father's hand. "But I don't understand. He loves his hydrangeas!"

Papa and Kit exchanged a look. "Let us not jump to conclusions. Perhaps it is the work of the wind, after all. We've had some dreadful storms all over recently."

"An odd-looking old place, isn't it?" observed Kit, peering up at the hall as they drew closer. No light reflected through the stark narrow windows, as if the grey flintstone façade had sucked up every thin November drop of it. Kit shivered. "And not altogether welcoming."

"No," agreed Papa slowly, returning the hall's frosty stare with one of his own. "Rather chilling, in fact."

Rollo remembered his own poor welcome and how he'd gazed up in dismay at the forbidding house. He'd nearly demanded the carriage be turned around. How strange that it now felt as much his home as Rossingley.

"It is warm inside," he assured. "Peat is so plentiful in these parts, and Fitz is unstinting with his fires. All the waterways we crossed on the road here are made from peat digging."

He was gabbling nonsense, and he knew it. But he would cry if he stopped speaking about normal things, and once he started, he didn't think he would stop. "There are fires in each of the receiving rooms and in all of the bedchambers too. Can you see? Up on the roof? Four chimneys at the front and another four at the back. Perfectly paired. You get a far better view of the front ones after we've rounded this bend. Broad and solid, like —"

There were five. Five chimneys at the front. Four were as he'd described, squat and compact, matching the four at the back. The fifth was shorter and thinner. It wavered in the breeze. And more strangely, it seemed to be on legs, two of them, long and untethered. Occasionally, the legs paced, unsteadily, one in front of the other as if walking along a balance beam.

Rollo screamed.

"It's...good God. It's Fitzsimmons," cried Kit. "He's up on the damned roof. Look! There!" He banged his fist hard on the ceiling of the carriage. "Faster!"

Rollo leaped from the carriage before the horses had even drawn to a halt. He raced up the gravel, his father not far behind.

"Fitz!" Rollo yelled. "I'm here! I'm coming."

If Fitz was aware of the commotion on the gravel below, he showed no sign.

"He can't hear us, poor man," the earl shouted. "He's facing the wrong way, and the wind direction is too strong."

"How does one get up there?" panted Kit at his shoulder. "Is there a staircase? A ladder?"

"I don't know." Rollo's breath caught in his throat as a sudden gust tugged at the figure on the roof. "Oh, God, he's going to fall."

The distant figure swayed, alarmingly close to the edge. For a dreadful moment, Rollo thought he might cast up his accounts.

"Fitz," he called. "Hold on. I'm coming!"

"You must stay calm," barked Kit, grabbing Rollo's arm. "No sudden movements. We don't want him to suddenly turn and receive a fright."

The front door flung wide, and Greaves came running down the steps, Berridge tottering behind.

"Thank heavens you're here, sir," Greaves called. "It's his lordship. He's been on the roof since sparrowfart, sir. Drunk as a skunk. I can't get him down, sir."

"I can't watch," sobbed Willoughby, hobbling to catch up. He buried his face into his father's neck. "He looks as if he's going to jump! Someone stop him!"

"No. He's not," interrupted a determined voice. "He's not going to jump, dammit. He's strong. He wouldn't."

As a rush of fire flooded his veins, Rollo recognised the voice as his own. "Because I won't let him. Greaves, tell me how I get up there."

"Through a skylight in the old nursery, sir."

Elbowing the footman aside then barging past Berridge as if he wasn't there, Rollo raced towards the house. Somewhere over his shoulder he heard his father snapping orders to Greaves before giving chase. Kit demanded the whereabouts of a set of ladders and sent Greaves rushing to find them. But there wasn't time for that.

Rollo skidded across the hallway. Smashed toy soldiers turned to crumbs under his pounding boots. Paint brushes and oil pots skittered in his wake. He took the stairs two at a time, lungs swollen like overfilled balloons.

"Rollo," the earl shouted behind him. "Slow down. For goodness' sake. Think about what you're doing."

"I know what I'm doing, Papa." Rollo rounded one corner and then another with his leg muscles straining. "I'm bringing one of best men there is down from that blasted roof!"

His breath sawed in short, harsh gasps. *Please*, he begged over and over, *please. Wait for me*. Each tortured beat of his heart bolted after the other in a messy confusion of anguish, terror, and regret. But mostly with ice-cold fury that this lovely, lovely man could, for a single second, believe that Rollo's love for him was not constant.

Chapter Twenty-Eight

ROLLO KNEW FITZ had climbed this roof many times over. And lived to climb down again. Fitz had confessed as much to Rollo himself. But surely, he'd never done it on a day as blustery as today. Hurtling up the back stairs, Rollo tripped over a second smashed decanter, the fumes racing him to the top of the house. The vibrations of his booted feet and those of his father hammered along the dark passages, beating time with the furious pumping of his heart.

As Rollo careened into the nursery, a sharp draught of air from the open skylight slammed into him. Better lit than the rest of the house, one wall of the room had been taken over by a large canvas propped against it, all grey stripes and tawny splodges. *Hopeless Last Dawn.*

Rollo gritted his teeth. *No.* Not if he had any say in the matter.

"Rollo," panted his father behind him. "The weather. The wind. Listen to it. It's too dangerous. Listen to sense, darling. You'll get yourself killed."

"No." Grasping the stepladder in both hands, Rollo scaled it, three rungs at a time. "I need to do this, Papa. I love him. Fitz needs to know that."

He shimmied through the narrow gap and swung onto a blessedly flat section of roof.

His father's anguished cries followed him up. "But you're petrified of heights."

As the skylight slammed down behind him like a gunshot, Rollo dropped to his knees clutching at roof tiles. Bugger, he'd forgotten that part. The skylight popped open again, and his father's blond head poked through.

"You're scared of heights," he repeated breathlessly. "You've always been scared of heights." A note of panic crept into his voice. "This is a high roof."

"Yes, I am," Rollo answered weakly. "And it is. Three storeys, in fact. But losing him terrifies me more."

"As losing you terrifies me," his papa begged. "Let me talk to him in your stead, darling. At least until he's in a safer spot."

"What? Do you want him to jump?" Keep calm, and don't look down, Rollo told himself. Keep calm. "Stay there, Papa. I'll be fine. I'm a grown man now. I can do this."

When Willoughby and he were small, their father had taken them to visit St Paul's Cathedral. Rollo remembered the trip well. They'd scaled the five hundred spiralling stone steps all the way up to the Golden Gallery to peer out across the whole of London. He'd squealed with delight, insisting he could see right to the ends of the earth. He remembered feeling as if he'd climbed the inside of a magical tiered cake, as if he could raise his hand and touch the sky.

And then he'd made the fatal error of leaning over the edge, dropping his gaze to the streets far below. Whereupon, his legs had promptly dissolved from underneath him, and Pritchard and two grooms had been summoned to lug him back down all those dizzily spiralling steps to the safety of Papa's waiting carriage. Once ensconced, he'd redecorated both the carriage upholstery and Pritchard's coat with his earlier eggy breakfast.

St Paul's stood over three hundred and fifty feet tall. Goule Hall was a mere three storeys. A nothing height really, or so Rollo told himself. In a second, when he'd caught his breath and pulled himself together, he'd hop across the slippery tiles, explain everything to his darling confused man, and they'd both be back down in the nursery before his papa had even rung for tea.

Daring to look up, Rollo spied his lover, one hand carelessly wrapped around a chimney stack. Fitz swayed lightly from side to side as he peered over the edge. Hot bile filled Rollo's mouth.

"Fitz!"

Awash with terror, Rollo repeated his name more gently, stifling the urge to scream it. "Fitz. It's me. I'm here."

Fitz tossed him a glance from over his shoulder, casually, as if Rollo had called his name in greeting across the packed lounge of White's. Even from six feet away, Rollo swore he could smell stale brandy on his breath. His lover had clearly abandoned all attempts at a rugged respectability several days ago. Straggly, matted clumps of red hair danced around his haggard, unshaven face. His untucked linens billowed like a kite.

And he swayed, God how he swayed, freely, with an apparent lack of fear, almost joyfully. Like an escaped beast let loose inside an empty ballroom, wild, untamed, and undaunted. As if the fires of hell lived in him.

Fitz lifted his hand from the chimney pot to wave a greeting, and Rollo's heart stopped. "A simple letter would have sufficed, pup. Would have saved you the trouble of coming all this way. Or are you come in person so that you may gloat? Do you wish to give me a helping push over the parapet?"

"Step away from the edge, Fitz." On shaky legs, Rollo stood, shuddering as a sharp gust of wind blasted through him. Bravely, he took a step forward, his eyes fixed straight ahead at his lover, whilst behind him, he heard his father cursing. "Why don't you come over here, Fitz, so that you don't have to shout?"

"No." Fitz turned away from him. "The view's much finer from here. I can see all the way to the ocean, beyond Beccles Ridge."

Rollo took two more paces forward. His belly roiled. Only three more baby steps and he'd be able to grab and hug the solid chimney stack paired with the one Fitz embraced so indifferently.

"Eight weeks I waited for you, pup —" Fitz sniffed the air like a hound picking up the scent of a fox. " — for news of your return. Waited and waited and waited. As if I were a damned virginal chit." He twisted, sneering at Rollo's pathetic attempts to shuffle closer. "You made a convincing show of love. I'll grant you that. Did dear Papa put you up to it? Or did he talk you out of it?"

"If only," grumbled the earl from the safety of the skylight. "Rollo, darling, please —"

"I wrote a thousand times, you ass! My...my brother's circumstances kept me at Rossingley, and the first thing I did was write to you. Willoughby had a dreadful fall from his horse. For days, weeks even, we believed he might not live. I penned letters to you every chance I got. We believe the first got caught up in an accident near Winchester. Papa and Kit think — and there is no other credible explanation — that Ralph Hart prevented the rest of my correspondence from reaching you. Out of spite."

Reaching the blessed chimney stack, Rollo sagged against it, seizing it around the middle. "So, you see, all this is for nought, nothing but a misunderstanding, thanks to the vagaries of the weather and the malevolence of a slighted wastrel. And now I've cleared that up, you should come down."

An empty brandy glass hung from Lyndon's fingers. He held it up to his face, the crystal catching the light as he studied it, then off-handedly tossed it over the edge. With a squeal of terror, Rollo squeezed his chimney stack even tighter.

Lyndon heaved a long-drawn-out sigh and rubbed at his bristly chin. "Or perhaps it is God's justice catching up with me at last. Everything I deserve."

"In the form of a slighted sodomite? That's nothing but self-pitying balderdash, Fitz! And you know it."

Fitz sighed again, stretching his neck from side to side. He sniffed at the air once more, pushing up his fluttering shirt cuffs. Then he turned away from Rollo, looking this way and that in the manner of someone about to step down onto a busy street.

Fear flooded Rollo anew. He broke out into a cold sweat. One stumble was all it would take. Just one small stumble.

"Please, Fitz," he begged, dropping to a crouch, not trusting his limbs to hold him up. "At least sit down. Here, next to me. Rest your legs. Surely, they must be weary by now."

Fitz shook his head sadly, looking out in the distance over Rollo's head. Then he turned back to contemplate the drop. "The devil fishes in my troubled waters, Rollo. There's nothing for you up here."

"Only my entire bloody future, you damned fool! Will I have to come over there and wrestle you down? I box, you know. And fence."

Fitz tossed his head back, letting out a bark of laughter. "Wrestle me? You weigh less than a stuffed goose. I could break your spine with one hand tied behind my back."

"Come over and give it a try, then. But be warned, I would kick and scream and never surrender. You can be sure of that. I would be a worthy foe."

"I daresay. But never have I encountered a foe more deadly than my own soul."

"Then you have never wrestled a determined Duchamps-Avery. Would you have me tumble over the edge with you? I shall follow you down, you know."

From somewhere behind, Rollo's father yelped.

A look of anguish crossed Fitz's features. "You wouldn't dare."

"Yes, I would. Please," Rollo begged again. "Come and sit with me, over here. You do not wish to do this."

"You are dismissive of my desires? You know my head better than I?" Lyndon licked a finger and held it up. "There's a biting easterly setting in. Brisk enough to send a man flying."

"Please don't," Rollo whimpered. Tears streamed down his cheeks. A couple of loose roof tiles rattled as another sharp gust weaved around the chimney pots. "Please don't say that."

His clammy hands gripping the chimney stack shook as he made an aborted attempt to rise to his feet.

Fitz smirked. "Is it the wind keeping you stuck over there, pup?"

Grinding his teeth, Rollo got one foot underneath him. "It is not the wind as you damn well know. It is my fear of heights."

"Ah, yes." Lyndon nodded. "I had forgotten. When you visited me in the nursery, you always sat on the window seat looking across at the gardens, but never directly down."

"Actually, I spent most of the time looking at you."

For a second, Fitz's features softened. Then his mouth twisted into a sneer. "Fear of heights is irrational, pup. Are you afraid of widths too? And depths?"

Despite his terror, Rollo's heart swelled. Sophistry at a moment like this! Absurd, and yet so typical of the man. Sucking in a breath, he shakily rose to his full height.

"Fear of falling then," he corrected, his voice cracking. Anything to keep Fitz distracted and talking. "It is much the same thing, is it not?"

"It's not the fall that scares you either," remarked Fitz. "It's the crunch and thud when you reach the bottom."

Rollo shuddered. He blinked several times, his vision blurring. Two Fitz's now appeared to be dancing on the edge of the roof, not one.

"Please, do not say that, Fitz," he whispered, though his voice sounded as if it was coming from very far away. His left leg had numbed, too, as though it were no longer there. He thought he heard his father's voice, urgently insisting on something. The grey sky faded in and out, little white stars dotting it as it merged with the flint roof slates like a vast, stormy ocean. "Please, Fitz, I cannot bear —"

*

ROLLO CAME BACK to himself, cradled in a pair of strong arms and ensconced in a solid, broad lap. Despite the sloshing in his belly and feeling like he might swoon again if he opened both eyes properly, he decided that he was so comfortable he never wanted to climb out of it. When he braved peeling his eyelids apart, he discovered he was still far too high from the ground for his tastes, though not near the edge. A howling wind whistled through his ears.

And yet, he'd never felt more secure.

Fitz's throaty voice rasped in his ear. "Heights are stupid things to be afraid of, pup." Soft lips pressed against his temple. "You should avoid them in future. Or you'll do yourself an injury."

Rollo would have had a smart retort for that if his mouth were working properly. Instead, he drifted in a half-asleep haze with the steady thrum of Fitz's heart against his cheek until he felt better.

"I'm afraid of many stupid things," he answered eventually. "Such as Willoughby doing pretty much anything from here onwards. And the peat bogs surrounding Goule. Sheep when they start that higgledy, gambolling run. This creaking house when darkness falls and the ghouls come out to play." He opened both eyes to find his lover's soft, dark, worried ones gazing down at him. "But…but losing you scares me more."

Fitz stroked his damp hair back from his face. "I tried, pup. I strived to return to how it was before you came. But…existing in such an empty, meaningless world felt so hopeless. No one needed me. I am not capable of such a pointless existence."

"No, but you are capable of love. You have so much to give."

"I am." Fitz kissed his forehead. "And I gladly gave it all to you. But then I realised it wasn't the giving that frightened me. I am afraid of not being loved back."

Rollo entwined his fingers in Fitz's. "Then be afraid no longer. Because you are much loved. And needed." He paused. "Very needed."

"I respectfully disagree."

"What about Will?" Rollo countered. "Who would read him Johnson's cheerless essays one day and Rodolfo's exploits the next, if not you? And give a highfalutin Italian count a rough Glaswegian accent, just to bring a smile to your oldest friend's poor face?"

Fitz's cheeks warmed with a tinge of colour. "He nearly choked to death the first time I tried it, from laughing so hard. Perhaps it would be wiser if I didn't."

"And no one except you would keep Berridge in employ. He can barely climb the steps to the front door, let alone the hall staircase. A lesser lord would have palmed him off years ago. And Simpson wouldn't receive any church support for his second project without your name adhered to it. The Elliot's grave markers would be strangled by weeds at the first hint of spring. Not to mention your beautiful hydrangeas."

Rollo sat up a bit, rallying. "In fact, the whole of Goule would suffer. You have no heirs, and your brother is far too busy to spend his time trekking all the way to Norfolk several times each year to ensure all is kept shipshape. The hall and the village would fall into disrepair and the people into poverty. Ripples would stretch far and wide. These folk aren't tin soldiers, Fitz. If one kills the commander, the entire regiment falls."

"All right, all right. You've made your point," Fitz muttered.

"Trust me, I've only just started. I have much more to say, especially about the duke. He needs —"

Fitz held up a finger. "That's where you're wrong. Benedict has no need for me. He is perfectly capable of being Ashington without my hindrance. And anyhow, if its support he's after, he has Squire warming his bed."

Rollo scoffed. "And Tommy Squire, born in the back alleys of Covent Garden, knows all about running a dukedom, does he?"

"Well, no —" began Fitz, but Rollo cut him off, apparently suddenly feeling much better.

"I shall support Willoughby in every way I can when he takes over from Papa, and gladly."

Fitz smiled at him gently. "Then I hope for his sake that your Willoughby has a strong character." He nuzzled against Rollo's ear, his mouth tracing the delicate flesh; Rollo felt he never wanted move again.

"You haven't mentioned you," Fitz whispered into it. "Sometimes I think this slight body hides within it the strength of ten men, but I fear I shall test all ten of them in years to come."

Rollo reached up to cup his lover's coarse whiskery cheek. "All ten of us would be bereft without you." He scratched his fingers against the bristly hairs. "I am your man, Fitz, until I draw my last breath."

"Then, God help me, I am yours."

They kissed, long and deep. Rollo clung to him, even though Fitz's mouth tasted like an uncorked cask of old brandy.

"It will be hard, this business of loving," he said as he came up for breath. "I am still young. And I am not always wise. And…and tend to speak my mind."

Fitz's mouth smiled against his. "Indeed, we shall often do battle with each other. I look forward to it."

"Talking of battles," Rollo pulled away to gaze about him. "What have you done with my papa?"

Fitz chuckled. "I sent him back down in search of a stiff drink and his lover's comforting arms. Never seen the man quite so distraught. Or dishevelled. Anyone would think a big, warm heart beat inside that pillar of ice."

"An enormous one," Rollo confirmed. "He was prepared to scramble across this roof in my stead."

Fitz's dark eyes twinkled. "In that case, I'd have definitely jumped."

"I put that argument to him." Rollo traced a line across his lover's strong jaw. "Being young and unwise, I decided to do it myself. And…" He wriggled a little. Truly, Fitz had a marvellous lap. "If you had received all my thousands of letters, you would see that I tried to explain my fears. I still have much to learn about life and…and I think that you have much to forget."

"And I think you are demonstrating your vast wisdom already."

Fitz's fingers travelling over the front of his trousers was distracting, but Rollo pushed on.

"Yes, but having you living here and my Rossingley life over there, and London somewhere else entirely, will be damned tricky to navigate on occasion. And we can't overlook that you appear to have made enemies of half the country. We'll have to sort that out and I daresay make the odd recompense for it, just as we will also have to accept that I'm a damned foolish youth desperate to enjoy a few seasons. I intend to be the pink of the *ton*. I am determined to get into all sorts of scrapes with Willoughby, which you may have to haul me away from. Undoubtedly, I shall quarrel with Papa when I do. And with you."

Fitz smiled. "All three of us will disagree on many things. Your father and I have yet to find common ground."

"You have more in common than either of you would believe. You just haven't discovered it yet. What I'm trying to say, in far too many words when so very few would serve as well, is that I would be an utter disaster without you. If you had tumbled from this damned roof and died, I would never have forgiven you."

Planting a last kiss on Fitz's mouth, he brushed himself down and reluctantly clambered off Fitz's lap. "And it goes without saying that the art world would have suffered enormously."

Fitz fought a smile, Rollo could see it tugging at his lips. His dizziness had passed, but he wasn't taking any chances; the skies were as leaden as ever and inside was calling. Reaching out a hand, he helped Fitz up.

"Say goodbye to the roof, Fitz. You shan't be seeing it again."

"You annoy me, pup."

"And I plan on annoying you every day for the foreseeable future." As he tilted his head up to meet Fitz's eyes, a spot of rain landed on his nose. "But if it's all the same to you, I'll make a start from the comfort of the house."

Chapter Twenty-Nine

THEY MADE IT as far as the nursery, then Lyndon could hold back no more. Desperate hunger for the touch of his lover's skin burned through his own. He pushed Rollo against a wall, and they kissed madly in a clash of lips and teeth and tongues. He began tearing at Rollo's clothes.

"I need to take you, pup."

"It's been far too long," gasped Rollo. "Eight weeks and a day."

He wrenched off his cravat and wriggled out of his linen, exposing the milky-white skin of his chest. His small rosy nipples pebbled; Lyndon pinched one between his thumb and finger, tonguing, biting and sucking at the other. Rollo groaned his approval, his hands busy at the fall of Lyndon's trousers.

"I need this." He ran his hand along the length of Lyndon's jutting prick. "I need you inside of me, tearing my soul apart with every thrust. These weeks without you, I have hardly imagined anything else."

Lyndon yanked down Rollo's trousers and drawers, scattering

buttons. He swept his hands across Rollo's flat belly and over his jutting hips. So smooth, so perfect. A body made for brazen display and wanton loving. But, above all, for Lyndon's mouth.

Sinking to his knees, he ran his tongue along the length of Rollo's slim, elegant cock. As Rollo writhed with pleasure, Lyndon's mouth watered. "Already, I'm destroying you in my head, pup."

His tongue travelled lower, and he sucked one of Rollo's tight ballocks into his mouth.

"You're already destroying me in the nursery too," Rollo moaned. His cock pulsed; when he made to squeeze it, Lyndon slapped his hand away.

"No. Keep away. I licked it; I believe that makes it mine."

Rollo chuckled hoarsely. His hands tangled in Lyndon's hair. "My spoiled, highhanded lord." He canted his hips, head tipped back, and his wet lips parted in surrender. Again, Lyndon tongued the crown of his cock, breathing in the musk of him, savouring the bittersweet pearls. Feeling it throb against his tongue.

"You're shameless, my love. How you thrust into my mouth."

He sucked harder and deeper, tracing a path behind Rollo's ballocks with his finger. Then he broke off, sitting back on his haunches to watch his lover's face. Another silvery pearl dripped down Rollo's shaft. "How do you get so wet for me?"

Rollo moaned again, biting on his lower lip. "I have no control over it. When your fingers touch me there, dignity and I readily part company." He hissed as Lyndon cupped his ballocks again, squeezing gently, then teased his prick with his mouth. "And if you persist, I shall also part company with my sanity. It shall stream down your throat."

With a last, lingering lick along the hard line of Rollo's shaft, Lyndon pulled off to plant bruising kisses the length of Rollo's body until, finally, he met with his lips. One day, he would manage a calm, measured seduction. He would unveil his lover's body with exquisite care. He would carry him to bed, whereupon they would tenderly pleasure each other until reaching a leisurely, shared crisis. But not today.

Clutching a fistful of blond hair, he spun Rollo to face the wall. "Spread for me, pup," he whispered hotly against Rollo's nape.

By God, the boy was beautiful. It was all he could do not to fall to his knees again, torn between the urges to sink his teeth into Rollo's juicy rump or his cock into the channel within. He licked his finger, then swept it across Rollo's hole, up and down, up and down, up and down, teasing the entrance. Then, without warning, he sank two thick fingers inside. A moan locked his throat at Rollo's shuddering response.

"You want more?" Lyndon breathed. "You want my prick?"

Rollo sucked in a gasp, pushing back on Lyndon's fingers, and he crooked them, finding the nubbin that made his boy cry out. "Yes," Rollo panted. "Yes."

Lyndon rubbed his bare shaft up against Rollo's arse, grasping Rollo's cock with his other hand. He pressed a path around the curve of his lover's perfect ear with his lips and nipped at the soft lobe. "Then you must ask me nicely, pup."

"Please," Rollo gasped. "Please. I beg you. My lord and captain."

In one short thrust, Lyndon slid inside. Even with oil, it was tight, so damned tight. He fought for control, his thoughts splintering. Rollo gasped.

"Am I hurting you, pup?"

"Yes. A little." Rollo sucked in a deep breath, then let it out between clenched teeth. "But it is exquisite. Indistinguishable from joy." He threw his head back on a long groan, and Lyndon felt something give. "You have stretched me to the fullest."

Rollo braced his hands on the wall as Lyndon cradled him. Though his little rocking movements grew in purpose, he wouldn't hurt his lover. Not even if he begged. Instead, he steadied them both, one hand wrapped around Rollo's chest, the other around Rollo's cock.

Clasped against the warmth and weight of his body and hardly moving inside it, the raging, savage force of Lyndon's climax raced towards him.

"I could die like this, pup," he breathed on a long slow thrust. "And I would never regret it. You against my hips, your taste on my tongue."

"Please don't," gasped Rollo. He twisted, his eyes flashing with amusement even as he winced. "I did not clamber upon that roof for you to die fifteen minutes later with me impaled on your cock."

Half a minute later, and his man was underneath him, cossetted from the hard floor by a dusty old dress, red as blood against the white of Rollo's skin. Linseed oil's earthy scent filled the air. Arguably a better use for it than daubed on Lyndon's useless canvases. This time when he slid inside, Lyndon's eyes never left his lover's.

"Spend with me like this," he urged. Lyndon pushed Rollo's knees higher, moving his dainty feet around the back of Lyndon's neck and pulling him in. Nothing lay between them except the sweat from their bodies. Rollo's damp hardness rubbed against his belly and Lyndon's ballocks tightened. As long as he had this — this creature in his arms — he was saved. "Spend with me now as I can hold back no more." Lyndon thrust deep and long, unravelled, unfettered, and undone. "My dearest pup, my love."

*

ROLLO WRIGGLED DAMPLY. "The entire Duchamps-Avery clan is here," he said.

"What?"

The entire clan? Knowing that Rossingley had witnessed him dancing around his chimneys was enough. Never mind the others. Lyndon very much prayed he'd misheard. Or was still half asleep and had dreamed it. Whilst the immediate effects of his morning's brandy excesses had evaporated several hours ago, its afterbite was catching up with him. His fabulous, insane exertions had left him limp, woollen mouthed, and craving his bed.

"The entire Duchamps-Avery clan is here," Rollo repeated.

Lyndon groaned. "Yes, I was afraid that's what you said."

Of all the words he yearned to hear spill from his lover's lips after Lyndon had bled him dry, he was not prepared for those.

"My father has brought along his lover, Kit Angel," Rollo added, as if that made it all better. "And you'll meet Willoughby at last. Half of our bloody servants have accompanied them, of course. My father doesn't travel light."

Lyndon would have been quite happy if the Earl of Rossingley never travelled at all.

"And…ah…if I'm not mistaken," Rollo continued, "As you were feasting on my ballocks, I believe I recognised the sound of another coach and four heading up the driveway. Admittedly, I was a tad distracted, but…could it be your own brother perhaps? His visit was due about now, was it not?"

Lyndon closed his eyes. Perhaps he could feign illness and avoid all of them. Particularly the ones who'd witnessed his theatrics on the roof. In honesty, he felt terribly foolish about it all and furious that he managed to let his black thoughts get the better of him.

That he came so close to losing all he held dear.

Lyndon groaned again. "Benedict will be accompanied by Tommy bloody Squire, I'd wager."

"I jolly well hope so," answered Rollo cheerfully. He delivered a sloppy kiss, then laughed with delight as Lyndon wiped it away. "Having everyone together will be such fun."

Lyndon gave a mournful sigh, refusing to let himself be so easily mollified by scrumptious kisses. "A slew of sodomites awaits me."

Rollo snorted. "You say it as if gangs of us roam the countryside."

"I'm starting to believe they do. Claiming unsuspecting, women-bedding lords as one of their own." Lyndon gathered a giggling Rollo up in his arms and kissed his forehead.

"You are one of our own," Rollo said. "You simply haven't come to terms with it yet. Don't worry. We shall have fully indoctrinated you by the end of the week."

"I'm surprised they're not here now, making a start. Certainly, they'll be wondering where the devil we've got to."

"I suspect that once Papa saw me safely in your arms, he retreated." Rollo giggled again, happily. "He's not widely known for racing up three flights of stairs."

"Bloody tulip."

Rollo's frivolous little waistcoat, a peach stripy thing, hung from the old rocking horse, flung there in a fit of lust. Lyndon had never owned an item like it. He never intended to either. "Can one…" he began, then hesitated.

In the past few lonely weeks, convinced Rollo would never return, his unhappy mind had brooded on this very subject a great deal.

"What I mean is…I label myself no more a sodomite than I would label myself an astrologer or a…a horticulturalist. I am a man who enjoys those things — stargazing and plotting my summer flowerbeds — as I enjoy sodomising you. Enormously. But…am I defined by it? So that I must carry that label in all that I do? One is not defined by a love of hydrangeas, for instance. Nor by a passing fascination with…with the Flaugergues Comet."

Rollo frowned as he considered. "Why do you ask? Does it concern you? Do you view us as lesser? Is that why you hid your urges for so long and made trouble for Benedict?"

"No," Lyndon answered truthfully. "Especially as I have come to accept, nay embrace, my own desires. This…" He gestured around the room at the discarded clothes and the rumpled red dress on which they lay — it made for an excellent blanket. "Is the most pleasure I have attained in my life thus far. My love for you and how we…make love to each other is a…a source of great pride as well as comfort."

Rollo tilted his head on one side, studying him, no doubt seeing scruffy whiskers, skin sallow from poor living, and two eyes resembling dark, bloodshot wounds. All redeemable though. Lyndon would turn over a new leaf starting tomorrow. As he'd rushed to Rollo's rescue up on the roof and the boy had lain faint in his arms, he'd decided he would jolly well like to live to a ripe old age, after all.

"For some of us," Rollo began carefully, "our sexual predilections imbue our every action. In our walk, in our speech, in how we view the world. My father, for example, is of that nature. As am I."

"You think nothing of donning a dusty old dress."

"Yes." Rollo smiled. "Though I am still a man and, should the occasion arise, I would willingly fight for our country alongside every other full-bloodied male."

He paused, choosing his words. "Your brother, Benedict, however, is not of my nature. He presents a more sober face to the world, befitting his standing as a duke. He does everything in his power not to draw attention to his private predilections. That is his choice, and because of it, the *ton* views him with fondness, as a man married to his estate. In so doing, the gossip mongers leave him alone."

He stroked a soft hand across Lyndon's chest and its thicket of russet curls. "You, my lord, are a man built in your twin's mould. You would not wish to flaunt your desires for a man outside of this household any more than you would covet living as a monk."

"No."

"And I wouldn't want you any other way."

As Lyndon indulged Rollo petting him, he mused on his good fortune. Being stroked and kissed was all well and good, but if he lay really still, his sated lover might nod off again. They could postpone leaving the nursery until they absolutely had to. Alas, after Rollo's mouth nuzzled his neck, he wriggled from Lyndon's grasp.

"You smell," the boy declared and wrinkled his nose charmingly.

"Like a troll," Lyndon replied, sniffing his bare armpit. "I haven't bathed for days."

"I adore your scent. But one can have too much of a good thing. Especially where guests are involved."

Lyndon scratched at his bristly chin. "I fear the state of my hair and whiskers might frighten our visitors too."

"Not half as much as the sight of you swinging from the chimney pots. But you might want to…ah…tidy them. Everybody will be congregating in the drawing room soon. It is time we went your bedchamber and spruced you up."

"I suppose we'll have to feed them all? And find them beds for the night and so forth?" Lyndon pouted. He wanted his lover all to himself and preferably spreadeagled on the hearth rug.

Chuckling, Rollo clambered to his feet, pulling Lyndon up by the hand. "It is traditional when people have travelled a certain distance to visit a person, yes. It is also traditional that one refrains from taking pot shots at them. But I'll leave that to you, my lord. As master of the house."

Chapter Thirty

GOULE HALL DIDN'T need a resident ghost spooking its guests, not when a living, breathing Berridge glided about the place like a wraith. As Rollo pulled the door to Fitz's bedchamber closed, after having escorted him down from the nursery and left his lover strict instructions to bathe, the servant materialised by his side. Rollo jumped five feet in the air.

"Berridge," he acknowledged stiffly, crumpled cravat in hand. "I was just…"

"Precisely, sir."

Rollo didn't need to look down at himself to know his waistcoat was askew. And he knew for a fact his trousers were sagging because Fitz had ripped the top fastening clean off. "I am…um…I am on my way to change for dinner."

His guilt hung heavy in the air. The scent of Fitz's release certainly lingered on his skin.

"Very good, sir."

Berridge stepped aside to let Rollo pass.

"I was just..." Rollo began again, then faltered. Damn it, he'd rescued a man from near death today. He didn't need to explain himself to anyone, least of all a servant. And anyhow, Fitz's household were loyal as the day was long, and today had proved to be very long indeed.

"Tell me, Berridge," he began instead, waving his ruined cravat around as if leaving his host's bedchamber in a state of undress was absolutely the done thing in smart circles. "His lordship has an unexpectedly full house this evening. I trust Cook is able to rustle something up for dinner? And my father and Mr Angel will require rooms, of course. Adjacent, if possible, as they will be sharing a...um...valet. My brother shall bunk with me, seeing as he still requires some assistance. And am I to understand that the duke and his entourage have also arrived?"

"Indeed, they have, sir. All is in hand."

With a brisk nod, Rollo marched towards the staircase, resisting the urge to run. As he placed a foot on the first tread, Berridge's quavery voice called after him.

"Shall I assume that his lordship's venture up onto the roof to... ah...adjust the loose chimney pot was a success, sir?"

Rollo halted. "A-A loose chimney pot?"

"Yes, sir." Berridge paused a beat. "Such a dreadful east wind today. It's no surprise something worked loose. I cannot imagine any other reason for him to have climbed up there, sir. Can you?"

"No," Rollo replied slowly. "I don't believe I can."

"Excellent, sir. I shall report his success to the remainder of the staff, if I may. So that they may sleep more easily tonight knowing all is safe and secure. Sir."

"You do that, Berridge. And you can reassure everyone that they will not be troubled by...ah...loose chimney pots in the future. No matter how severely ill winds blow. From here on, I shall be personally seeing to it myself."

"Very good, sir."

His interaction with Berridge, combined with leaving Fitz to complete his toilette alone, *trusting* him to be alone, sapped the remainder of Rollo's strength. Thankfully, he'd have a moment or two to rest. He found Willoughby all by himself in the drawing room, his leg propped on a pouffe.

"I've been stranded here," Willoughby announced cheerfully. "After all the excitement, Papa and Kit have retired for a 'lie down' — we know exactly what that entails — and the duke and Tommy have taken themselves on a tour of the grounds."

Rollo collapsed onto the settee next to him with a sagging groan, as if he'd never rise again. "I'm fagged to death," he declared. "Saving lives is such hard work, Willoughby."

"You were incredibly brave crawling all over that roof. What with you so hating heights and all that."

"I was, wasn't I? I didn't even think about it until I was up there. All I could think of was rescuing and talking some bloody sense into my poor Fitz."

"So brave," cooed Willoughby as Rollo nestled against him wearily. "And may I also say, so terribly stupid. One slip, and we'd have been scrubbing bloodied bits of you out of the cracks in the cobblestones for days."

Rollo shivered as if still up on the roof at the mercy of the winds. "It was nothing," he lied, "for a courageous sort such as myself."

Willoughby gave him a sharp prod. "Rolly, I've seen you baulk at slightly charred toast. Spill the beans. How on earth did you manage to talk him down?"

Rollo shivered again, recalling how his mind had fumbled for the magic words to make Fitz see sense, how they'd utterly failed him, how he'd seen his future teetering on the edge of a fifty-foot drop and been powerless to prevent it falling.

"Oh, you know how it is." He waved his arms expansively. "Lashing of charm, mostly, sprinkled with devilish cunning. I find any difficult situation can be handled with grace and dignity if one is equipped with the right tools."

Willoughby snorted. "You swooned, didn't you? Go on, admit it."

"Ugh." That was the problem with owning a twin brother. They knew you far too well. "Oh, all right then, yes. It was damned horrific. One second, I was pleading nonsense at him, positive he was about to leap to certain death. The next, I woke up drooling in his lap like a rabid dog and trying to prevent my pent-up fear from dribbling down my thigh. Fitz said he caught me just before I bashed my skull on the lead chimney flashing."

Willoughby squealed with laughter. "Only you, Rolly, could make a drama such as this all about you. Kit owes me a sovereign."

Rollo squawked. "You wagered on me? When I was risking my veritable life?"

"No, of course not. Not until after you disappeared back inside. But we had to do something to pass the time whilst you and your old man were swiving the living daylights out of each other in the nursery. Next time, for all our sakes, skip the theatrics and go straight to the reconciliation part. Papa's poor heart was on the cusp of giving out."

A warm feeling came over Rollo. It was all over, thank God. Willoughby was safe, Fitz was safe, Rollo himself was safe. And they were all together, under the same sturdy (if a little high) roof. He yawned widely. "I'm going to take a nap. I've earned it."

"All right." Willoughby sighed. "Though it's very dull of you. I'll wake you at dinner. Unless, of course, anyone else requires heroic rescues before then." He tutted. "Lashings of charm. Honestly, Rolly. As if you thought I'd ever fall for that."

*

"ROLLO, MY SWEET."

As he floated across the drawing room, the Earl of Rossingley's deceptively light tones roused Rollo from the depths of blessed oblivion.

"It was a loose chimney pot, that was all," he answered sleepily, getting his defence of Fitz in early. "Rattling in the wind."

"So Berridge has informed us." His papa, resplendent in peridot silk, took a seat across from him as Kit helped them both to a small sherry. "The plausibility of his scheme is beyond reproach."

"Yes," Rollo agreed, "I thought so too."

"Then the truth shall forever remain within these four walls." His father hummed. "Do you believe this afternoon's activities are likely to reoccur?"

A few of them Rollo planned on repeating later that evening, but he didn't think that was his father's question. "No. I believe now that he and his brother are fully reconciled, and I have returned to his side, Fitz will stay quite well."

"Excellent." The earl regarded Rollo thoughtfully. "However, you must convey the message from me that if ever he suffers...ah...loose chimney pots again, he has plenty of experienced, supportive friends he may call on."

A few minutes of silence followed, during which Rollo tried to retrieve snatches of the lovely dream he'd been having. His lover had featured, naked too, though the details were annoyingly vague.

"But what should one do about this Ralph Hart character?" mused the earl too loudly for him to ignore. "Surely some form of chastisement is in order. One can't go about helping oneself to other people's personal correspondence. It's against the law of the land, isn't it?"

In Rollo's opinion, Ralph Hart should be strung up by his hairy ballocks. He didn't say so, of course.

"I suppose it's entirely up to Fitz how he decides to respond," answered Kit. "Though I would have thought ploughing one's way through acres of Rollo's lovelorn scrawl punishment enough."

Even Rollo found himself smiling. As Kit and Papa's idle chatter swung back and forth, with Willoughby adding his own points of view, he could almost imagine he was snoozing back in the library at Rossingley. For a third time, he contentedly closed his eyes, letting his thoughts drift once again in the happy direction of his beloved. For all of half a minute.

"Rollo, my sweet."

"Yes, Papa," he answered tiredly.

"May I make the observation that your taste in men is singularly…unique."

"You may. Yes."

His father's wise sermons all started a little like this. Rollo braced himself. Papa had had time to come up with a dozen reasons in the name of self-preservation and protection of the Duchamps-Avery's good standing as to why Rollo should abandon Fitz, and he'd no doubt be correct about every single one of them.

Which was not the same as Rollo agreeing with him.

His head throbbed. The last few days, nay, weeks of fear, not to mention his escapade on the roof, had left him weak-limbed and feeble minded. Yet from his father's tone, the subject seemed not quite finished.

"Yes, Papa," he repeated without opening his eyes. "Fitz *is* unique. And you yourself taught me that a Duchamps-Avery doesn't allow unique, extraordinary men to wither away quietly. Especially when they cherish one's own peculiarities and forgive one's mistakes. And I am trying to think of a more precise way to explain it, but the only words I can find are that I love him. Without reason and unreasonably. Fitz is not perfect, as today has shown. Not even close. Yet all that has done is make me love him all the more."

Whilst they all digested that, Rollo took a deep breath, then ploughed on. Standing up for himself had got him into this mess in the first place. But if he hadn't, he would never have met Fitz. He didn't regret it for a second.

"Whilst Rossingley and my family will always be home," he continued, "from now forward, it is no longer my only home. And if Fitz is greeted with a cool reception at Rossingley, or if there are whispers about him in *ton* circles, if he is not a welcome guest in the smartest houses, then I shall survive here at Goule on his love alone. For the remainder of my days. Because it is enough to nourish me."

A profound hush ensued, during which Rollo dared not open his eyes. He didn't need to; his father's scrutinising pale gaze bore through his eyelids anyhow.

A log popped in the fire. Next to him, awaiting the earl's response, Willoughby flinched. Rollo felt for his hand as the moment stretched. The earl didn't answer straight away, and Rollo hadn't expected him to. If anyone understood the value of a suspenseful pause, it was their wily father.

Eventually, though, the eleventh earl cleared his throat. "Understood. And bravo, darling. I couldn't have put it better myself."

*

GOD, FITZ WAS handsome when he smiled. But also, when he wasn't smiling. Like now. When he was scowling. And filling the doorway of his own drawing room. Chatter ceased as everyone turned to look at him. The Duke of Ashington was first to stride over.

"Lyndon," he said, greeting him warmly. Then, "Thank God you're—"

"Benedict," Lyndon returned. "And, yes. I am. I apologise for any distress I may have caused."

As an awkward pause stretched, Rollo, trapped on the settee on the other side of the room, discussing the history of Goule with Will Elliot, experienced a pang of despair. The scene was all too reminiscent of that blasted solicitor's office in Norwich. So stiff. So bloody clogged. Hadn't they put all this nonsense behind them?

And then, just as he was about to make his excuses to Will, something extraordinary happened. And though Rollo believed it impossible, his love for his man swelled a little more. Raising his arms as Rollo had so painfully instructed, Lyndon took a step forward, clasped his twin's shoulders in both of his large hands, leaned closer, and embraced him in an almighty hug.

"I am…so very pleased to have you here at Goule," he said. "You and Squire are so very, very welcome."

"Yes! I meet him at last!" Willoughby gave Rollo a nudge, beaming from ear to ear. "That hair is magnificent. You didn't tell me your man is a veritable Viking."

"The best of Vikings," Rollo whispered back. "If he had a beard, it would be drenched in tears." Still embracing, and less clumsily by the second, Ashington and Fitz exchanged a few private words. Ashington even gave a soft laugh. Rollo's chest ached with pride.

"But by Jove, he's fierce," added Willoughby. "That expression on his face when he walked in. So…smouldering. As though the devil himself lived on his back."

"Yes." It was one of Rollo's particular favourites too. "Sometimes, I believe he does harbour the devil. But how I relish the thrust and parry."

"I bet you do," murmured Willoughby with a snort. "And I think that feeling is reciprocated. His gaze has been searching for you since he walked in."

Rollo chuckled, rising to his feet. "Then it's time we went over and rescued him from Papa. I think that's a friendship which will have to develop cautiously. Come on. Let me help you up. I'm desperate to introduce you to each other."

"Fitz!" Rollo exclaimed as Willoughby finally made it across the room. He had an overwhelming urge to pat his lover down, preferably using his mouth, but restricted himself to a brief touch on the other's arm. "May I present my brother, Lord Cavendish."

Willoughby nodded. "Very pleased to make your acquaintance, Lord Lyndon. But Cavendish will do. Or Willoughby, seeing as we're going to be firm chums." He smiled brightly at Fitz who stared back at him, dumbstruck. Perhaps being in the presence of the Duke, Rollo's father, and Willoughby at the same time was proving too much after all that had gone before.

"Willoughby responds to pretty much anything," interjected Rollo to break the silence. "I have a whole host of designations for him; hop-along, donkey —"

"There are two of you," Fitz blurted. His uneasy gaze flicked between Rollo and his twin. "I knew it, of course. It's a foolish thing to comment upon. But...I hadn't given it conscious consideration until you...you are both here in front of me."

He studied them some more, eyes darting from one to the other, before a glimmer of a smile tugged at the corners of his mouth. "And I believe that it is only because one of you is regarding me so anxiously and hopping from foot to foot as if I might say something outrageous, that I can tell the difference."

"Willoughby is the one of us with the crutch," Rollo said helpfully. His pleasure at seeing Fitz's small smile bloomed in his soul like a dozen red roses.

"And he has less sauce, I'd wager."

"Indeed," crowed Willoughby. "The more we get to know each other, you will come to see that you have chosen the wrong brother, dear Fitzsimmons. The annoying one." A sudden flush painted his cheeks. "Except for the small, crucial fact that I...you know, I... God,

I've cornered myself, haven't I?"

"It's because Fitz is so scary," soothed Rollo. "He's trying not to be, but sometimes he forgets the effect his austere countenance has on a person. One has to plunge through it regardless. And sometimes, he—"

"He's still standing here," Fitz interrupted, using *the voice*. "And he employs that austere countenance to good effect to put young pups in their place." He nodded at Willoughby. "Call me Fitz. Your brother does. It makes me feel more…"

"Human?" Rollo supplied.

Fitz's smirk suggested he would pay for that impudence later. He could hardly wait.

"Father was wondering what you might do to punish that mail coach chap, the one who stole Rolly's letters," said Willoughby. "I think Rolly has a few ideas, but none suitable for drawing room discourse."

"I'm going to find him work," answered Fitz, surprisingly. "Especially as I intend to spend much more of my time in London and elsewhere than I have of late." He threw Rollo a fond look. "Which means Will Elliot will need assistance and company. Ralph Hart is not an entirely stupid man. He has enough wit to keep Will amused and, furthermore, to drive him wherever he chooses to go."

Fitz cast his gaze over to his old friend, currently engaged in a healthy discourse with Kit. "I'm determined that he gets out more. Whether it will be joining me occasionally in London or visiting his spurious relatives in Norwich. If indeed, they exist."

"I think you've met your match," whispered Willoughby after Fitz moved on to greet Will Elliot over by the bookshelves. They watched as he bent and kissed Will on each cheek as though it was the most natural thing in the world. "I think I shall enjoy your Fitz's company very much."

"I'm so pleased you like him," declared Rollo. He assisted his brother back to the settee and arranged the pouffe to his liking. "He's going to have so many allies in the *ton*. People will be buying tickets to join our party."

He took up the seat next to Willoughby. Will and Fitz were soon joined by the duke and their father. Ashington nodded at something the earl was saying, then laughed out loud and patted him on the shoulder.

"Our dear papa collects people," commented Rollo. "Have you noticed? He gathers oddities. Outcasts."

"Ashington is hardly an outcast," Willoughby pointed out. "He's the most powerful duke in the land."

"No, maybe not Ashington. Though he regards Papa as a wise older brother. Together, they are a force to be reckoned with. But Kit, and Tommy. And before he's had chance to object, Fitz will be drawn into the fold, you'll see. Will Elliot is as good as a member already. All oddities."

Willoughby nodded his agreement. "Yes, I suppose he is. And even Pritchard, in his way."

Rollo laughed. "I didn't say Father was perfect."

Chapter Thirty-One

LYNDON RAN HIS hand along the top of the mantel, his fingers coming to rest at the base of Major General William Ponsonby, of the 1st Dragoons. The hour was late. Will had been found a bed for the night, and Rollo had disappeared to assist his brother. Lyndon smiled to himself. Having Willoughby around would take some getting used to. The boys were peas in a pod.

Their father, the earl, still wasn't quite Lyndon's cup of tea, in the same manner that Lyndon himself and Tommy Squire would never quite be bosom chums either. They'd rub along though, for the sake of Benedict. Lyndon could manage that.

He yawned, ready for his own bed. It had been a day of two halves (the second by far more palatable than the first), the kind of day that would live inside him forever.

The smooth pewter soldier cooled his warm skin. Ponsonby had been a worthy adversary. In fact, during Lyndon's long exile, every single soldier in the 1st Royal Dragoons had kept him well occupied. He rather fancied he might not have made it through without them.

Rollo awaited him in his bedchamber. Soon, Lyndon would climb the stairs and join him, whereupon, despite his exhaustion, he intended to twist that supple, little body into the kind of knots keen fishermen only dreamed of.

For the last time, he hefted Major General Ponsonby in his palm. The toy had a nice, solid weight to it. It was a shame to say goodbye, really, but the battle was done. He'd have Greaves tidy them all away tomorrow. Settle them into a new home inside the old toy chest, nestled inside the warm folds of an unfashionable red dress. A dream come true for most serving soldiers. His bow and quiver of arrows could be stowed in there, too, though he'd still enjoy a snifter or two of brandy of an evening. Even his dear boy couldn't rid him of *all* of his bad traits. Pissing in the fireplace, though, he probably shouldn't push his luck with that one. Young Rollo Duchamps-Avery's tongue might be mostly laced with honey, but his eyes could kill without ever drawing blood. And right now, they'd be demanding a gallon of his if he didn't get up those damned stairs.

On that note, Lyndon pressed his lips to the proud general. Then, after carefully placing him back on the mantelpiece at the head of his men, he headed for the door.

Acknowledgements

I'd like to thank my publisher, NineStar Press, and above all, my editor, Elizabetta, for her endless patience and encouragement. Any historical inaccuracies are mine, not hers!

About the Author

Fearne Hill is a British writer of queer romance and the winner of the 2025 Lambda Literary Award for LGBTQ Romance. When she's not crafting characters who fall hard and kiss slowly, she works as an anaesthesiologist. She lives in the deepest Dorset countryside with her beloved spaniels.

Email
fearne.hill@fearnehill.com

Facebook
www.facebook.com/fearne.hill.50

Facebook Group Fearne Hill's House
www.facebook.com/groups/1172459269938382

Twitter
@FearneHill

Instagram
www.instagram.com/fearnehill_author

Other NineStar books by this author

The Last of the Moussakas

Rossingley Series

To Hold a Hidden Pearl

To Catch a Fallen Leaf

To Take a Quiet Breath

To Melt a Frozen Heart

To Mend a Broken Wing

Regency Rossingley Series

To Tempt a Troubled Earl

To Defend a Damaged Duke

Coming Soon from Fearne Hill

To Save a Scoundrel's Soul

Regency Rossingley, Book Four

Most of Squire's well-heeled patrons were unaware of the private room tucked away from the clamour of the main floor. The air was a comforting blend of cologne and aged leather, and a fire smouldered lazily in the hearth, sending shadows dancing across the rich mahogany wall panels. A thick Persian rug, worn smooth by years of use, stretched across the floor.

Only a very select handful of gentlemen were privy to it. That Tommy Squire, his older cousin and boss, had admitted him to this rarefied group was a privilege Mickey Maurice felt he'd waited for half his life. He had no intention of squandering it.

A wingback armchair, positioned by the hearth, boasted tasselled cushions and a whiff of superiority. Tommy's darkly handsome lover occupied it—Benedict Fitzsimmons, fourteenth Duke of Ashington. Tommy's innocent lordling, all grown up.

Seated opposite and of fairer, slighter frame, yet no less imposing, was the eleventh Earl of Rossingley. His own lover, Kit Angel, stood before a window draped in thick velvet curtains the colour of midnight, looking out onto a rainy St James. He sipped from a brandy balloon, the leaded crystal catching the flickering firelight as if he were cradling a cup of glittering diamonds in his palm. On the deep, inviting sofa sprawled the duke's brother, Lord Lyndon Fitzsimmons, a scapegrace whose fearsome reputation would soon be in tatters if the Honourable Rollo Duchamps-Avery, a blond wisp of a young man, stayed curled up in his lap for much longer.

Tommy sauntered to the drinks trolley and poured himself a generous snifter of brandy. Mickey envied him his poise amongst all these toffs; he wasn't sure he'd ever get used to it. He hovered close to the door, feeling like an imposter and slightly ill at ease in his evening attire. Though thoroughly accepted into the group since Tommy had spruced him up, taught him some *ton* manners, and then insisted he mingle with society, Mickey still half expected one of the gentlemen demand he bring them a fresh decanter or call for a carriage.

"We're unduly popular this evening, given the poor weather," Tommy remarked to no one in particular. "Have been all week."

"That's because all the chaps are blackballing White's," piped up Rollo Duchamps-Avery from his cosy seat. Both his lover, Fitzsimmons, and Duchamps-Avery's father, Rossingley, regarded him fondly. "Willoughby thinks they should call in the runners to sort out the thefts before things get out of hand."

Rossingley smiled indulgently. "It sounds as if Willoughby needs a reminder of the first rule of a gentleman's club."

"Yes, yes, one doesn't talk about the doings of a gentleman's club," Duchamps-Avery chorused. "Which is all very cloak-and-dagger and everything, Papa, but someone is stealing trinkets worth several hundreds of pounds. This isn't a spot of card sharping to liven up a dull wintry evening, you know. It's grand larceny!"

Fitzsimmons nudged him. "And the second rule?"

Duchamps-Avery gave his lover an adoring, if exasperated, look. "Yes, all right, all right. One *still* doesn't talk about the doings of a gentleman's club." He relaxed down into his cosy seat again.

"And even more so when the culprit is purported to be a

gentleman himself," Fitzsimmons added, frowning.

"How many thefts have there been now?" This was from his brother — the duke — his deep brown gaze keen.

"The pilfering of Bannister's pocket watch brings the total up to five," Kit clarified from over by the window. "Three further items were reported to be taken from ladies' reticules at Mrs Bowman's gala dinner." A small smile crept across his face. "And before anyone says it, no, I wasn't present on any of the occasions."

"Yet no thefts reported here at Squire's," Tommy pondered. "If the pilfering at Mrs Bowman's exonerates White's household" — he shot Mickey a meaningful look — "then there is only one conclusion to draw."

"A gentleman thief is at large," agreed Fitzsimmons on behalf of them all.

"Yes. And, so far, he's keeping his hands to himself when he visits here," said Tommy. "Unless, of course, he's not a member."

"If they had their wits," Ashington commented, "White's would ask for a gander at your members list to see if any newcomers have recently joined their establishment but not yours."

He smiled faintly as if he knew his lover well. Mickey guessed how Tommy would respond to a request like that too. A members list such as Tommy's falling into the wrong grubby mitts could turn the tide of empires. Far more than an inventory of gentlemen's names and subscriptions, if there was a mote of dirt, gossip, or murk to be found, then it was recorded on the list and locked up tight in Tommy's office upstairs.

"Which I'd decline to produce." Tommy nodded thoughtfully. "Though snooping at theirs would be interesting, just in case the bounder tries his luck here."

"I… um… may have already looked into it," Mickey offered, and his neck heated. He tended to stay quiet unless addressed directly, a habit Tommy patiently tried to eradicate. Along with Sidney—Tommy's muscle—Mickey had spent most of the morning bribing, cajoling, intimidating, and charming one of White's less loyal and far too naïve secretaries.

As all heads turned in his direction, he flushed even harder. Even Rossingley, who so far had stayed quiet, seemed impressed. Tommy, on the other hand, tensed.

"Tell me you came to no harm, that no one threatened you."

Mickey rolled his eyes. Anticipating Tommy's needs was literally his job. "Sidney accompanied me. The poor fellow we spoke to is probably still cowering in a darkened room somewhere."

"That's my boy," praised Tommy. "Out with it, then."

Mickey gritted his teeth. He wasn't Tommy's 'boy' any longer; he was twenty-one years old! Nonetheless, he tried not to preen. If lumbering, granite-hewn Sidney was Tommy Squire's shield, then Mickey Maurice prided himself on being his sword. He was his older cousin's fixer, his eyes and ears, and Tommy's most ardent admirer, excepting the duke. Tommy Squire had dragged himself up from the gutter by his bootstraps, then returned five years ago to fetch Mickey. Starting as a lackey, then a footman, he was now Tommy's right-hand man and, as such, rubbing shoulders with the *ton*. God knew when he'd get used to it. Or be allowed out and about to do his job without Sidney in tow.

"White's hasn't signed any new members in the last month," Mickey confirmed.

Tommy pursed his lips. "Disappointing."

From the wine table at his side, Mickey retrieved a document. "So, with Sidney's able assistance, I pressed my source a little harder."

"Excellent." Tommy turned to where the duke already pretended to examine his nails. "You might want to close your ears, my love."

"As usual, I shall deny all knowledge." Devoted to the service of his family and dukedom, Ashington preferred to overlook some of his lover's murkier business matters. The others, however, were agog.

"Over the last two weeks," Mickey began, "three members of White's who haven't been sighted for several years reappeared." He passed the list of names over to Tommy. "The top one, I believe, we can exclude. Sir George Shippam. Sixty-one years of age, he spends most of the year at his hunting lodge in Cambridgeshire studying rare minerals."

"Gadzooks, I assumed he was dead," interrupted Rossingley. "My father and he were once great chums. Not heard that name in aeons."

"No," Mickey answered, gaining in confidence. "He's a bit of a recluse, by all accounts, and is only visiting town to deliver a series of lectures to the Royal Society."

"And half-inch purses?" Tommy raised an eyebrow. "Unlikely."

"Very unlikely," Rossingley agreed. "Unless said purses are adorned with rare turquoises and morganite."

"My thoughts too." Mickey pointed to the second name. "This next chap is an American, a Mr Chesterton, hailing from Virginia. Not shown his face for over fifteen years, had been crossed off the members list for good. However, having completed a tour of Europe—last stop Florence—he arrived in London six days ago, intending to stay for the season and to see his daughter safely married off to the Marquis of Talybridge."

"Talybridge?" spluttered the duke "How old's this Chesterton's daughter? Talybridge must be over fifty, if he's a day."

"That, I didn't ascertain, Your Gra—Ashington."

Mickey wasn't sure he'd ever get used to being on such familiar terms with a duke, despite his vague memories of Ashington as a shy youth, stealing visits to the molly house. "Talybridge has also been touring Europe recently. Chesterton and he travelled back together with the daughter in tow. The wedding date is set for the first day of the New

Year. The marquis vouched for Chesterton's temporary membership — they are friends of old, apparently — and the marquis's own records show him to be beyond reproach."

"I'd wager they show him to be a bore and an oaf," muttered the duke.

"Bitter and spite-fuelled," agreed his brother, Fitzsimmons.

"Odious," offered Kit from over by the window.

"But oh, so very, very titled and so very, very rich," finished Rossingley. "Which, to an avaricious papa seeking a match for his daughter, sadly makes his age an irrelevance." His pale eyes glittered. "Correct me if I'm wrong, Ashington, but the Ashingtons and Talybridges have never seen eye to eye, have they?"

"No," conceded the duke grumpily. "When I was a small child, our two families quarrelled at a summer shooting party, held at Ashington. I have very little recollection, of course, but the families have hardly spoken to one another in public or private since."

"Quarrelled over what?" asked Rollo, curious.

"Our father tended to be tight-lipped on the matter," Fitzsimmons said. His own lips pursed as he stroked his fingers through Rollo's fine blond hair. "His mother — our grandmother — sadly died during the same weekend."

"An unhappy coincidence?" Rossingley queried.

Fitzsimmons hesitated before answering, glancing at his brother. "We believe not. Safe to say that our grandfather always gave the Talybridges a wide berth and tended to spit whenever one was close by."

"Such intrigue," Rollo mused. "And what a delightfully uncouth way to express one's displeasure." He grinned up at Fitzsimmons, his stern lover. "If you cease stroking my hair, I may adopt it."

"Will this be Talybridge's second or third wife?" Rossingley directed this to Ashington and Fitzsimmons. "One quite loses track."

Mickey cleared his throat. Once the three of them began gossiping, it could go on for some time. "Our final candidate is far more interesting," he declared. "The Honourable Valentin Beauregard, Vicomte de Verdille. There's very little in White's records, except that he was last sighted in London five or six years ago. Allegedly, he has been living the high life in various European cities since."

"Never heard of him," Tommy stated. "Slippery?"

"As coal tar soap," conceded Mickey.

"He's a French vicomte," drawled Rossingley. "Slipperiness will have been his principal source of nourishment since suckling at his nursemaid's tit."

CONNECT WITH NINESTAR PRESS

WEBSITE: NineStarPress.com

FACEBOOK: NineStarPress

X: @ninestarpress

INSTAGRAM: NineStarPress

BlueSky: NineStarPress

THREADS: @ninestarpress